Give the Devil His Due

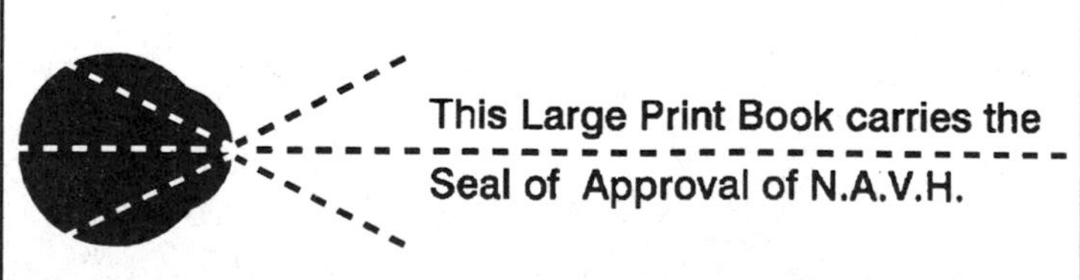
This Large Print Book carries the
Seal of Approval of N.A.V.H.

A TAROT MYSTERY

GIVE THE DEVIL HIS DUE

STEVE HOCKENSMITH
WITH LISA FALCO

THORNDIKE PRESS
A part of Gale, Cengage Learning

Farmington Hills, Mich • San Francisco • New York • Waterville, Maine
Meriden, Conn • Mason, Ohio • Chicago

This is a work of fiction. Names, characters, places, and incidents are either the product of the author's imagination or used fictitiously and any resemblance to actual persons, living or dead, business establishments, events, or locales is entirely coincidental.

Thorndike Press® Large Print Mystery.
The text of this Large Print edition is unabridged.
Other aspects of the book may vary from the original edition.
Set in 16 pt. Plantin.

LIBRARY OF CONGRESS CATALOGING-IN-PUBLICATION DATA

Names: Hockensmith, Steve, author. | Falco, Lisa, 1970- author.
Title: Give the devil his due / by Steve Hockensmith ; with Lisa Falco.
Description: Large print edition. | Waterville, Maine : Thorndike Press, a part of Gale, Cengage Learning, 2017. | Series: A Tarot mystery | Series: Thorndike Press large print mystery
Identifiers: LCCN 2017009850| ISBN 9781432838720 (hardcover) | ISBN 1432838725 (hardcover)
Subjects: LCSH: Psychic ability—Fiction. | Psychics—Fiction. | Tarot—Fiction. | Large type books. | GSAFD: Mystery fiction. | Occult fiction.
Classification: LCC PS3608.O29 G58 2017b | DDC 813/.6—dc23
LC record available at https://lccn.loc.gov/2017009850

Published in 2017 by arrangement with Midnight Ink, an imprint of Llewelyn Publications, Woodbury, MN 55125-2989 USA

Printed in the United States of America
1 2 3 4 5 6 7 21 20 19 18 17

Give the Devil His Due

PART 1
READINGS

COPPE
COUPES
1
CHALICES
COPAS
KELCHE
BEKERS

"Have a drink . . . on me," you hear someone say. And you look over, thinking, "Oh, god — who's the creep?" But what you see is a giant hand poking out of a cloud to give you a grail. *SURPRISE!* It's the universe, and that's not a cosmopolitan it's offering you out of the blue. It's something much deeper, much truer, much more transformative (though a really good cosmo can come close). You could even call it your destiny. But do you recognize the gift for what it is or do you slap the cup away — and only realize later that you were dying of thirst?

Miss Chance, *Infinite Roads to Knowing*

I believe it was the noted paranormal researcher Ray Parker Jr. who best summed up my feelings about hauntings: "I ain't afraid of no ghost," he so sagely put it.

While I don't agree with everything Mr. Parker had to say on the subject — bustin', for instance, *doesn't* make me feel good — I am, like him, not afraid of any ghosts. Because I don't believe in them.

Which is why, when I found myself talking to a dead man recently, I didn't scream, didn't faint, didn't reach for the phone. (Who you gonna call? No one, if you're me.) I just tried to do a little mental recalibration.

"Hello, Biddle," I said. "So . . . you're not dead."

"Not so you'd notice."

He grinned at me, eyes twinkling.

The wrinkles on his lean, dark face were new. The gray in his neatly trimmed beard was new. The beard was new, for that matter. But the grin was the same, and the twinkle, too.

This was no ghost.

Biddle was alive.

Biddle had never been dead. (I know that usually goes without saying when someone's alive, but this was a special case.)

Biddle was standing in the White Magic Five and Dime, the occult-themed tourist trap/fortunetelling parlor I'd inherited from my con-artist mother, smiling at me. *Twinkling,* damn him. As if he were just an old friend who'd popped in for a surprise visit.

Which he was, I suppose. Only this old friend had been my mother's lover and literal partner in crime. And the surprise visit was coming thirty years after I'd seen him marched into an Ohio cornfield by some very unhappy (and well-armed) gangsters, never to return. Until now.

Once upon a time, I'd wept for him. I'd missed him. I'd let him go. And now he had the gall to just stroll out of Hell and come to my little shop in Berdache, Arizona, and *twinkle* at me?

So wrong.

And so Biddle.

And as I had that thought — *This is so Biddle* — the reality of it finally hit me fully.

■ ■ ■ ■

Imagine —

You're in line at the grocery store, and you notice that the chubby dude behind you with the cart full of eggnog and Reindeer Chow is Santa Claus.

There's a knock at the door, and when you answer it, waiting on your porch with an earnest expression and a copy of *The Watchtower* is the Easter Bunny.

You go to the DMV to renew your driver's license, and you realize that the familiar-looking goblin who's processing your paperwork is Mrs. Gollumina, the imaginary friend you had when you were six.

It was kind of like that.

Never let them see you sweat, Biddle used to tell me. *While you're at it, don't let them see you blink. Hell, don't even let them know you need to* breathe.

I'd tried to live up to all that, even after he was gone. And I'd done a pretty good job at it, actually. But you know what?

Screw it.

We need to sweat. We need to blink. We need to breathe.

So I let myself.

Biddle never told me not to let my knees

turn to Jell-O, but I let that happen, too.

"I'm just going to go over here and sit down, if that's okay," I said, and I wobbled, suddenly sweating and blinking and panting, toward the small waiting area in one corner of the shop. When I reached the couch there, I managed to turn around and drop back onto it about a half second before my legs gave out.

"How's it goin'?" I said.

I wanted to sound nonchalant.

I didn't.

Biddle was looking at me forlornly now, twinkle snuffed out.

"I'm sorry, sweetie," he said. "I didn't know how to do this. Calling, sending a letter, emailing — none of it felt right. But I guess I should've given you some kind of warning."

I tried to take a deep breath, but I was still panting, my lungs barely expanding before I was puffing the air out and sucking in more.

"Sweetie." That's right. That was what he used to call me. He couldn't use my real name because I didn't have one. Was I Cindy this week or Jan? Marcia or Alice? Sabrina or Jill or Kelly? Whatever it was, my mother would make me change it in a couple weeks — right around the time she changed her own.

I turned toward the big fish tank near the couch. At the bottom was a porcelain pirate ship, and in its little hold was an airtight container packed with two and a half pounds of chalky ash — all that remained of my mother.

At least Mom wouldn't be rising again like a slasher movie axe murderer. I'd seen the body. She was dead dead *dead.*

I finally caught my breath. I might have even smiled.

"Don't worry about it, Biddle," I said. "You ripped the Band-Aid off, that's all. I'll be okay."

I still didn't sound nonchalant, but I didn't sound like I was hyperventilating either.

I patted the plush chair beside the couch. "Come on over and tell me what you've been up to the past thirty years."

Biddle's twinkle rekindled. He almost looked proud.

"Oh, you know," he said as he started toward me. "This and that."

He let his gaze wander around the store, taking in the display tables and shelves stocked with rune stones and crystals and spell kits and guidebooks to numerology and astrology and the vortexes that supposedly swirled in the desert nearby. To his credit, he didn't laugh, even though I'd learned what he thought of such things a long, long time ago.

"Ahh . . . the competition," Biddle said to me once when he saw Jimmy Swaggart (or maybe it was Jim Bakker — I could never tell those TV preachers apart) sermonizing on a motel television. "You know the difference between him and a palm reader? Between him and *us*?"

I'd shrugged.

Biddle patted the top of the TV. "He's on here."

Then he changed the channel, and our president at the time — the one who'd spent years acting in movies before he started doing it behind a podium — appeared on the screen.

Biddle had laughed.

"Same goes for him," he'd said.

Ancient history. But the more things change . . .

Biddle slowly eased himself into the seat beside the couch. He wasn't just older now. He seemed thinner and even shorter. He was dressed like an old man, too — in an untucked short-sleeve shirt and baggy khaki slacks and blindingly white sneakers that looked perfect for a morning cardio walk around the mall.

The Biddle I remembered was fond of black turtlenecks and leather jackets and tailored three-piece suits, and he'd filled them out to perfection. He'd been half Shaft, half James Bond.

Or maybe he hadn't. Maybe that was just who I'd wanted him to be — the surrogate father I'd cobbled together from the movies and TV shows that had raised me as much as he or my mother did.

So I could add "What are you *really* like?" to the long list of questions I had for him. That one would have to wait, though. Another was elbowing its way to the front of the line.

"Why now?"

"Three guesses," Biddle said.

I nodded.

One guess was plenty. And it wasn't even a guess.

"How'd you find out she was dead?" I asked.

"Oh, I tracked her to this place years ago. Never actually came here, but I used to check on her new name from time to time. Finally saw one of the headlines I expected — 'Local Fortuneteller Arrested' or 'Local Fortuneteller Killed' — it was gonna be one or the other in the end." Biddle looked around the shop again. "Happened right here, didn't it?"

I jerked my head toward the back of the building. "There. In the room where we do readings."

Biddle cocked an eyebrow at that "we."

I ignored it.

"So you read that she'd been murdered," I said. "And then you read that her daughter had taken over her business."

"Exactly. And I decided to come see if her daughter *was* her daughter. You could never tell with that gal. Used to pick up the most interesting partners."

Biddle smiled.

I frowned.

"Oh, *shit,*" I said.

My mother's last partner had been Clarice, my teenage half sister. Like me, Clarice didn't know who her father was. Unlike me, she thought she might: she'd found pictures of Biddle that Mom had squirreled away, and — him being black and her being half black — she'd jumped to conclusions. I hadn't had the heart to tell her the man she thought was her father was dead, and now I didn't feel like explaining that he wasn't dead but he wasn't Dad either, and I'd known the latter all along.

"What's wrong?" Biddle said.

I stood up. "You gotta go."

"What? Why?"

"Because a complicated conversation is about to get a lot *more* complicated if you don't get out of here before a certain someone walks in."

The front door opened, and someone walked in.

Biddle gave me a wide-eyed look that said, "The certain someone?"

I shook my head.

I'd been about to close the shop for the night when Biddle appeared, and in my surprise I'd forgotten to lock the door and turn off the neon OPEN sign in the window. And now we had a customer: a balding, paunchy, stoop-shouldered man about Biddle's age. He looked like the kind of tourist who usually gets dragged in by a wife hunting for souvenirs for the grandkids back home.

"Come on, Frank," Grandma would usually be saying. "I bet the stuff in here will be half what they charge over in Sedona. I mean, just *look* at this dinky town . . ."

(I really couldn't blame the deal-hunting grandmas, given the words my mother had someone stencil on the front window under the shop's name: DIVINATION * REVELA-

TION ★ BARGAINS.)

"Hello," the old man said to me.

"Hi. I'll be right with you." I turned back to Biddle. "The best burritos in Berdache? That's easy: we've only got two Mexican places, and the Department of Health just shut one of 'em down. The other is El Zorro Azul. Turn left on your way out and you'll hit it in two blocks. I think they're open till eight, so you've got plenty of time."

Biddle pushed himself to his feet. "I just hope their margaritas are as good as their burritos — and that I can find a pretty senorita to share a few with me."

Biddle gave me a grin and a wink, and the plan was set: we'd meet at El Zorro Azul at eight.

It was like old times. Talking to each other in a way only we understood. Putting one over on the rest of the world. Playing games with lies.

"Well, thanks for lookin' into your crystal ball for me," Biddle said as he headed toward the door. "It's good to know sinkin' my savings into the bikini carwash is gonna pay off."

"And don't you worry, Mr. Sanford — that rash is going to clear up, too," I said. "Happy days are here again."

"Indeed they are, sweetie. Indeed they are."

Biddle stepped around the other old man and left the shop.

I just stood there staring at the door for a moment, trying to make sense of my feelings.

Seeing Biddle again had stirred up something that wasn't entirely sadness and wasn't entirely anger but was entirely bad. After half a minute trying to pin it down, I finally realized what it was.

No, I ain't afraid of no ghost. But Biddle alive — and back in my life? For some reason *that* scared the shit out of me.

COPPE
COUPES
2
CHALICES
COPAS
KELCHE
BEKERS

So you meet Marie Antoinette at Oktoberfest, and maybe you've pounded enough beer to drown a small Chihuahua and maybe a lion-headed hawk is pooping in your stein, but none of that matters, dammit. You're not going to let anything distract you from this special moment: it's love at first sight. Or lust at first sight. Or maybe you're just excited because it looks like she might give you her beer. Whatever. The important thing is this: you've just encountered someone who's about to have a huge impact on you. So pay attention — and try not to puke on her dress.

Miss Chance, *Infinite Roads to Knowing*

I kept staring at the front door, lost in thought. So lost in thought, actually, that I completely forgot about the old man who'd walked into the shop after Biddle.

Eventually he cleared his throat, and I turned to find him standing by one of the display tables, looking at me with a somber expression that made it plain he'd come to the White Magic Five and Dime with a question of soul-shattering importance.

"Could I use your john?" he said.

I pointed to a bead-draped doorway near some display cases. Beyond it was a hall leading to the back of the building.

"That way. On your right."

"Thanks."

The old man pushed through the beads with the hint of a scowl on his wrinkled face (he obviously wasn't a groovy love beads kind of guy) and headed up the hall. I calculated the odds of him actually buying something when he was done. They weren't good. All I could do was hope he hadn't just come from El Zorro Azul.

I started toward the neon OPEN in the window, meaning to turn it off before more last-minute customers could pop in. Just before I reached it I heard footsteps behind me, coming up the hall. The old man had barely had time to unzip his fly, so I figured I knew who it was.

"How was school today?" I said.

I turned to find a willowy, dark-skinned teenager slipping through the beads to join me in the store. Behind her was another girl, this one with lighter skin and short-cropped electric blue hair.

Clarice and her girlfriend, Ceecee.

"The usual," said Clarice.

"Boring," said Ceecee.

"Well, at least it's Friday, right?" I said.

Clarice rolled her eyes. "Woo hoo. Friday night in Berdache. We can either stay in and watch Netflix or pound Budweiser in the desert with the football team. Decisions, decisions."

"Netflix," said Ceecee. "Definitely Netflix."

Clarice stepped behind the shop's counter, opened the cash register, and gave the day's takings a sorrowful look. "I hate to say it, but we did better when Mom ran the place. A lot better."

"First off, if you hate to say something, maybe you shouldn't say it at all," I told Clarice. That got me another eye roll. "And secondly, Mom was doing so much better because she was running cons on the customers. I'd probably be making more money if I was a sociopath, too, but I just didn't get lucky like that."

Ceecee peeked over Clarice's shoulder at the money in the till. She was enough of a regular around the place to know that what she was seeing wasn't impressive.

"You should let Marsha work more hours," she said. "She's a better salesman than you."

Marsha had been one of my mother's marks. Now she was the White Magic Five and Dime's assistant manager. (Not that she had much to manage: she was the shop's only official employee. But "assistant manager" sounds so much better than "woman I pay to hang out around the store because she needs a job and I feel guilty about how my mother treated her.")

"I can sell stuff when I'm in the mood," I said.

"Exactly." Clarice waved a hand at the mystical/spiritual grab bag that was the

White Magic Five and Dime — Buddhas beside runes beside crystals beside crucifixes. "And you're never in the mood because you don't believe in any of this stuff."

I nodded at the hallway. "Ixnay on the on't-day elieve-bay."

The girls both stared at me blankly. Clarice served as their spokesman.

"Chuh?" she said.

"Doesn't anyone know pig Latin anymore?" I whispered. "There's a customer in the bathroom."

"Oh. I thought maybe it was your boyfriend," said Clarice.

Ceecee smirked at her. "But which one?"

"It's so hard to keep track with her, isn't it?" Clarice said. She looked at me and shook her head. "You hussy."

Usually I didn't mind Clarice teasing me about the men in my life. I loved it, actually. A little sister giving me shit about my love life — it felt like one of the most normal things that had ever happened to me.

Now wasn't the time for normal, though. It's hard to be in the mood for playful repartee when your very abnormal past suddenly invades your paranormal present.

Subject change ahoy!

"Have you two had dinner yet?" I asked.

"Yes," said Ceecee.

"No," said Clarice.

They looked at each other.

"She's about to tell us to take a twenty from the register and get something to eat if we're hungry," Clarice said. "And that means we can get something a lot better than your mom's macaroni."

"Oh. Right."

They turned toward me again.

"No, we haven't had dinner," said Ceecee.

"Well," I said, "why don't you take a twenty from the register and get something to eat if you're hungry?"

Clarice slipped a hand into the cash drawer. "Told ya."

"You can go anywhere but El Zorro Azul," I said. "And I said you could take *a* twenty. Singular."

"Oooo — hot date tonight?" Clarice asked as she returned the extra bill she'd palmed.

"Not hot. But a date, yeah."

"Victor or GW?" Ceecee asked.

"She said it wasn't a hot date, so that means GW's out," Clarice said. "It must be Victor."

Ceecee nodded as if that made sense.

As far as the girls were concerned, poor

Victor Castellanos had three strikes against him.

Strike #1: He was a gym teacher at their high school.

Strike #2: He was boring. (Or so Clarice and Ceecee had decided. I tried to tell them that he brought his mother along on dates and was uncomfortable about the rotten roots of our family tree because he was *nice,* not boring. They couldn't see the distinction.)

Strike #3: He wasn't GW Fletcher.

GW they liked because he was a little younger and a little cuter and not a teacher at their school and definitely not boring. The fact that he was interesting because he was a petty criminal didn't faze them. (How much did it faze *me*? I hadn't decided yet.)

Since I didn't want the girls anywhere near El Zorro Azul, I knew exactly what to tell them about my "date."

"You're right. I'm seeing Victor again."

Clarice groaned. "Don't fall asleep in the salsa."

"You just don't appreciate a mature, solid man," I said.

"You got that right," Clarice shot back.

She and Ceecee looked at each other and burst out laughing.

As their guffaws faded to snorts, the front

door opened, and I turned to find a middle-aged man walking into the shop.

I used to think my gaydar was pretty good until it took me most of a week to figure out that Clarice and Ceecee were a couple. But my copdar — *that* I still had faith in. And it started pinging loud and clear.

Maybe it was the man's aggressively middle-of-the-road clothes. (Blue oxford, unwrinkled chinos, gray New Balance sneakers.) Maybe it was his standard-issue, close-cropped, two-guard-on-the-clippers Supercuts hair. Maybe it was his physique — lean and surprisingly fit for a late-fortysomething. (Don't put too much stock in that old doughnut-scarfing lard-ass cliché. That's strictly for rent-a-cops and old timers watching the clock till retirement.) Maybe it was the way he slid into the store without making eye contact.

And maybe it was the best way to spot cops of all, according to Biddle.

"Listen to your gut," he used to tell me. "If it tells you someone's a cop, you tell your feet to start moving."

I glanced over at Clarice. All she had to do was raise an eyebrow an eighth of an inch for me to know her copdar was pinging, too. Mother had taught her well.

So who was the handsome (I noticed the

longer I looked) fifty-something dude pretending to peruse our buy-one-get-one-free voodoo dolls? He wasn't local. I'd have seen him — and, given his looks, remembered him.

Berdache, Arizona. Population: 4,567 — only a dozen of them cops. *SaaaaLUTE!*

Maybe the guy worked for the DA or the state CID. In the last two months I'd gotten mixed up in two murders — quite the crime wave, by Berdache standards. Perhaps the powers that be wanted to see if they could ship me back to Chicago.

Or this might have been a more unofficial — and unsavory — sort of visit. My mother hadn't been the only con artist working the fortuneteller angle around town. There was a whole family of competitors, the Grandis, and they didn't appreciate that I'd been trying to make amends to the very suckers they and Mom had been bilking. They'd already tried to take me down twice — could be the Gray Fox (who'd moved on to a box of pewter pentagrams now) somehow was going to make it thrice.

There was another possibility, too; one I wasn't ready to let myself seriously consider just yet because it was too damned depressing. I could blow up that bridge when I came to it . . . if it wasn't rubble in the river already.

All this whizzed through my mind in about six seconds. As of second number seven, I knew what I was going to do about it.

I pointed at the mystery man.

"He's the one, right?" I said to Clarice.

She nodded firmly, though she couldn't have known what the hell I was talking about.

"He's the one," she said.

Like I said: Mom trained her well.

"He's the one *what*?" said Ceecee, who obviously *hadn't* been trained by our mother (lucky girl).

The man looked over at us with a "Who . . . me?" expression on his face.

"Congratulations," I told him. "You're our one-hundredth customer of the week."

"Oh? Do I win something?" the man asked with a guarded smile.

It looked like he expected me to say something like, "Absolutely — you've won 10 percent off any purchase of two hundred dollars or more!"

Instead, I said this: "Absolutely — you've won a free tarot reading."

The man looked surprised. I think it was the word "free" that really shocked him.

"You two don't mind sticking around to keep an eye on the place a few more minutes, do you?" I said to the girls.

Of course, I was really asking them to stick around to keep an eye on *me.*

"No problem," Clarice said.

"Anything for the one-hundredth customer of the week!" Ceecee enthused.

She'd been a little slow to catch on, and now she was eager to make up for it. I could only pray she wouldn't wink.

I walked to the doorway to the back hall and pulled back the beads across it.

"This way," I said to the man.

I stood there with one arm crooked in the classic "after you" position.

The man hesitated before walking past me up the dimly lit hallway. It had only been a pause of a couple seconds, but it told me something important.

He was as wary of me as I was of him.

"First room on your left," I said as I followed.

We passed some of the posters Mom had hung on the wall: large prints of the more empowering tarot cards. The Star. The Sun. The Lovers.

Between Temperance and Strength was the door to the bathroom, which was still closed, with a light visible inside.

I'd forgotten all about the old man. So much for hoping it was just his bladder that needed emptying.

Thanks, Mom, I thought. If I hadn't been working so hard to turn around the bad karma she'd left behind, maybe I could've put up a NO PUBLIC RESTROOMS sign.

The man turned into the small room — it was really more of a glorified walk-in closet — where we did readings. In it were two chairs, a small table, and a low bookshelf topped with an honest-to-god crystal ball.

The man sat in one chair. I sat in the other. Between us on the table was a deck of tarot cards.

"Shuffle," I said, nodding at the cards. "And before we begin, I'll need to ask you a few questions."

"Perfect," the man said as he reached for the deck. "I have some questions for you."

The man told me this: his name was Mike Brown and he was a certified public accountant from Bridgeville, Delaware, passing through Berdache on his way to a convention of model railroad enthusiasts in Flagstaff.

Translated: boring boring boring, and don't ask too many questions or you're going to end up learning more about model trains than you ever wanted to know.

I gave the guy points for a smart cover story.

His questions for me were just as carefully bland:

"How long have you lived here?"

"What's it like?"

"Do you like it?"

"How did you become a fortuneteller?"

I kept my answers brief but not brusque:

"A few months."

"Mostly quiet."

"It's nice."

"Family business."

"Mr. Brown" (yeah, right) didn't seem annoyed by my lack of chattiness. He'd relaxed a bit after settling into his seat — maybe because the room was too small for anyone to sneak up behind him — and soon he had a small, sly smile on his face as he shuffled the cards. A you-know-that-I-know-that-you-know-what's-really-going-on-here kind of smile.

Except of course I *didn't* know what was really going on. But I knew how to get some clues.

"Think of a question you have," I said. "Then give me the deck."

"A question? Okay." Brown's smile widened. "How's my trip going to go?"

He handed me the cards, and I started laying out my go-to spread: the Celtic Cross.

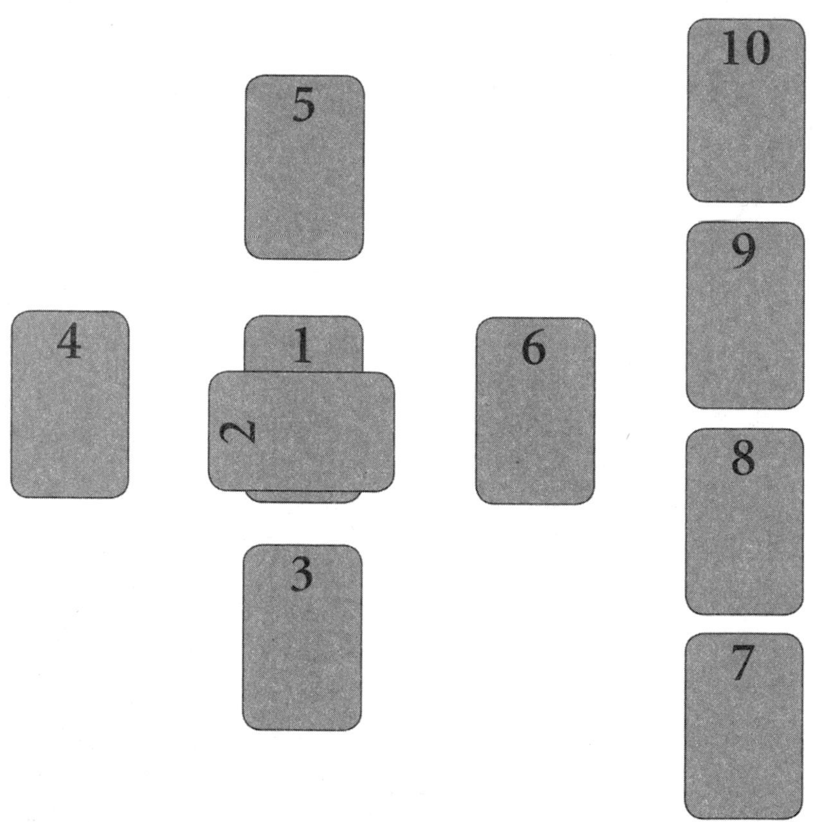

"So this'll show me the future?" Brown asked.

"Maybe."

" 'Maybe'?"

"Some people think the cards can be used for divination. Some think they're just a useful mirror of our past and present."

"What do *you* think?"

"I think there's a lot I don't know."

"You don't talk like any fortuneteller I've ever heard before."

"Want your money back?"

Brown snorted out a gruff laugh. "Point taken."

I reached for the card at the center of the spread — the only one that was covered by another — and flipped it over.

"This is the big picture," I said. "Your overall situation."

"Wow — looks like my mom was right about me all along," Brown said wryly. "I'm a knight in shining armor."

"I don't know about that, but you are on a quest. You're looking for something."

Brown stiffened, his wariness returning in an instant.

"Oh?" he said. "What am I looking for?"

"Well, Cups is the suit of emotion and harmony. Maybe . . . love?"

Brown smiled again, but it was a grim, tense smile now.

"Now you *do* sound like every other fortuneteller," he said.

"Let's see what I can do about that."

I turned over the second card — the one that had been covering the first.

"Hey, it's my old buddy," I said. "I get this a lot myself."

" 'The Fool'? The universe trying to tell you something?"

"Always," I said. And I believed it — which was new.

Just a few weeks before I would've said that the only thing the universe has to tell us is this: "You're on your own, pal." After I took over the shop and started pretending to read tarot cards, though, I changed my mind. I still didn't believe in a warm and fuzzy universe that dropped helpful hints for finding our bliss. But when it came to the cards, I wasn't pretending anymore.

"The card in this position reflects your current situation. The state of your quest," I said. "You're making progress, but there are challenges ahead that you don't see. Dangers even. The dog — that's someone trying to warn you. But you're not listening."

"So I'm supposed to give up? Is that it?"

"I didn't say that. I said be careful."

Brown narrowed his eyes. "I hope that's not the only thing your cards are going to tell me."

"Let's see."

I turned over the card in the position below the first two.

"This is the root of what we're looking at — what your quest is growing out of."

Brown peered down at the card. "Drinking? Or flying lion heads?"

"A relationship. Not a romantic or emotional one, though; the card's reversed. So that thing you're looking for — you're doing it for someone, but not because you love them. Maybe it's part of your job . . . ?"

"Some of my clients do have extremely

complicated ledgers," Brown said tersely.

It was the "tersely" that told me how close I'd come to the truth. The next card got me even closer.

"And there we go. This is the recent past, and that's the universe handing you a nice big lump of money — or the chance to get your hands on one, anyway. Is this making more sense to you now?"

"Yes and no," Brown said grimly (which is a lot like saying something tersely, only now you're scowling). "I'd like to know what the point is."

"Wouldn't we all?"

Brown straightened up in his seat, body tense, gaze hard.

"No. Really," he said. "What is your point?"

"It's not *my* point, it's the cards'. But if you're in a rush all of a sudden, we can hurry them up."

I flipped over the next card.

"For possible outcome: the Wheel of Fortune. That's a simple enough message. What goes around comes around. I hope you've been a little ray of sunshine everywhere you've gone. Moving on to the near future . . ."

"Cups again. The five this time. Sorry, but do you see how many of those cups are knocked over? This is a card about being bummed because things didn't go your way. It's not looking good for your quest. So let's see how you might handle that. This next card is just about *you.*"

"Looks like your mom wasn't that far off about you after all. You're the Knight of Swords. You've been looking for new challenges, adventure, the chance to prove yourself. A battle to fight — or a quest! But the card's reversed. You're overconfident. In fact, you're about to fall right off your horse. Or maybe it's already falling on you. But let's take a look at what's around you.

Maybe that'll be a rosier picture."

"Sorry. Rosy it isn't. The Seven of Wands is all about conflict, and it looks like you're going to be surrounded by it. Now, the next card — it's in the position most readers call 'hopes and fears,' which I still don't totally understand, to be honest with you. But let's see what we've got."

"Looks like 'hope' to me. Unless you fear a victory parade . . . and I'm guessing you don't. So you're hoping to ride home in triumph, a conquering hero. I know: 'Duh,' right? But remember the near future card? The Five of Cups? That's not matching this. So let's take a look at the last card: the ultimate outcome."

"Ooo. That right there is what they used to call 'the agony of defeat.' It's not looking too good for your quest — or for any of your plans, really. You might want to . . . what?"

Brown was scowling at me, arms crossed, head tilted.

It was a look that said *enough.* And didn't say it nicely.

I had no idea how long he'd been staring

at me like that. I'd become so absorbed in the cards, I'd stopped watching the person they were telling me about.

That was a first. And a last, I promised myself.

"Keep your eye on the birdie," Biddle used to tell me. The birdie being your pigeon. Your mark.

In other words: *Stay on your damn toes, kid.*

The cards had given me a pretty good idea what "Mike Brown" might be. But they couldn't tell me what he was going to do next.

"So that's all I'm going to get from you?" he growled. "Mumbo jumbo and threats?"

"I haven't threatened you."

"Yeah, sure. You were just telling me what the cards said, right?"

"Exactly."

"Fine. Have it your way."

He stretched a hand out toward the heavy crystal ball on the bookshelf . . .

. . . and took one of the business cards I kept beside it in a little plastic holder. He glanced down at the card, then tucked it into his shirt pocket.

"You'll be hearing from me again, *'Alanis.'* "

Brown stood and began striding away.

"I really wasn't threatening you," I called after him. "I was just calling 'em like I saw 'em."

I heard the man scoff as he stomped through the shop. After the front door had opened and closed, Clarice and Ceecee appeared in the doorway to the reading room.

"What was that all about?" Ceecee said.

"Who sent him?" said Clarice.

I answered both questions at the same time.

"I have no idea."

Which wasn't true, strictly speaking. I had an idea. I just didn't like it.

"Anyway — no use worrying about it now," I said. "It's closing time. Did that old guy ever come out of the restroom?"

Ceecee furrowed her brow.

"Old guy?" said Clarice.

"Oh, god," I groaned.

I got up, stepped past the girls, and headed down the hall to the bathroom. The door was still closed, the light still on inside.

"Excuse me," I said. "Sir? Are you . . . uh . . . are you almost finished?"

There was no response.

I knocked softly.

"Sir? Everything okay in there?"

Still no response.

"Great," I sighed.

I steeled myself, then put my hand on the doorknob and turned.

The door was unlocked.

Thank god for small favors. We weren't going to have to kick the door in.

I pushed it open assuming I was going to find the old man slumped over on the john, trousers around his ankles. I assumed wrong.

The old man wasn't dead. He was gone.

COPPE
COUPES
3
CHALICES
COPAS
KELCHE
BEKERS

The DJ just put on "We Are Family," so you grab your goblet and hit the dance floor with your gal pals. It's time to celebrate the deep, strong bonds that only family and the best of friends share, and you should revel in it while you can. Time might turn those grapes overhead into red, red wine, but some are bound to sour, too. And you won't necessarily know which have gone bad until you've taken a taste.

Miss Chance, *Infinite Roads to Knowing*

We checked the little office at the back of the house. We checked the apartment Clarice and I shared upstairs. We checked the other bathroom and the closets and the parking lot out back. We even checked under the beds. (Just because the guy we were looking for was a senior citizen didn't mean he wasn't a perv.)

Nothing. The old man was gone.

"Did you look *in* the toilet?" Clarice asked me. "Maybe he fell in."

I gave that the flat "ha ha" and eye roll it deserved.

"I bet he just turned the wrong way and went out the back door by mistake," Ceecee said. "Or he was too embarrassed to go out the front way, so he sneaked out."

"You're right — it had to be one or the other," I lied. Then I went right on lying by adding, "It doesn't matter anyway. I'm sure we'll never see him again."

We were back upstairs in the apartment's little living room, and Clarice dropped back onto the couch like she was doing the Nestea plunge.

"It's that other guy that weirds me out," she said. "The cop or whatever he was. When he left he was totally, like, 'I'll be back.' "

Clarice croaked out "I'll be back" Arnold Schwarzenegger–style, so that it sounded like someone simultaneously saying "aisle bebock" and belching.

Ceecee squinted at her, obviously mystified.

I was now old enough to see the day when the average teenager (Clarice didn't qualify) couldn't spot a *Terminator* reference. My time had clearly passed. If we'd been Eskimos, I would have crawled out onto the ice to die.

First things first, though.

I walked over and pushed Clarice's legs off the couch.

"Up," I said.

"Hey!" she protested.

I grabbed her hands and pulled her to her feet. "Out."

Clarice yanked her hands free.

"Okay, okay! We'll go! *Geez,*" she said. "I've never seen you so excited to get together with Victor."

"What can I say? My loins are on fire, and only your gym teacher can quench the flame."

That had the intended effect.

"Ewww!" cried Clarice.

"Ugh," said Ceecee.

They turned and scurried out of the room.

"Have fun!" I called after them.

"You'd better not be up here gettin' busy with Victor when I come back!" Clarice said.

"No promises!"

There was another "ewww" as the girls scrambled down the stairs, then I heard them turn and hurry out the back door. Once they were gone, I just stood there a moment listening to the utter silence, waiting to be certain it *was* utter silence and that I was totally alone.

When I was sure, I began giving the place the once-over again, slowly this time. Looking for anything out of place, which might have been pointless, given that I lived with a teenager. What was *in* place? Still, I needed to try.

Had half the drawers in the kitchen been left open before? (Yes, actually.)

Had Clarice's dirty clothes been spread over that much of the floor? (Again, yes.)

Had the painting of poker-playing dogs

over the television been slightly askew? (Apparently my mother had developed some pretty questionable taste in art in the years we were apart. And again, yes — the painting was always a bit crooked.)

I checked the apartment upstairs, I checked the office downstairs. Everything was a mess. But it looked like *our* mess. That was the problem with messes, though. They were so messy. If someone added to it, it was hard to spot.

I vowed to keep the place more orderly in the future — and immediately scoffed at myself.

Living with a teenager, remember?

I re-vowed to hire a cleaning lady. *That* was a promise I could keep.

Again, I found myself just standing there for a while. Not listening for anything this time. Trying *not* to listen.

"You know what's going on here," a part of me was saying.

"Just sit right back, and you'll *la la laaaaa,*" the rest of me was singing with its fingers in its ears. "A tale of a *la la laaaaa* . . ."

It didn't work. I could still hear that other part of me — the part that was cynical and suspicious and really, truly didn't want to be. Not now. I'd have to find another way to block it out.

And then it hit me. Just the thing — and it was time to head in that direction anyway.

Musical me switched to a new tune.

"*La la laaaaa la-la* in Margaritaville . . ."

The margaritas were on the house. Lupe, the night manager at El Zorro Azul, had a superstitious uncle who'd been slowly handing over his savings to a local "psychic" called Madame Jezebel. (I hadn't learned Madame Jezebel's real name yet, but I knew her family all too well: she was one of the Grandis who'd been my personal Unwelcome Wagon ever since I'd come to Berdache.) I hadn't been able to convince Lupe's uncle not to trust fortunetellers, but at least I'd transferred his trust to one who wouldn't bilk him: me. He got free weekly readings; I got free drinks. It was a good deal.

Too good this particular night. I was on my third margarita and my second basket of chips before I realized Biddle was late.

My blood turned to ice. (Which wasn't a huge change, seeing as it was already 50 percent margarita.)

What if he wasn't coming?

What if I'd been too guarded, too standoffish with him?

What if he'd changed his mind and left town?

What if something happened to him after he left the store?

What if he'd just slipped into the booth beside me and I was so preoccupied — not to mention buzzed — I hadn't even noticed him come in?

"I like this place," Biddle said. "You always get the best Mexican at a hole in the wall. 'Course, half the time you get Montezuma's revenge, too."

I looked at him in the dim light. (Lupe kept the lights low, probably to make it that much harder to notice what a hole in the wall the place really was.)

"You came," I said.

I'm sure Biddle was impressed with the observant adult I'd grown up to be. "You came." "So . . . you're not dead." Just call me Sherlock.

"Of course I came," Biddle said. "I see you again after all these years and I'm gonna stand you up at a Mexican joint?" He squinted at me, then pointed at my half-empty margarita glass. "How many of those have you had?"

"How 'bout I show you?"

I turned toward the cash register at the front of the restaurant. Lupe was hanging out there, watching us out of the corner of her eye. I waved her over.

She was a plump, pretty fiftysomething, and Biddle turned his smile on her as she came our way.

"I'd like to get Jefferson caught up with me," I told her when she reached our table. "I'll pay."

Lupe swiped a hand at me. "Your money's no good here."

She turned and walked away.

"Only time I ever heard that was when I was trying to pass a queer fifty," Biddle said. "Looks like you've already got some friends in this town."

I nodded. It was true — and I was still getting used to it.

I'd never had friends growing up. We never stayed in one place long enough for me to find any. Even if I had, the friendship wouldn't have lasted long. My mother would have seen to that.

"A friend?" she'd scoffed at me once, as if I'd asked why I couldn't have a unicorn or a magic wand. She pointed at the motel TV. On the screen Dr. McCoy and Mr. Spock were arguing about something while Capt. Kirk tried not to roll his eyes. "There's all the friends you need. And they'll never stab you in the back either. Because they can't."

"I used to think I didn't know how to make friends," I said to Biddle. "But in Berdache, it just seems to . . . happen."

"Maybe it's those vortexes they got in the desert around here. Makes everyone extra groovy."

Biddle eyed me in an amused/bemused sort of way. Berdache was the poor man's Sedona — a slightly seedier New Age tourist trap — and Biddle was obviously wondering how much I'd swilled of the mystical Kool-Aid.

"Not everyone around here is groovy, that's for sure," I said. "As for the vortexes, all they seem to do is make certain people extra gullible."

Biddle's smile broadened. He liked that answer — as I'd known he would. Maybe one day I'd tell him the part he wouldn't like so much.

How much of the mystical Kool-Aid had I guzzled? When it came to the tarot, at least, I was starting to swallow more and more.

Lupe returned to the table with three margaritas on a tray. As she began lining them up in front of Biddle, he shot me an incredulous look.

"You trying to give an old man diabetes?"

Lupe laughed.

"Enjoy," she said, and she turned and walked away.

I picked up my glass and held it out toward Biddle.

"A toast," I said. *"In vino veritas."*

Biddle picked a glass and lifted it up.

"That Spanish?" he asked.

I shook my head. "It's Latin for 'bottoms up.' "

We clinked glasses and took a drink. Or seemed to.

When Biddle put his margarita back down, I gave it a quick look to make sure some had actually gone down his throat. Some had.

My eyes were only on Biddle's drink for a fraction of a second. But a fraction of a second was all he needed.

"You want to know what's really on a man's mind . . . ," he began.

". . . put some booze in his liver," I finished for him.

Biddle looked pleasantly surprised that I'd remembered one of his little mottos.

"You remember that after all these years?"

"Oh, yeah. I remember. A lot. If there's one thing you can say about growing up with you and my mother, it's that it was *memorable."*

The pleasant went out of Biddle's surprise.

Uh-oh, the look on his face said. *Here it comes* . . .

I reached out and patted his hand. It was the first time I'd touched him that day, I realized. It was almost a shock to know for certain that he was real.

"The good stuff I remember all has one thing in common," I told him. "You. You made it bearable, Biddle. I'm glad that I can finally thank you for that."

Before he could react, I gave his hand a squeeze, then drew mine away.

"So," I said, "how *are* you alive? The last time I saw you, you were about to be whacked in a cornfield."

Biddle looked relieved by the change of subject, even if it was to what I can only assume was one of the worst nights of his life.

"There was a lot of confusion when you and your mother escaped," he said. "It gave me a chance to escape, too, and I sure as hell took it. After that, I figured it was for the best for us to stay split up. A black grifter traveling with a pretty white partner and her daughter? Those guys would've found us again within a month."

"What were they after you for, anyway? And whatever happened to them?"

Biddle took another drink — a big one. When he put the glass down, half of his first margarita was gone.

"That was just old business, sweetie," he said. "It's all forgotten now."

I had my rebuttal all lined up. It was going to be quite eloquent, too.

"Oh, yeah?" I was about to say, but Biddle didn't give me the chance.

"Tell me about *you.* How did you and your mother get away?" he added quickly.

So I told him. And just as I was wrapping it up — thinking I'd circle back to his "old business" and my "Oh, yeah?" — he asked me what happened next.

So I told him. And just as I was wrapping it up — thinking I'd circle back to his "old business" and my "Oh, yeah?" — he asked me what happened next.

So I told him. And just as I was wrapping it up — thinking I'd circle back to his "old business" and my "Oh, yeah?" — he asked me what happened next.

Etc.

Etc.

Etc.

It might have been the margaritas that got me rolling. But it was the expression on Biddle's face that kept me going.

He looked like he really wanted to know

— like he was *dying* to know — and I realized I was dying to tell him. About how I finally escaped from Mom. The years I spent drifting alone, struggling to make sense of the "normal" world. The safe, secure, dull, lonely life I'd eventually made for myself as a telemarketer in Illinois. And how I'd finally escaped from that, too, thanks to the White Magic Five and Dime.

I'd never shared the whole story with anyone, either to protect myself or to just keep from freaking people out (which was another form of protecting myself, of course). The only person I'd come close to telling everything to was . . .

I stopped. I wasn't sure how much time had gone by, but Biddle's margarita glasses were all empty, and so was the new one Lupe had brought me while I had been talking.

"What is it, sweetie?" Biddle said.

"There's a compliation . . . compelnation . . . *complication,*" I said. (Four margaritas, remember?) "We need to discuss it tonight. Before we go any further with . . . whatever this is."

Biddle didn't look surprised or wary. But then again, he wouldn't. He was a pro.

Forget being cool as a cucumber, he used to tell me. *You've gotta make that damn cucumber look like a speed-popping hophead compared to you.*

"Complication?" he said to me now.

I nodded. "I'm living with my sister."

Biddle raised his eyebrows at that, but in a way that seemed more curious than surprised.

"Sister?" he said.

I nodded again. "Well, half sister. I guess Mom tried to find a replacement for you at some point, because she's half black . . . which is why she thinks you're her father."

Biddle's eyes widened in a very uncucumbery kind of way. Even a pro has his limits, I suppose.

"Say what?"

"She found some old pictures Mom had of you, and she assumed they were of her dad," I explained. "It didn't seem like there was any harm in letting her go on thinking that. But if she were to see you walking into the shop . . . I think the term for it these days is 'awkwaaaard.' "

Biddle lifted one of his glasses and tried to take a drink. When he remembered it was empty, he put it back, shook his head, and sighed.

"Awkward is right. We'll have to figure out a way around that, though. I'd like to meet her." Biddle flashed me a grin. "Any daughter of Athena Passalis is worth knowing."

Athena Passalis had been the last name my mother worked under.

I couldn't quite bring myself to return Biddle's smile. He'd reminded me of one of the biggest questions I had for him; one I wasn't quite ready to ask.

What did you ever see in that bitch, anyway?

"How's it going, guys?" Lupe called to us from the front of the restaurant.

We were the only customers still there, and Lupe wasn't just hovering by the door, she was holding it open.

Hint hint.

"I think it's time we called it a night," I said. "Thanks, Lupe."

I slid from the booth and started to stand. When my butt was six inches off the seat, my knees suddenly remembered all those margaritas and went wobbly on me. I managed to remain upright by steadying myself with a hand on the table.

I threw a sidelong glance at Biddle to see if he'd noticed. He was pulling a twenty from his wallet and dropping it on the table, seemingly oblivious. Which didn't mean he *was* oblivious, of course.

"You don't have to do that," Lupe told him.

"Honey, in my day if you didn't pay for

your own drinks, you were a floozy," Biddle said. "I'm just protecting my reputation."

Lupe laughed.

Biddle winked at me.

He'd reached the age where he could play Foxy Grandpa. I assumed he could play Cranky Cuss and Addlebrained Oldster, too, when it suited him.

The roles had changed, but he hadn't. Not deep down. That I was sure of.

I took a deep breath, stepped away from the table, and was relieved to find my knees in a more cooperative mood.

Biddle and I walked out into a crisp, chilly desert night.

"So," I said. "What now?"

"I figure I'll go back to my motel room and catch a little TV. Nothing sobers you up faster than watching the news. Then I'll probably call it a —"

"What now for *us,* Biddle."

"Oh. Well. I feel like we still have a lot of catching up to do. A lot to talk about. I'd like to keep at it . . . if it's okay with you."

I pretended to think it over just to call his bluff. "Come on — like I'm going to let you get away again after one round of margaritas," I said. "There's so much I'm dying to know."

We smiled at each other awkwardly, then

hugged even more awkwardly.

I pulled out one of my business cards and tucked it into his shirt pocket.

"Call me before you pop in next time, alright?" I said.

Biddle laughed and nodded. "Want a ride home?"

"Nah. It's a short walk and a beautiful night."

"You sure?"

"The fresh air will do me some good. See ya 'round, Biddle."

"Alright. See ya 'round, sweetie."

We went our separate ways.

It was 9:30 at the latest, but Berdache was a ghost town. The streets were empty, the store fronts dark. The only sounds were my footsteps on the pavement and the lonely howls of a dog in the distance. All that was missing was a tumbleweed blowing down Main Street.

It was perfectly peaceful, perfectly calm. The perfect place and time to do some serious thinking.

Too bad about all the tequila.

With each step, my head grew lighter, my thoughts fuzzier.

In vino veritas.

In margaritas . . . what's Latin for barf?

It would've been worth the wobbly knees and churning stomach if I'd learned something useful. Instead, there was only one takeaway that I could see: the old "get into someone's brain via their liver" trick wouldn't work on Biddle, and I needed to get my shit together.

I know. That's two takeaways. My math skills had gone out the window somewhere in the vicinity of margarita #3.

As I stepped off the corner of Furnier Avenue and Fourth Street, less than a block from the five and dime, the night's perfect peace and calm was obliterated by the roar of a revving engine. I turned toward the sound and saw a dark car racing up Furnier. It was the right time of night for drunks — just look at me — so I played it safe and stepped back onto the sidewalk.

The car rocketed around the corner and shot through the intersection exactly where I would've been if I'd kept heading home.

"Asshole," I muttered.

The car screeched to a stop.

"Whoa," I said. "Bad driving. Great hearing."

I stood there staring at the car, not quite able to blink the license plate or the make into focus, and waited for the driver to pop out and yell either "Sorry!" or "Who are you calling an asshole?"

But after a moment, the car simply roared off. It zipped right at the first corner, and a few seconds later I heard the squeal of tires as it took another fast turn. I started across the street, shaking my head.

When I was halfway across the intersection, I heard the distant squeal *again,* but louder this time. The rumble of the engine was growing louder now, too.

I glanced back and saw the car racing up Furnier Avenue. The driver had circled the block.

I darted to the other side of the street and hopped behind a lamppost just to be safe.

The car careened through the intersection, missing me by less than six feet.

The driver didn't stop this time or zip right at the first corner. Instead, the car just kept speeding up Fourth Street, the taillights fading into distant red blurs before disappearing altogether.

I stepped away from the lamppost and looked up at the bright white stars in the cloudless sky.

"Really? Again?" I said to the universe. "I've been trying to be *nice,* and you give me this?"

It had been three weeks since anyone tried to kill me. I'd been hoping for a longer break — like maybe a lifetime — before somebody gave it another go.

No such luck, apparently. The only question now was how much time I'd have before it happened again.

The stars had no comment.

I trudged upstairs to the apartment over the shop, wondering if I should call in backup. If there was one consolation from this latest murder attempt (and *man* it was depressing to find myself thinking about a "latest" murder attempt), it was that it had been pretty incompetent. What kind of killer can't run down a drunk woman in the street? That seems like the kind of thing you'd master in Hit Man 101: Intro to Assassination.

Still, even a crappy assassin can get lucky. And there were innocent bystanders to think of. Clarice and Ceecee were still out on the town, apparently — the five and dime was locked and dark when I came in — but I couldn't help picturing what might happen if the *next* murder attempt happened when they were around.

Who could I call, though?

Victor the straight-laced gym teacher? He already thought I was trouble . . . maybe more than I was worth.

GW the crooked hustler? He was trouble himself.

The police? The locals hated me. (Those murder attempts had come with actual murders attached.) And anyway, call them and I'd have lots of 'splainin' to do — too much.

Biddle? He was the reason I had so much 'splainin' to do . . . and I still didn't even know everything there was to 'splain.

I sank back onto the couch in the little living room and sighed.

I was on my own — which was alright. Been there, done that, went into therapy for it. (Although I was still skipping the therapy.)

My eyes settled on the poker-playing dogs over the television. One of them was holding four of a kind. Lucky son of a (literal) bitch.

Then I noticed something odd about the painting he was in.

It was straight.

The last time I'd seen it — and the five hundred times I'd seen it before that — it had been crooked.

I hopped to my feet and pulled out my phone.

Someone had searched our place. I was sure of it. What I didn't know: whether she or he was still around. I didn't intend to be alone if I got an answer I wouldn't like.

I started to call Victor. I stopped.

I started to call GW. I stopped.

I started to call the phone an indecisive idiot. I stopped.

It wasn't the phone's fault.

I started to call Victor. I didn't stop.

"Hello?"

"Hey, Victor, ol' buddy, ol' pal. Whatcha doin'?"

There was a pause. Not a long one, but long enough to be noticed.

"Not much. Catching a game I DVRed," Victor said. "Uh . . . what are you doing?"

It was the pause that did it. And the wariness in his voice. And even the phrase "catching a game I DVRed." It sent a chill through me. For his sake.

Victor belonged in Sunshineland, where the nice people live. I wasn't going to drag him over the city limits into Shitsville, USA. Not again.

"I need you to help me," I said. "What did I get when we were at Il Finto Italiano with your mom last week?"

"Um . . . you mean what did you order?"

"Yeah. I can't remember."

"Uh . . . eggplant parmesan?"

"That's it! It *was* eggplant parmesan,

Clarice! You gotta try it! It was incredible! Thanks, Victor — you're a lifesaver."

"That's really all you wanted?"

"Yup. Sorry to call so late. Enjoy the game, champ!"

I hung up.

I called GW.

"Alanis! Whazzup?"

"Hey, GW, ol' buddy, ol' pal. Whatcha doin'?"

There was no pause. No wariness. No DVRed game to watch. Just:

"Whatever you need me to do, ol' buddy, ol' pal."

COPPE
COUPES
4
CHALICES
COPAS
KELCHE
BEKERS

Your cosmic bartender is at it again. “Here you go,” he’s saying as he offers you a cool, refreshing cup of Opportunity. “On the house.” But you’re too focused on the empty cups before you — the past — to even see it. You’re so convinced happy hour’s over for you that you’re missing your chance to keep it going. Too bad. Because even the Hand of Fate gets tired after a while, and sooner or later that drink’s going down the drain.

Miss Chance, *Infinite Roads to Knowing*

GW told me he could be over in twenty minutes. But there was no way I was going to just hang out alone until he showed up.

My only choice for company was the competition.

I'd noticed the lights on in the House of Arcana, the occult store directly across the street from the White Magic Five and Dime. I'm pretty sure that Josette Berg, the woman who owned the place, didn't see herself as competition to anyone for anything: in her world there were enough good vibes and rainbows for everybody. Paying customers, of course, can be a little harder to come by, yet Josette had always treated me as a friend, not a rival. I didn't think she'd begrudge me a late-night pop-in.

As I headed across the road (after looking both ways four times), I sent a text message to Clarice.

THINGS HEATING UP HERE. [FLAME EMOJI] CAN YOU STAY AT CEECEE'S TONIGHT?

I could guess what Clarice's response would be.

ICK!!! [YUCK-FACE EMOJI]

But grossing out my little sister was a small price to pay for keeping her out of harm's way.

A call came in while I still had the phone in my hand.

VICTOR CASTELLANOS, it said on the screen.

Maybe the game wasn't very exciting. Or maybe even the good citizens of Sunshineland become suspicious when they get late-night calls about eggplant parmesan.

I wasn't in the mood to figure out which. I didn't answer.

Before heading into the House of Arcana, I paused for a deep breath of crisp night air to clear away the last of the lingering tequila buzz. It was mostly gone already. Nothing sobers you up faster than a break-in and a murder attempt. If you could bottle it, you'd be a millionaire.

"Alanis! I haven't seen you in days! How are you?" Josette said when I walked into her shop. As usual, she was dressed in full

Earth Mother uniform: flowing paisley print kaftan, oversized bead necklace, dangling hoop bracelets, frizzy gray hair flowing free.

"You need us to call the cops?" growled the pot-bellied, bushy-mustached man standing beside her.

Josette's husband, Les, was *not* big on good vibes and rainbows. Or me.

I couldn't blame him. Not only was I the competition, there was the whole two-murders-in-two-months thing. I used to wonder why anyone spoke to Angela Lansbury on *Murder, She Wrote.* Every time you said "good morning" to her, your chances of being bludgeoned to death doubled. Now I was in danger of becoming Berdache's Jessica Fletcher.

"No need for the police," I lied. "I just dropped by to chat."

"That's too bad 'cuz we were on our way out," Les said. He turned to his wife. "Right, babe? Don't wanna miss *Blue Bloods.*"

"Oh, that can wait," Josette said. "We've always got time for Alanis."

She smiled at me.

Les glowered. It was obvious he'd rather spend his time on *Blue Bloods.* Or staring at the wall. Anything but me.

"Just promise there won't be any voodoo

talk," he said. (Les may have been married to a tarot reader, but he wasn't a practitioner — or even a believer — himself.)

I held up three fingers, Boy Scout oath–style. "No voodoo talk. I'll keep it strictly earthbound. For instance: did you guys happen to notice someone sneaking around the five and dime tonight?"

Les rolled his eyes. "Here we go. I'm calling the cops."

"Really — it's not a big deal," I said. "It's just that I thought I heard something outside my place. I might just be getting paranoid, though. Things *have* been a little weird since I came here."

Les began to reply — it was even money on whether he was going to say "no kidding" or "you're tellin' me" — but Josette cut him off.

"I didn't see anyone," she said. "How about you, *honey*?"

The *honey* seemed to be a reminder to Les to play nice.

"No. Me neither," he grumbled. "Want me to go take a look?"

"Thanks, but you don't have to do that," I said. "I've got a friend coming over. I'd just like to hang out and talk until he gets here, if that's okay."

"Of course it is," said Josette.

Les started stomping off.

"I'm gonna look around," he said.

Given the choice between talking to me and bumping into a prowler in the dark, he apparently preferred the latter.

When he reached the door, he looked back at us and said, "And no freebies!"

Then he made his escape into the night.

"It *has* been a while since we did a reading," Josette said. "How about it? On the house."

They were always on the house, which was another reason Les resented me. Not only had Josette been giving the competition all kinds of tarot-reading tips, she'd been doing it for free.

Tonight she probably thought it would be a good distraction for me. In reality it was just the opposite: it was a chance to make some sense of what was happening, and I took it.

"That sounds great, Josette," I said. "There are a few things I've been wondering about."

Josette smiled, pulled a deck from a pocket (who knew kaftans had pockets?), and put it down on the sales counter in front of her.

"Any particular spread?" she asked me.

I picked up the deck and started shuffling.

"My friend'll be here soon, so we don't have a ton of time," I said. "How about a modified Celtic Cross? Six cards?"

"Good choice. What's on your mind tonight?"

I tried to boil it down to something simple (and vague).

"The past," I said. "And the present. And the future."

I put down the cards.

Josette picked them up and started laying out the six-card spread, still smiling.

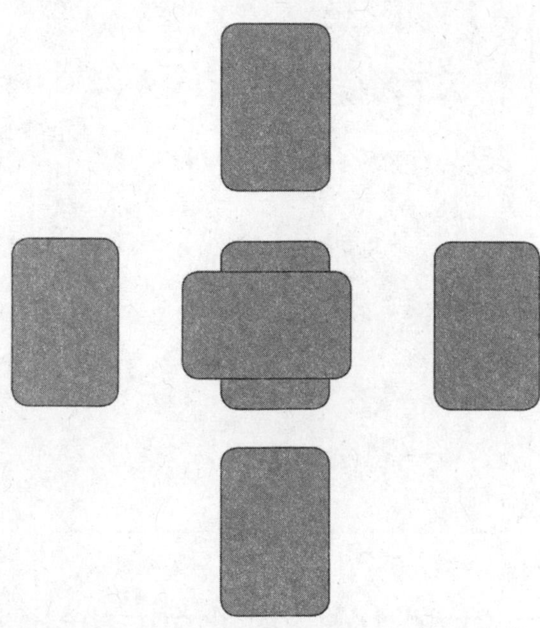

"The past, the present, and the future, huh?" she said. "Perfect. That's exactly what the cards like to talk about."

She reached for the covered card at the center of the spread — the one that represented *me* — and turned it over.

"You wanted to talk about the past," Josette said. "Well, there it is. You're thinking of another time — a time when you were young and maybe there was someone you looked up to or who took care of you. But see how the children are dressed? He's a peasant, and she looks like a little princess. It's like a fairy tale. How realistic is this memory of yours? Have you been idealizing something — or someone — you shouldn't?

"Now the crossing card. The issue you're dealing with."

"The Eight of Swords — you know what that means: you're a prisoner; you feel powerless. So, in combination with the Six of Cups, we're seeing that something from your past — something maybe that you've romanticized to some extent — is still exerting influence over you. And that's got you feeling trapped.

"Moving down to your unconscious, or the root of the problem . . ."

"The Queen of Wands. A domineering woman with a familiar. The black cat. Since we started off with the Six of Cups — the past — I'm assuming they're in your past, too. But though the queen may be gone, she's still with you. You carry her around with you everywhere you go. And she's still on her throne because she still has power over you.

"Now we'll move to the *recent* past. And we see . . ."

"Speak of the Devil. We were just talking about feeling trapped, and there it is again. Chains. Prisoners. So something that used to control you — some unhealthy relationship you were in — is back in your life again. Now, you know that the Devil doesn't have to represent an individual. It usually doesn't, in fact. But it *can* be a person. And when it is, all those other things the Devil can stand for — dysfunction and lies and materialism — are going to be part of the package. So in other words, watch out.

"You know what's next. The conscious mind . . . and what it might lead to."

"Hmm. It's just you and me, so I'll admit

it: that's a bit of a stumper. The Eight of Cups reversed. Well . . . see the hermit moving on alone, leaving the cups — the emotions, the relationships — behind? Maybe that's what you think you've done. Maybe it's what you think you'll need to do. But being reversed, the energy is blocked. Walking away might not be so easy. Like we've been seeing: the past is harder to escape than you thought. That makes sense, right? Tell you what — full money-back guarantee if it turns out I'm wrong.

"Alright, final card. The near future. And . . ."

"Darn. I was hoping for something a little more empowering. I need to learn to stack the deck, don't I? Well, you know what this means. The things that keep us awake and worried. Nightmares. Anxiety. Bad news . . . coming soon. But on the bright side . . .

"Uh . . . um . . .

"At least this reading was free, right?"

■ ■ ■ ■

"Was that helpful at all?" Josette asked as she slipped the deck back into her pocket. "With the past, the present, and the future?"

"The past and the present, yes. It put things in perspective," I said. "As for the future . . . I guess I'll hope you got that part wrong."

I heard the door to the shop open behind me, and I turned to find a glowering Les marching back in.

"Got your prowler," he said. He jerked his thumb over his shoulder. "Caught him skulking around outside the five and dime."

A slim, dark-haired man in a flannel shirt, jeans, and weathered cowboy boots stepped inside.

"He didn't catch me skulking around, actually," he said. "*I* caught *him.*"

"Like hell you did," Les huffed.

"Thanks for coming, GW," I said.

George Washington Fletcher grinned.

"I'm just disappointed it took a B&E to get you to call me again," he said.

"So you two are old friends?" Josette asked.

I heard concern in her voice, and I knew what put it there.

Was this the Devil she'd seen in the cards?

Josette had no idea how many Devils I knew.

"GW's a *new* friend," I said. "He was very helpful during all the hullaballoo last month."

"Oh, he was, huh?" Les said. He scowled at GW.

"The hullaballoo" was the last murder I'd been mixed up in.

"What do you do for a living, 'GW'?" Les asked.

"I'm a freelance financial security consultant," GW said. He jutted an elbow toward me. "Shall we?"

I thanked Josette and a still-scowling Les and took GW's arm.

" 'Freelance financial security consultant,' huh?" I said once GW and I were outside. "Cute."

"Well, people do have a better idea of their financial vulnerabilities once I'm done."

I picked up where Les had left off, scowl-wise.

"Hey, I gave up a *very* promising Friday night because you said you needed help," GW said. "Don't get all judgey on me."

"Sorry. You're right."

I turned away to check the road. There were no headlights zooming toward us, no distant screeching of tires.

I started tugging GW across Furnier Avenue.

"What's the rush?" he said.

"I'll show you when we get upstairs."

"Ooo. Suddenly my Friday night sounds pretty promising again."

I shot GW another glare.

"Now that one I deserve," he said with a grin.

I shook off the glare and rolled my eyes and smiled. In less than a minute, GW had reminded me of all the reasons I had to *not* call him. Still, I was glad he was there.

Just before we got to the White Magic Five and Dime, my phone pinged. It was a text from Clarice.

ICK!!! [YUCK-FACE EMOJI]
BUT HAVE FUN . . .

I saw that I had one voicemail message, too. It could wait.

Once we were inside the five and dime, I gave GW the Reader's Digest Condensed Books version of my day.

Biddle comes back from the dead.

Some kind of cop pops in for a reading.

An old man flushes himself down my toilet.

A driver tries to go Mad Max on me.

And the capper —

I held out my hand toward the painting over the TV.

"Dogs start playing poker?" GW said.

"No. They've been doing that for decades. What's new is the way that painting's hung. It was crooked when I left the house tonight. Now it's straight."

"You think someone cased the joint?"

"Yes," I said. "Do freelance financial security consultants really still say 'cased the joint'?"

"No. These days they say 'got the 411 on the hizzouse.' "

"Or they would if they were Snoop Dogg and it was 1999."

"Maybe I'm not as up on FFSC lingo as I used to be. Did I mention I'm going straight?"

"No. Are you?"

"I just mentioned it, didn't I?"

"Yes. *Are you?*"

"Would I lie to you?"

I gave GW a look.

"Let me rephrase that," he said. "Would I lie to *you*?"

I didn't drop the look.

"Let me rephrase that again," he said. "Why do you think people are sneaking into your house to straighten your velvet paintings?"

"I don't know. But I don't think it's a coincidence *when* they started."

"It's about Diddle?"

"It's about *Biddle.*"

"That's what I said," GW lied. (It didn't take long to get an answer to *that* question.) "Anyway, there's not much we can do about it tonight. It's after 10 o'clock. The whole town's half asleep on the couch watching *Dancing with the Stars.*"

"Blue Bloods."

"Whatever. The point is, Berdache is dead. Practically the whole state's dead. We can figure out what to do in the morning."

"You're right. We may as well call it a day."

"Sounds good to me," GW said. He plopped onto the couch, picked up the remote control, and flicked on the TV. "So . . . *Dancing with the Stars* or *Blue Bloods*?"

I snatched the remote from his hand and hit the power button.

"Try *Searching the House Again,* followed by *Making Sure No One Can Get in.*"

"Aww. Those sound boring," GW said.

He followed me downstairs anyway.

■ ■ ■ ■

We searched the house again. We made sure no one could get in. Then we headed upstairs.

GW went straight to the couch.

"Got any popcorn?" he said as he stretched out again.

"Sure. Help yourself."

GW sat up and stared at me.

I was heading for my bedroom.

"You're going to sleep?" he said.

I nodded. "It's been a long day. A long, *weird* day. With four margaritas. I'm cashed."

"I was hoping we could discuss the situation further. Fill me in more on the backstory. Hash out how we want to proceed."

"Over popcorn?"

"Well . . . afterwards we'd chill."

"Sorry. I'm not in a chilling mood. There are extra pillows and blankets in that closet over there, or you could just sleep in Clarice's room. She won't be back tonight. See ya in the morning."

I stepped into my bedroom.

"Alanis," GW said.

I stepped back out.

"I'm glad you called me . . . even if it was

just 'cuz you need a cheap bodyguard," GW said. "But wouldn't I do better guarding if you kept your body closer to mine?"

GW gave me his most charming grin. It was a pretty good Sly Rogue Special — 7 out of 10 on the Han Solo scale.

It wasn't good enough.

"Adjoining rooms will be close enough for now," I said. "Good night, GW . . . and thank you again for coming."

I went back into my bedroom and closed the door.

Despite the long, weird day and the four margaritas, I couldn't fall asleep right away. Instead I lay in bed thinking. About Biddle. About my close call with the (almost) hit-and-run car. And about the man eating popcorn (I'd heard the popping) on my couch not thirty feet away.

GW's smile hadn't changed my mind about where he'd spend the night, but it did make me feel more guilty about asking him to come over. Yes, he was a "freelance financial security consultant." Yes, he was a Sly Rogue. But he'd backed me up before, and now he was doing it again, all because . . . why? He liked me?

Yet I kept him at a distance. I hadn't called in weeks. And I wasn't so tired now I couldn't get up and chill with him a *little.* But I didn't.

Was I just using him? Or was I afraid to let him get close because of the other Sly Rogues I'd had in my life? Was I so intent on not being my mother I'd pass up a chance at a decent guy? Well, decent to me, anyway.

And speaking (or at least thinking) of decent guys, I still hadn't even listened to the message from Victor. Shouldn't I haul myself back out of bed and . . . Buck Rogers and Scrappy-Doo . . . naked at school on the first day of class?

I'd drifted into dreams.

I was jerked out of them by the sound of distant pounding.

Someone was knocking on the front door. Hard and steady.

Rap-rap-rap.

Pause.

Rap-rap-rap.

Pause.

Rap-rap-rap.

It was a knock I knew well.

GW knew it, too.

"Think they're here for you or for me?" I asked him when I stumbled out of my bedroom.

GW sat up and brushed popcorn crumbs

off his chest.

"It's your place," he said. "And I haven't done anything. Lately."

"Because you've gone straight, right?"

"Well, I'm trying."

Rap-rap-rap.

Pause.

Rap-rap-rap.

"Tell you what," GW said. "Why don't you get the lay of the land while I do a little reconnoiter around the perimeter?"

"In other words, why don't I go talk to the cops while you see about sneaking out the back?"

"I like how I put it better."

Rap-rap-rap.

Pause.

I sighed.

"Fine. We'll do it your way," I said.

I started toward the stairs.

GW cleared his throat.

When I glanced back at him, he dropped his gaze to my legs.

"Forgetting something?" he said.

"Oh. Right."

I wasn't wearing pants.

You never know what you'll get if you pay me a visit before my first cup of coffee.

Rap-rap-rap.

"Alright, alright! I'm coming!" I shouted.

I ran back into my bedroom, pulled on some sweatpants, and headed downstairs. GW followed me as far as the hallway at the bottom of the staircase.

"FYI," he said, "if they *are* looking for me, I ain't here."

He gave me a thumbs-up.

Rap-rap-rap.

I headed up the hall toward the front door.

Rap-rap.

Pause.

There was no third knock this time. The cop saw me coming.

And I saw him.

I almost turned around and ran back upstairs.

No, I thought. *Not already. Not when we'd just found each other again . . .*

I forced myself to open the door and say good morning to Daniel Burby, the Berdache Police Department's one and only homicide detective.

"You're not here to pick up a fresh bag of healing crystals, I assume," I said.

Burby was baby-faced but utterly stone-faced, too. He usually looked like a constipated eighth grader. This morning was no different.

"Can I come in?" he asked flatly.

"Of course."

I moved back to let Burby in (and keep myself between him and GW at the end of the hall, though he'd probably ducked out of sight already).

"What can I do for you today, Detective?" I said.

Burby pulled the front door closed behind him.

"Do you know a man named Robert Dryja?"

Not already not already not already not already.

"The name doesn't ring a bell. Why?"

Burby reached inside the jacket of his baggy Men's Warehouse suit and pulled out a small, clear plastic bag. He held it up for me to see.

Inside it was a business card.

Seeing * Guiding * Helping
★ THE WHITE MAGIC ★
Five & Dime
455 Furnier Avenue
Berdache, Arizona
(928) 522-2137
whitemagic5dime@yahoo.com

"Mr. Dryja was found murdered this

morning," Burby said. "And this was in his pocket."

COPPE
COUPES
5
CHALICES
COPAS
KELCHE
BEKERS

Bummer, dude. Just look at all that Kool-Aid someone spilled. And it was grape — your favorite flavor. So go ahead and give yourself a moment to wallow. That's what this card's all about. Oh, the waste. Oh, the mess. Oh, the humanity! But guess what's right behind you: more goblets! Are they filled with your beloved Kool-Aid? Or is it Country Time Lemonade or Crystal Light or perhaps even the dreaded Tang? You won't know until you stop focusing on the catastrophe you think is before you and take a look around.

Miss Chance, *Infinite Roads to Knowing*

I locked my knees so they wouldn't wobble. A couch and chair were just a few steps away, in the store's waiting area, but I wasn't going to use them. Not with Burby already staring at me like "I did it! Love, Alanis" had been written on the back of that business card in Biddle's blood.

"Oh my god," I said. "Who was he?"

"That's what I'm trying to work out," Burby said, sliding the bag with the business card back into his suit pocket.

"How was he killed?"

"Violently."

Little prick. As if I hadn't figured that out myself.

Some of my anger and disbelief and sorrow must have showed, because Burby narrowed his eyes.

"You sure you didn't know him?" he said. "Robert Dryja? Bob? Five foot ten? One hundred and eighty pounds? Forty-eight years old?"

That did it. I couldn't keep my knees locked any longer. If I didn't sit down, I was going to fall down.

I stumbled to the waiting area and dropped onto the couch.

Burby recognized the shock. What he did see was the *relief.*

"What is it?" he said. "You do know him?"

"White guy?" I said. "Short grayish hair?"

"Yeah. That's right."

I didn't say "whew!" — that'd be a bit of a giveaway — but I definitely felt it. For the second time in less than twenty-four hours, Biddle had risen from the grave.

It was the customer who'd set off my cop radar the day before who was dead.

"A man matching that description *was* in the store yesterday," I told Burby. "And now that I think of it, he did take a business card. But he didn't call himself Robert Dryja. I think he said his name was Brown."

"What did he want?"

I shrugged, which didn't count as a lie in my book. For that you usually need words. And hey — I *didn't* know what Dryja/Brown had wanted. Just that he'd been after *something.*

"He poked around a bit, got a reading, then left," I said. "He told me he was an accountant from back east. Maryland or Delaware — I don't remember which. He said he was here for a convention in Flagstaff. Model trains."

"What?"

"That's what he said the convention was about. Model trains."

"And you believed him?"

"People who build model trains don't have conventions?"

"So you're saying that my murder victim came to see you and lied about who he was and why he was in the area? But he has no connection to you, and you have no idea who he really is?"

"No. I'm saying a man who seems to meet the description of your murder victim got a reading in my store, and he said his name was Brown and that he was an accountant who'd come to Arizona because he likes model trains. That's it. How you interpret that is up to you."

Burby glared at me. His interpretation was written all over his face.

Bullshit.

"You seem pretty shook up by the death of a total stranger," he said.

"He was one of my customers. I was talking to him just yesterday. I'm not supposed to react to his *murder*?"

That shut Burby down, but it didn't shut him up. He had more questions to ask.

What time had "Mr. Brown" come into the White Magic Five and Dime? (Around 7.)

Did he say why he'd come in? (No.)

Was he alone? (Yes.)

Burby didn't bother asking how the reading had gone, which was fine by me. I do a spread for a guy who's about to be murdered, and I don't scream and yell, "Run for it!" It didn't say much for my skills as a fortuneteller. I did remember telling him his trip wasn't going to go as planned, but in hindsight that was a bit of an understatement.

Burby scribbled in a notebook as I spoke, then flipped it closed and put it in a coat pocket.

"Alright — that's all for now," he said. "I'll be back if . . ."

I think he wanted to say "I find out you're lying."

He settled for "I have more questions."

He turned to go but stopped when he reached the door.

"You know, you've got a bad habit of poking your nose into police business," he said. "This time leave it to the professionals."

He didn't wait for a response. He just left.

He wouldn't have liked what I had to say anyway.

"What a tool," I heard GW say. "He has a big-enough stick up his ass to start his own 84 Lumber."

He stepped through the hanging beads that separated the hallway from the rest of the store.

"You okay?" he asked as he came toward me.

"Yeah. I am now."

"For a second there, I thought your ol' buddy Biddle was toast."

"He still might be. Whatever's going on, he's in the middle of it, which means we're in the middle of it with him."

GW came to a sudden, stiff stop.

"What do you mean?" he asked warily.

" 'We' as in me and Clarice, GW, not you and me," I told him. "People came into this place yesterday — into our *home* — looking for something. And now one of those people is dead. Until I figure out what's going on, Clarice and I aren't safe."

GW cocked his head and gave me a wry "here we go again" look.

"What about leaving this to the professionals?" he said.

I sighed.

"Unfortunately, when it comes to Biddle's world," I said, "I *am* the professional."

COPPE
COUPES
6
CHALICES
COPAS
KELCHE
BEKERS

Aww, ain't that cute? That sweet peasant boy is giving the little lady of the house flowers. That's just how it used to be, right? The children of the nobles and the serfs playing together? Darling little princesses eagerly accepting the affections of adoring slaves? Or is that just how we choose to remember it? Are we forgetting the callouses on the boy's hands, the mud on his boots, the resentment on his face? Think hard. Nostalgia's great at creating both pretty pictures and crummy history.

Miss Chance, *Infinite Roads to Knowing*

For a moment, it looked like GW was about to say, "Well, good luck with that. Call me when it's over." The front door of the five and dime was less than twenty feet away. A dozen steps and he'd be free of the whole mess.

Instead, he walked over and sat beside me on the couch.

He didn't touch me. There was no hand on the knee, no arm around the shoulders. But just by plopping his butt down beside mine, he'd made a statement.

Here I am. With you.

What now?

"I'd call Biddle if I could," I said. "But I don't have a number and I don't know where he's staying or what name he's using. So I'll have to start from the other direction."

"Which is?"

"The dead guy. Dryja. He was looking for

something connected to Biddle — probably following Biddle to find it. And other people are looking for that something, too."

"How do you know that?"

"*Somebody* made the dead guy dead."

"Yeah. But isn't it kind of obvious who that somebody could be?"

It *was* obvious. Blinking-neon-sign obvious. Bat-signal-over-Gotham obvious. "Why hasn't Liberace ever gotten married?" obvious. Yet it still took me a moment to see it.

"Biddle?" I said. "No. That's not his style."

"How can you be sure? You told me you haven't seen the man in, like, thirty years. When you knew him you were a kid. He was nicer to you than your mom was, so you have fond memories of him. That doesn't mean he's a good guy."

"He's not a good guy. He's a grifter through and through."

"Hey, grifters can be good guys!" GW protested. "In their own way."

"You didn't let me finish. He's a grifter . . . but not a killer. You know there's a difference."

"Sure, there is. But grifters get themselves in some pretty gnarly situations, like when more than one person wants the same thing, say. What if Biddle and Dryja got into it over the whatever, and Biddle killed the guy in self-defense?"

I shook my head. "Biddle's got three decades more mileage on him than Dryja did. If they 'got into it,' I doubt it would be Biddle who walked away. And even if that is how it went down, it just makes it all the more important to find Biddle before he gets into it with somebody else."

"Alright. So where do we begin?"

I smiled at the "we." Grifters *can* be good guys, in their own way.

And then a voice came to me. The voice I heard in my head almost more than my own.

Biddle. Talking to me when I was a kid. Telling me why drifting from town to town with him and my mother, never going to school, was actually the best education I could ask for.

"Readin', writin,' and 'rithmetic aren't so important," he'd said. "All you really need to know is geometry."

"Geometry?" I'd asked — as he'd known I would.

"Angles, sweetie," he'd said with a grin. "Always be calculatin' the angles."

So I calculated.

If A = Something People Wanted . . .

And B = Dryja . . .

And C = Biddle . . .

And D = GW . . .

A − B − C + D = D + A = $$$

Or something like that. I still suck at 'rithmetic.

As for angles — those I tried to push out of my head, other than the one GW had asked about.

Where to begin?

"Well, seeing as I'm about to ignore a direct warning from the police and interfere in an active homicide investigation, I may as well start where I'm probably going to end up," I said. "I'll call my lawyer."

When I inherited the White Magic Five and Dime from my mother, I also inherited a black Cadillac, approximately $50,000, around two dozen enemies (most of them either graced with Berdache PD badges or the last name "Grandi"), and one Eugene Wheeler.

Eugene had been Mom's lawyer, but he'd had no idea what a piece of work she really was. If he had, he wouldn't have stuck around for me to inherit. Eugene's so straight he makes your average Rotary Club member look like Caligula. He tolerates me because he knows I'm trying to make amends for my mother's wicked, wicked ways — even if that means resorting to them myself from time to time.

"I'm on the sixteenth hole and I'm five under par, so this better not be something that'll throw me off my game," he said.

This in lieu of "hello" or "good morning" or even "what do you want now?"

"I'm just calling to gossip," I said.

"Gossip?"

I could practically hear Eugene's scowl over the phone.

"Sure. It'll be fun," I said. "Which Kardashian's getting divorced next? Who or what is Lady Gaga dating? Is it true what they say about Aunt Jemima and the Pillsbury Doughboy?"

"Alanis —"

"Didja hear about the murder in town last night?"

"Oh," Eugene said.

There was a pause. Then a sigh.

"Enquiring minds want to know," I said.

"Well, they'll have to enquire somewhere else. I don't know anything about it. I don't *want* to know anything about it. And if you're about to tell me that I, as your attorney, *need* to know something about it, I'm going to say, 'Save it for the arraignment.' "

"Don't worry, Eugene. You don't need to know a thing. I just thought you might have been dishing with your friends at the courthouse again."

"It's Saturday morning, Alanis," Eugene said. "And I don't 'dish.' "

"Sorry. No. Of course not. You network with your colleagues . . . some of whom occasionally drop useful tidbits about events of the day."

"Well, no one's dropped any tidbits on me about any m— activity of that sort. Alright? Can I get back to my game now?"

"Who are you playing with?"

"The pastor of my church. I've told him about you, actually. Want me to put him on? I bet you and he could have a truly illuminating conversation."

"Uh-oh! A customer! Gotta go!"

I started to hang up, but Eugene managed to get in the last word.

"I'm billing you for this!"

"That sounded productive," GW said.

"Hey, it was worth a try. If he'd heard something, maybe I wouldn't have to do this."

I opened the Web browser on my cell phone and typed in "hotels Berdache Arizona."

"We're getting a room?" GW said.

I didn't dignify that with an answer (though I did dignify it with a brief glare).

"Robert Dryja wasn't a local, and his body was found within the jurisdiction of the Berdache Police Department," I said. "Therefore . . ."

"He was probably staying at one of the hotels in town. Gotcha. So what are you gonna do? Call every one and ask, 'Any sudden vacancies?' "

"Pretty much. How would you do it?"

"Ancient Chinese secret." GW pulled his cell phone from his jeans pocket. "But I'll bet my way's faster."

"You're on."

GW stalked off up the hallway, hunched over his phone.

I picked the first hotel listing that came up and hit *CALL.*

"Arizona Sunset Inn; how may I help you?"

"Hello, could you connect me to Robert Dryja's room, please? I think he checked in there recently."

"I'm sorry, I can't do that. You don't have a direct number you could try?"

"He's not answering his cell phone. Why can't you just put me through?"

"I'm not allowed to. I'm sorry."

"But he *is* there?"

"I can't say that either."

"Look, I'm his goddamn wife and I'm

goddamn pregnant and my goddamn water just goddamn broke and I can't find the goddamn keys to the goddamn van and he's at some goddamn hotel instead of at the goddamn house because we had a goddamn fight about what to name a goddamn kid who's not even goddamn born yet. Put me through!"

"I really am sorry, ma'am. But honestly, I'm not even supposed to say who *isn't* here."

"Oh, goddamn!"

Click.

"BestRest Suites; how can I help you?"

"Hello, could you connect me to Robert Dryja's room, please? I think he checked in there recently."

"I'm sorry. I can't say if anyone by that name is staying here or not."

"Really?"

"Really."

"You couldn't even say, 'Sorry, wrong suites'?"

"No. It's BestRest policy not to give out guest information of any kind."

"Oh, come on. The Beanie Baby that Bob's been after for twelve years is finally on eBay, and the auction ends in eight minutes. If he doesn't put in a bid *now,* he's gonna lose his shot at Luau the Pig."

"I'm sorry. There's nothing I can do."

"Well, you've made BeanieGranny94 very happy. Looks like she's gonna get Luau for less than $200."

Click.

"Class Act Motel."

"Hello, could you connect me to Robert Dryja's room, please? I think he checked in there recently."

"Call him yourself."

"I am calling him myself."

"Call him on his own phone."

"He's not picking up."

"That ain't my problem."

"Listen — I'm Mr. Dryja's neurologist, and I just saw an X-ray of his skull that looks like a plate of scrambled eggs. One sneeze and the man could be wiping his brains off his face with a Kleenex. I need to speak to him immediately or his life's not worth a —"

"Ain't. My. Problem."

Click.

"Devil's Ridge Lodge, your desert oasis of luxury living. How may I help you?"

"Hello, could you connect me to Robert Dryja's room, please? I think he checked in there recently."

"Oh. Uh. Um . . ."

Bingo.

"May I ask what you're calling about?"

"This might sound weird; I don't know. I hope it does. I met Mr. Dryja yesterday, and this morning someone told me . . . well, let's say I heard a disturbing rumor about him. And I was calling to see if it was true."

"I'm afraid I can't say anything about that."

"Oh my god. So it *is* true!"

"I'm really not supposed to talk about it. I'm sorry."

"Oh, that's okay. I totally understand. I'm sure everyone there must be completely freaked out. You know — him being drowned in the lobby fountain like that."

"What? Is that what people are saying?"

"It's what I heard."

"Well, it's not true. He was out in the . . . I'm sorry, ma'am, but like I told you: there's nothing I can say about that. Have a nice day, and don't forget to check devilsridge lodge.com for special offers on our fine dining and luxury accommodations."

Click.

GW came striding back into the store's

front room with a triumphant look on his face.

"He —," he began.

"Was staying at the Devil's Ridge Lodge," I said. "They found his body outside."

GW gave me a round of polite golf applause.

"But," he said when he was done, "do you know *where* he was outside? Or in what condition?"

"If I did, I would've said."

"Then allow me." GW cleared his throat. "Robert Dryja was found in the parking lot, behind the wheel of his car, shot in the head."

"How do you know that?"

"I told you before. Ancient Chinese —"

"You know someone who works the local hotels," I said. "Who is it: a thief? A hooker? A dealer?"

"All of the above, actually," GW said. He didn't seem to know whether to feel embarrassed or proud. "You know how it is. Friends in low places. I called around till I found one who was on the prowl when the body turned up. Screaming, sirens, flashing lights — that gets noticed at a place like the Devil's Ridge Lodge. It's the swankiest place in town."

"Gasp!" someone said.

And I don't mean someone gasped. I mean someone walked through the front door, stopped, and said "Gasp!" good and loud.

I should have seen it coming. Clarice worked in the shop from 10 to 4 on weekends, but I'd forgotten all about that. (Murder tends to give me a one-track mind, I've learned.)

I turned to find Clarice and Ceecee gaping at GW. They both seemed to be focused on his hair, which completely confused me until I glanced over at it myself.

GW's short, dark hair was mussed and unruly, one side matted down, the other a potpourri of little cowlicks.

In other words: the man had a wicked case of bed head.

Busted — or so the girls thought. I'd kicked Clarice out for some quality time with Victor (supposedly), and when they come back the next morning it's (seemingly) obvious I spent the night with another man.

Clarice didn't say, "Why, you little minx, you!" but given the smirk on her face, she may as well have.

"GW's helping me out with a little situation," I said.

"Oh?" Clarice replied archly.

"You can help, too," I went on.

"Oh?" Clarice said again, minus the sarcasm.

"First, call Marsha and see if she can come in for a shift today. I can't stick around to do readings."

"Clarice can do the readings," Ceecee said, folding her arms and leaning against a nearby bookshelf. "She is a world-renowned expert on tarot cards, you know."

Ceecee grinned. Her round, cherubic face and bright blue hair were directly beside a tarot guide prominently displayed on the top shelf: *Infinite Roads to Knowing* by Miss Chance (aka Clarice and my mother).

I shook my head. "Sorry, but I think most customers are going to be a little skeptical about a fortuneteller who looks like she ought to be using her crystal ball to see the answers to tomorrow's math test."

"But —," Ceecee began.

"Second," I said, "we got a name for that nosy parker who was in here yesterday. See what you can dig up on him."

" 'Nosy Parker'?" said Ceecee.

"The cop or whatever he was," Clarice explained. "What's the name?"

"Robert Dryja."

Clarice rolled her eyes. "Great. May as well be Joe Smith. Does he spell his last name with an 'ew' or an 'ou'?"

I shrugged. "Sorry. No idea."

"Even better," Clarice grumbled.

"And third," I said, "I'm expecting an important phone call at the store soon. If you pick it up, pass along my cell phone number."

"What's it about?" Clarice asked.

"The little situation."

"Which is . . . ?"

"Little. But very situational."

"Fine; be that way. Who'll be calling?"

"A man."

"That's all I get? 'A man'?"

"A seventy-something African American man."

"Better. And his name is . . . ?"

"Not important. And he won't give it to you anyway."

Clarice sighed. "So when this unnamed seventy-something African American man calls about the little situation —"

"He might not know about the little situation."

Clarice sighed again. "So when this unnamed seventy-something African American man calls about whatever he's going to call about, give him your cell phone number."

I nodded. "See? It's not that complicated."

"No. Just annoying."

"You should trust Clarice more," Ceecee told me. "She can handle way more than you let her."

"When I was her age, I *was* handling way more. And I shouldn't have been." I turned to GW, who'd been quietly watching the conversation with a studiously neutral look on his face. "Shall we?"

GW rubbed his stubble-covered chin. "Well . . . I guess I don't have anything better to do today."

He followed me up the hall.

"Hey! Where are you guys going?" Clarice called after us.

"Out" was all I told her.

The truth — "to a hotel" — just wouldn't have sounded right.

COPPE
COUPES
7
CHALICES
COPAS
KELCHE
BEKERS

Welcome to the world's weirdest bar — the one in your head. What's on tap? Oh, the usual: snakes, dragons, laurels, diamonds, castles, heads, some kid from *Peanuts* trick-or-treating as a ghost. But there's no bartender. If you see something you want, you have to reach out and grab it. That's the only way you'll pull one of those kooky visions out of the clouds and into the real world. It's BYOD here: Bring Your Own Dream. Then make it come true by doing something.

Miss Chance, *Infinite Roads to Knowing*

The Devil's Ridge Lodge seemed way too upscale for Berdache — or a murder in the parking lot. It was on the north side of town at the exact spot where civilization (such as it was around there) gave way to desert. The terrain was rocky and parched, yet the hotel was trying awfully hard to look like a chalet in the Alps, with a broad, sloping roof and decks ringing the second and third floors. It may have been 80 degrees in the shade that day, but looking at the place still made you want to pull on a knit sweater and sip hot cocoa by the fire with people named Heidi and Hans.

I cruised by a few times, searching for any sign of Berdache's finest, before pulling into the lot out front. I parked as far as I could from the entrance without being obvious about it.

"Think any of your friends in low places are around?" I asked GW.

He shook his head. "They're not morning people. Or afternoon people, for that matter."

"Of course. Creatures of the night. They've returned to their subterranean lairs till the sun goes down."

"Something like that. They'll probably steer clear of this place for a while, day or night. It'll be getting a little too much attention for their taste."

"Guess that means I'll have to get the scoop on last night the old-fashioned way."

"A séance?"

I rolled my eyes.

"Sorry," said GW. "Tea leaves?"

"Actually —," I began.

"You were thinking you'd go to talk to *him,*" GW finished for me.

He jerked his head at the carport in front of the hotel. A stubby, tanned man was stationed by the entrance in a white, short-sleeved shirt and brown slacks.

"Now I know why you got all dolled up before we left your place," GW said. "You wouldn't get far with a bellman looking like this."

He flapped a hand at his own well-worn flannel shirt and jeans.

I hadn't gotten *that* dressed up — my cashmere turtleneck and corduroys were pure L.L.Bean bourgeois. Yet that was enough to make me look like the Lady of the House (probably a McMansion), while GW would have been the guy who mowed the lawn.

"The clothes alone wouldn't get us what we need," I said. "It's the accessories that make all the difference."

I picked up the pleather purse I'd brought with me and got out of the car.

The bellman smiled cheerfully as I walked up. He had stumpy legs and short but muscular arms and a blocky head covered with a mop of graying hair. Put him in a white tuxedo and he wouldn't have looked entirely out of place yelling "De plane! De plane!" from a bell tower.

"Good morning," he said. "How can Hector help you?"

I looked around. "Hector?"

The bellman pointed at the nametag pinned to his shirt.

HECTOR, it read.

"Oh. Right," I said. "Well, I think we can help each other, actually."

Hector looked puzzled, but in an eager-to-please way, like a dog that has no idea what you're saying but is pretty sure your next words are going to be either "good boy" or "walk." If he'd had a tail, it would have been wagging.

"I heard what happened here last night," I went on. "It's probably all over the news by now."

It didn't have quite the same effect as "bad dog," but it was close. Hector's shoulders slumped, and the smile slid off his face.

"Ah," he said. "That is too bad."

"You know what that's going to do to business."

I nodded at the sliding glass doors leading to the hotel lobby. About thirty yards beyond them a tall gray-haired man stood behind the front desk alongside a plump young woman. The man was pointing at something on a computer screen that obviously made him deeply unhappy, which just as obviously made the woman deeply uneasy. Neither of them were looking our way.

"Looks like the cancellations have already begun," I said.

Hector glanced back at the front desk, then let out a deep, weary sigh. His tips for the day, the weekend, the week, maybe the next several *months* were going up in smoke before his eyes.

"This is how you help?" he said to me.

"No. This is."

I opened my purse and held it so Hector

could see inside.

Resting on top of my keys, billfold, and spearmint Tic Tacs was a roll of tens I'd taken from the emergency cash stash in the White Magic Five and Dime.

"That does look helpful," Hector said. "But Hector would never betray his employers."

"Laura's not asking him to."

Hector squinted at me a moment. Then a sliver of his smile returned.

"You are Laura," he said.

I nodded. "Laura Holt, private investigator. All I'm looking for is information, and whatever I learn won't go any further than my client."

"And who is that?"

I crossed my arms, cocked my head, and said nothing.

Hector's smile grew a little larger.

"You would never betray *your* employers," he said.

"Exactly. We're peas in a pod, Hector. You can trust me to be discreet."

The bellman thought it over a moment. Then he raised a stumpy arm and pointed at the rocky red bluffs on the horizon.

"Hector has to give directions a lot," he said. "Sometimes there is a generous tip."

"I understand."

I started to reach into my purse.

"When we are done," Hector said.

He started to lead me out toward the road. As we walked, he swung his little pointed finger this way and that, as if he were describing the advantages and disadvantages of different roads.

"Hector used to work at a very nice hotel in Sedona," he said. "Then late one night, an old man died in one of the hot tubs. A heart attack. Gone like *that.* And nobody noticed till morning. The old man boiled for hours. 'Hotel Stews Senior Citizen' — that is a headline people won't forget. The place was closed within a year, and it took Hector three more months of looking to find this job." Hector sighed again. "It's been very nice here, too."

"You don't have to explain to me."

"But maybe I want to."

We'd walked all the way out to the street by now, and Hector stopped and pointed to the right. He frowned and shook his head as though warning me away from some particularly chintzy tourist trap down the road.

"I think you had better start asking your questions. There's really not much to point at around here."

"Right. The man who was killed — Robert Dryja. Was he a guest at the lodge?"

"Yes."

"What do you know about him?"

Hector turned and pointed to the left.

"Not much," he said. "He arrived yesterday afternoon at 2:10. He only had one suitcase — a 29-inch gray Samsonite Aspire spinner — so he didn't need any help getting his luggage to his room, which was probably on the third floor because that's where Mr. Raffel, the day manager, has been putting most of the single business guests. From the smile on Mr. Dryja's face and the way he looked around when he walked in, it was obvious that he was not used to staying at such nice hotels. He had an early dinner in the lodge's restaurant with another guest, an angry conversation in the lobby with *another* guest, and a drink in the lodge bar with an attractive young lady who was not a guest. He was shot in his rental car — a black BMW 528i sedan — which was in our parking lot. No one has reported hearing the shot, which means the murder probably occurred between 11 p.m. and 4 a.m., when there is no bellman on duty. The police have been looking for his wallet and his cell phone, which weren't on his body, in the car, or in his room. And he liked nuts and beer."

"Nuts and beer?"

Hector turned to the right again. There was nothing to be seen there but cars on the road and a gas station and a church and distant houses and even more distant cliffs. Nothing to point at unless someone said, "Say, you guys got a big bunch of nothing around here anywhere?"

Hector pointed anyway.

"There was a minibar in his room," he said. "Mr. Dryja drank two Amstel Lights and ate both the mixed nuts and the macadamia nuts. That added $44 to his bill."

"You know, Hector, it's a good thing you didn't know much about this guy. If you knew a lot, I'd be here all week."

I put a confused look on my face and pointed to the left. If the hotel manager was watching us, he'd think Hector was trying to give directions to the dumbest tourist on earth.

"What do you know about the two guests Dryja talked to?" I said. "Not much, I hope."

"No. Not much. The man from the restaurant is Mr. Pichler. He also arrived yesterday afternoon and is staying in our Presidential Suite on the fourth floor. He had two suitcases — matching black 32-inch Rimowa Salsas, very pricey — and did not seem so impressed with the lodge. He is around sixty years old, has long white hair he keeps in a ponytail, has a German accent, and is a generous tipper. The other man arrived yesterday evening with only one small, cheap carry-on bag. He is also around sixty and is heavy and bald. Just looking around the lodge seemed to make him angry somehow. I did not speak with him, but his last name sounds something like 'Buttsiac.' That's what Dryja seemed to call him during their conversation in the lobby. It got a bit loud."

"Could you tell what they were arguing about?"

"No. But Mr. Dryja looked surprised that the other man was there. And money was mentioned. And a grout connector."

"Did you say 'a grout connector'?"

Hector nodded.

"Is that a thing?" I asked.

Hector shrugged.

"Okay. The woman," I said. "Tell me about her."

Hector went back to pointing. "There's not much Hector can say."

"I think you and I define 'not much' differently, Hector."

"No, really. I barely saw her. All I know is that she is not tall and not short and not heavy and not skinny." Hector closed his eyes and concentrated. "And she had blond hair. Shoulder length. And a round face. Big cheeks, like a baby. Big glasses, too. And she was dressed like a professional, not like someone on vacation."

"You mean dressed like a professional or dressed like 'a professional,' " I said. I winked. "I'm winking, by the way."

Hector's eyes popped open. "No! Like a real no-winking professional! Blouse, skirt, heels. We don't have 'professionals' at . . . . hey. That's strange."

"What is?"

"That, that! What I'm pointing at!"

"You've been pointing at nothing for the last five minutes."

"Well, now I am pointing at something! Look!"

I looked.

To our right, perhaps 150 yards away, was the parking lot of the First United Methodist Church of Berdache. In it was a single car — a dark blue sedan of some kind — parked near the road. Light glinted off something inside it from behind the steering wheel.

"I think that woman is looking at us with binoculars," Hector said.

I squinted. I couldn't see the woman or

the binoculars — just a fuzzy blob in the driver's seat and a glimmer that could have been sunlight bouncing off polished glass. But I'd come to appreciate Hector's powers of perception. If he'd said he saw Fat Albert and the Cosby Kids mooning us from the Goodyear Blimp, I'd have believed him.

The dull, distant twinkle of light disappeared, and a moment later the car screeched out into the road and roared away from us. The sound of it was very, very familiar.

At least this time the driver didn't try to run me over.

"Whoa," Hector said. "So it really is like that for you."

"Really like what?"

Hector hummed a few bars of the theme song from *The Rockford Files.*

"You're not going to chase her?" he asked me.

The car was almost out of sight already. I wasn't going to catch it unless it ran out of gas in the next ten seconds.

"I don't do car chases," I said.

Hector looked disappointed.

"But everything else in *The Rockford Files* is 100 percent accurate," I added.

Hector cheered up.

"What did she look like?" I asked him.

"The woman in the car? I don't know. She was too far away."

"How'd you know she was a woman?"

"She was just . . . woman shaped, you know? I'm sorry I can't tell you more than that."

The car disappeared into the distance. With it went any reservations I'd had about getting GW involved. I needed backup — and I needed to start keeping it closer, too.

"You have nothing to apologize for, Hector," I said. "You've more than earned your tip."

I opened my purse, pulled out the roll of bills, and handed it to Hector.

He was a true pro. The money disappeared so quickly he may as well have waved a wand and said "Presto!"

"Thank you, Miss H—"

"Hector," I cut in, "your memory is amazing. But don't you think you could learn to forget certain things from time to time?"

Hector gave me a sly grin.

"Probably . . . whoever you are," he said. "As long as I'm being forgetful, are you sure you can't tell *me* what's really going on?"

I truly can't — because I have no damn idea seemed like a disappointing answer. So instead I said, "Give *me* a $300 tip, and I might tell you."

Hector nodded.

"Have a nice day," he said, and he turned and headed back to his post in front of the hotel.

Another response I didn't want to give: *It's way too late for that.*

Why be sour? And anyway, Hector had been chock full o' leads. I'd taken the initiative and gotten results. Maybe things were looking up.

I walked back to my car. Or tried to, anyway.

It was gone.

COPPE
COUPES
8
CHALICES
COPAS
KELCHE
BEKERS

See the hermit? He's movin' on up (movin' on up) to the top (movin' on up). Not to a deluxe apartment in the sky, but close. He's heading to the mountains. He finally got a piece of the pie (or eight honkin' gold goblets, anyway), and now he's looking for a fresh perspective. Will he find it in the jagged peaks on the horizon or would he be better off staying safe and sound in the lowlands? There's only one way he can answer that. He has to grab his staff and go — and there ain't nothin' wrong with that.

Miss Chance, *Infinite Roads to Knowing*

Reaction #1 to discovering that your car is gone (and your supposed backup/partner with it): *Shit.*

Reaction #2 to discovering that your car is gone (and your supposed backup/partner with it): *I* knew *I shouldn't have given up on Victor so easily*!

Reaction #3 to discovering that your car is gone (and your supposed backup/partner with it): *Shit shit shit!*

Reaction #4 to discovering that your car is gone (and your supposed backup/partner with it): *And I've still got the keys in my purse, too. Credit where credit is due — the guy's good.*

Reaction #5 to discovering that your car is gone (and your supposed backup/partner with it): *Shit shit shit shit SHIT!* (Accompanied by clenched fists and stamping feet.)

Reaction #6 to discovering that your car is gone (and your supposed backup/partner with it): *This is not a disaster. The stakes are too high for me to become emotional over such a minor setback. I will take a deep breath, set aside my feelings of anger and betrayal, and proceed in a calm, rational manner that advances me toward my true goal.*

Unfortunately, I never quite reached Reaction #6.

"Shit shit shit shit SHIT!" I spat, clenching my fists and stamping my feet.

I managed to stop myself, but not because I found peace with being stabbed in the back. I just didn't like being stared at.

"Isn't 'shit' a bad word, Mommy?" said the wide-eyed, pigtailed kindergartener who'd just hopped out of a minivan parked nearby.

Her mother and father shooed her toward the hotel.

"Just keep walking, Brittany," Mommy whispered.

Daddy pointed at the sky. "Ooo — that cloud looks just like Dora the Explorer!"

Brittany reluctantly tore her gaze away from me and looked up.

"No, it doesn't," she said.

"Just . . . keep . . . walking," Mommy grated out.

"Sorry!" I called after the rapidly retreating family. "You're right, Brittany! It *is* a bad word!"

"Look!" said Daddy, doubling his pace and pointing at the clouds again. "It's the Cat in the Hat!"

"No, it's not," said Brittany.

Then they were too far away for me to hear them anymore. Which meant they were too far away to hear *me.*

"Shit," I sighed one last time.

Never mind finding a killer. I couldn't even keep track of my own Cadillac.

I pulled my cell phone from my purse, about to call Clarice and Ceecee for a ride. (Which was really calling Ceecee for a ride. She was the one with a beat-up 2003 Crown Victoria. The only wheels Clarice owned were on a skateboard that never left the back of her closet.)

On my phone's screen were two text messages. The first was from Victor.

DID YOU GET MY VOICEMAIL?

That could wait.

The other was from one "Jacques Strap," number blocked.

DENIED TO PET MYSELF SOMETHING MORE APPROXIMATE CLOTHS. BLACK SOUP!☺

That could wait, too. There were more

important things to do than figure out which bored eleven-year-old was crank-texting me.

I called the White Magic Five and Dime.

"Stuffin' Stiffs'n'Stuff Taxidermy and Party Supplies. Enid speaking," Clarice said.

Caller ID: *such* a double-edged sword.

"Put Clarice on, *Enid,*" I said. "I'm not in the mood for Stuffin' Stiffs."

"Fine. But are you in the mood for major scoopage?"

"That depends. Is it good news major scoopage or bad news major scoopage?"

"Neither, as far as I know. But it is very interesting major scoopage."

"That goes without saying. It's major scoopage. What is it?"

"Robert Dryja is a private detective."

"And a cop!" Ceecee threw in from (by the muffled sound of it) over Clarice's shoulder.

"Dryja is a cop *and* a private detective?" I asked.

"He *was* a cop, *now* he's a private detective," Clarice explained.

"In Philadelphia!" Ceecee added.

"Can you just let me do the talking, please?" Clarice complained.

"Why not put her on speaker phone so we both can talk?" asked Ceecee.

Clarice and I answered her at the same time.

"I hate speaker phone," I said.

"She hates speaker phone," said Clarice.

My sister and I still had a lot to learn about each other, but some things she'd picked up on fast.

"So," I said before there could be any more speaker phone talk, "how'd you find him?"

This time it was Clarice and Ceecee who spoke at once.

"We hacked the International Association of Police Unions database," said Clarice.

"He has a website," said Ceecee.

There was a moment of silence. I assumed some glaring was going on a couple miles away.

"Um . . . what Clarice said," Ceecee mumbled meekly.

"Well, very impressive, ladies, no matter how you did it," I said. "I'm looking forward to hearing more. But that's actually not what I was calling about."

"Oh god — are you in jail again already?"

"I have been in jail *once* since you've known me, Clarice. Why would you think I'd be in again?"

"I don't know. 'Cuz a private eye's been poking around and now you're up to something with GW?"

"Ah. Alright, you got me: jail's not a bad guess. But that's not it. I need Ceecee to get her car and . . ."

My voice trailed off as I spotted what looked like a familiar car heading up the road toward the hotel.

Right make. Right year. Right color.

Wrong car?

". . . check all the fluids and the tire pressure," I said when it turned into the parking lot.

"What?" said Clarice.

I thought I heard a "Huh?" or "Chuh?" from over her shoulder, too. It was hard to tell without speaker phone on.

"Make sure Ceecee checks her fluids and tire pressure," I said. "Proper maintenance is step number one on the road to automobile safety. Did you hear that, Ceecee?"

"Sure, Alanis. If you say so," I heard Ceecee say.

"What were you *really* calling about?" said Clarice.

"Sorry," I told her. "Wrong number."

I hung up just as my black Cadillac came to a stop beside me.

GW rolled down the window and leaned out from behind the wheel.

"What'd I miss?" he said.

"A lot. Most recently, me traumatizing passing children because *my car had disappeared.*"

GW furrowed his brow in confusion. "You didn't get my message?"

I furrowed my brow right back, then unfurrowed it.

"Of course. You're Jacques Strap."

GW bowed his head. "At your service, mademoiselle. It seems to me our mutual friends the police wouldn't approve of what we're doing, so I thought I should switch to a burner phone I happened to have — just in case."

"Do you always 'happen to have' a spare burner phone on you?"

"Not always. Just usually."

"Yeah, well, thanks for telling me. And a decoder ring would've come in handy, too."

"What do you mean?"

I called up the text message from Monsieur Strap and started to show it to GW. As I leaned toward him, I finally noticed something odd: he'd traded his grungy flannel and jeans for a preppy red polo shirt and cargo shorts.

" 'Denied to pet myself something more approximate cloths. Black soup!' " GW read aloud. He grinned. "It was supposed to say, 'Decided to get myself some more appropriate clothes. Back soon!' But I was typing as I drove."

"Of course." I rolled my eyes. "Autocorrect."

"At least the smiley face came out right."

"So . . . do I want to know how you upgraded your wardrobe so quickly?"

"Not really."

GW's polo shirt and shorts were, I'd noticed, slightly darker than they should have been.

They were still a little moist — because (I assumed) the laundromat dryer he'd just snagged them from hadn't been quite done with its load.

I stifled a sigh.

My chosen partner was unpredictable, unreliable, and unethical.

But he was also smart enough to guess what was next and dress accordingly.

He pointed at the hotel. "We going in?"

I nodded. "We're going in."

GW flashed me another grin, then got out of the car. His well-worn cowboy boots had been traded in, too: he was now wearing a pair of big, clunky sandals that were both a little embarrassing and completely appropriate for someone dressed like a J. Crew model.

They weren't the kind of thing you'd find

lying around a laundromat. GW was quite the fast worker.

"I knew you were getting good leads out of the bellman. He was talking to you long enough to give you directions to Timbuktu," he said. "That's why I figured you could spare me for a few minutes."

"Well, you figured wrong — and you missed your chance to hear someone say 'follow that car!' in real life."

GW's grin wilted. "What happened?"

I told him about the woman who'd been watching me — and the alarmingly familiar car she'd sped off in.

"She was looking at you through *binoculars*? In broad daylight?" GW said. "Not exactly subtle."

"Neither is running people over. Apparently subtle isn't her style."

Sincere wasn't really GW's style, but he looked me in the eye as if trying his best to give it a shot (or fake it).

"Sorry I wasn't around for that, Alanis," he said. "I won't leave you alone again."

They were reassuring words — and for some reason they made me wince. Maybe because they sounded so much like something Biddle would have said. Or should have.

I clapped my hands together. "Alright,

then — I've spent enough of my day loitering around a parking lot. Time to head inside."

"What are we looking for?" GW asked.

"Not what, who. Dryja was seen talking to other guests at the hotel yesterday: a rich European guy named Pichler and a schlubby American with a name that sounds like Buttsiac."

"So what are we gonna do, knock on doors until one of 'em answers?" said GW.

I wrapped an arm around one of us and tugged him toward the hotel.

"Something like that," I said.

I knocked on a door. But not just any door.

Hector had said Pichler was in the Presidential Suite on the fourth floor. So after bluffing our way through the lobby (no one questions you when you're white and well dressed and look completely, obliviously comfortable doing whatever you're doing), we got in the elevator and headed up. Of all the guest rooms on the fourth floor, only one had double doors and no number. It was at the end of one of the hallways, too, tucked away from the other rooms.

Voilà. Presidential Suite. So I knocked.

No one answered.

I knocked again, a little louder.

Still nothing.

GW cupped a hand to his ear. "Is that opportunity knocking?"

Translation: *Should we let ourselves in?*

I shook my head. "Let's keep this legal for as long as we can."

GW tugged at the collar of his polo shirt. "It's a little late for me."

"You're just borrowing that. We'll return it when we're done here."

"Yeah, right," GW scoffed.

Then he saw I wasn't joking.

"Great. Just what I need," he said. "A good influence."

He sighed — and smiled.

I turned and headed for the elevators. It was time to look for the other man Hector had told me about.

If we couldn't find him . . . well, we'd see how long I'd stay a good influence.

Hector had said the manager was putting "single business guests" on the third floor, so that's where we went. GW stayed by the elevators. I started roaming the halls.

"Yes, hello," I heard GW saying into his phone. "I'm looking for a guest of yours. I think his name is Mr. Buttsack."

"Buttsiac," I muttered.

"I had a lovely conversation with him

yesterday here at Cheney Garden Supply — I'm Pat Cheney, by the way — and he ended up buying quite an assortment of flowers and decorations," GW went on. "But when he left he totally forgot his new garden gnomes. I just noticed them sitting here by the counter. They're really adorable. One's dressed like a ninja and the other one's holding a little sign that says 'Protected by Gnome Security.' Get it? Like 'home security'?"

"Get on with it," I grumbled.

"Anywho — could you put me through to Mr. Buttsack's room?" Pause. "Oh, that's okay. I understand." Pause. "Absolutely. I don't mind." Pause. "I'm on hold."

That last part was for me.

I froze. I listened. And because even upscale hotels have thin doors and loud phones, I heard it.

The warbling chirp of a ringing phone. Down the hall to my left.

I moved toward the sound as quickly yet quietly as I could.

I'd only gone a few steps when it stopped.

Damn. Buttsiac must have been near his phone when it started ringing.

I kept going. Slowly, head cocked. Straining for the sound of a man's voice.

"Wait . . . what?" someone said. "My

gnomes?"

I stopped in front of room 322.

"I don't know what you're talking about," a man behind the door said. "I wasn't in any gardening store yesterday, and I didn't buy any gnomes. Yes, of course I'm sure!"

There was a sharp clatter of plastic on plastic — a phone being hung up hard.

GW stepped up beside me. He was already slipping his own phone into one of the pockets of his cargo shorts.

"Mr. Buttsack, I presume?" he said softly.

"Buttsiac," I said.

I raised a fist to knock on the door. And froze.

"What?" GW whispered.

I took him by the arm and marched him twenty feet up the hall.

"Who are you?" I said, looking him up and down.

GW blinked at me. "I'm GW."

"No. Who are you going to be to *him*?"

I jerked a thumb back at room 322.

"Oh," GW said. "Who are *you* gonna be?"

"I'm still deciding. But at least I've got options." I waved my hands in front of my clothes, *voilà!*-style. "I could pass for a professional on the job. You look like a vacationing dentist."

"I'm supposed to look like a vacationing

dentist."

"I know. But why would a vacationing dentist be knocking on Mr. Buttsiac's door?"

GW blinked again. "To remind him to floss?"

I took a deep breath. I already knew what I had to do when I pulled GW away from the door. I already knew it was stupid, too, but I was about to do it anyway.

"Wait by the elevator until I'm inside," I said.

"What? No way you're talking to this guy alone. He could be the killer."

"Which is why I need to talk to him. And I'm betting I won't get word number one out of him with Dr. Birkenstock, DDS, hanging out with me."

"Alanis, not five minutes ago you were pointing out what a dumb mistake I made by letting you out of my sight. Now I'm supposed to leave you alone in a hotel room with a murder suspect?"

"Exactly. It's impressive how quickly you grasp the plan."

I spun GW around and pushed him toward the elevators. "Get out of sight."

GW stopped himself and spun around. "Alanis . . ."

I was already marching up to room 322.

I glanced over my shoulder and saw a scowling GW shaking his head and mouthing one word.

No.

I mouthed one word back.

Go.

I raised my fist again.

GW shook his head harder.

No.

I shooed him away.

Go.

GW started toward me.

I knocked on the door.

COPPE
COUPES
9
CHALICES
COPAS
KELCHE
BEKERS

Would you just look at those cups? “Be the first one on your block to collect ’em all!” the ads said, and this guy went and did it. Maybe he had to pound down a bunch of thousand-calorie milkshakes in the process (he sure didn’t get those jowls doing bench presses at the gym), but it was worth it. Now he owns the entire Golden Chalice Collection, and man, does it make him proud. Self-satisfied, even. Downright smug, actually. Well, he should enjoy it while he can. Those cups are empty — and so is his victory. When his first coronary kicks in, the Golden Chalice Collection won’t be able to call 911.

Miss Chance, *Infinite Roads to Knowing*

"Can't you see the thingie on the knob?" the man behind the door said.

In fact, I had seen the thingie on the knob. *DO NOT DISTURB,* it said. I just chose to ignore it.

"I'm sorry, sir. I don't mean to disturb you," I said. "I just want to speak with you a moment."

"Sounds disturbing to me!" the man barked.

"*He* sounds disturbed," GW said under his breath.

I shooed him away again.

"Alright, I'll go. But if that guy murders you, don't come crying to me," he whispered. "I'll be nearby. If you need me, the signal is screaming your head off."

With that he spun around, skulked up the hotel hallway, and disappeared around a corner.

I turned back to the door.

"Please, sir," I said. "Just open the door and you'll see that there's nothing disturbing about me."

There was a muffled shuffling sound, and the door rattled ever so slightly.

The man was looking at me through the peephole.

I stared ahead earnestly, pretending not to notice.

"I promise not to take up too much of your time, sir," I said. "Please?"

"Who the hell are you, anyway?" the man said.

"I'm a journalist. Carla Kolchak, Independent News Service."

The door did more than rattle now. It thumped. Hard.

The man had kicked it.

"Disturbing!" he yelled.

"I'm sorry."

"*Very* disturbing! You people! Already!"

There was another thump against the door.

"Jackals!"

"I'm not a jackal, sir," I said. "I swear."

"Buzz off!"

"Fine. I'll just put you down for a 'no comment,' then. *That* never seems incriminating."

The man went silent. So silent, I could

hear a TV playing to my left that I hadn't noticed before. I looked toward the sound and found an owlish gray-haired woman gaping at me from two doorways down.

"Sorry for the noise," I said. I slipped the *DO NOT DISTURB* sign off the knob and gave it a little wave. "Try putting one of these on your door. It might help."

The woman ducked back into her room.

When I turned back toward the door to room 322, it was opening.

"Alright. Come in," muttered the jowly, stubble-faced, bed-headed man now facing me — Mr. Buttsiac, I presumed.

He was sixtyish, shortish, roundish. And fuming, with no -ish about it.

"Thank you," I said.

As I walked past him into the gloomy, underlit room — the blinds were drawn and only one small lamp was on — he snatched the *DO NOT DISTURB* sign from my hand and hung it back on the knob.

"Not that this thing does any damn good," he grumbled.

He leaned out into the hall and looked first one way, then the other. Satisfied that we weren't being observed, he closed the door, turned to face me, and crossed his arms over his chest, blocking the only way out (excluding a quick trip through the window). He might have looked like the Black Knight guarding a bridge — "None shall pass!" — if he'd only been a foot taller and wearing dark armor instead of a baggy sweatshirt and saggy dad jeans.

He didn't look much like a killer, either. But then again, few killers do. It's one of the things that can make catching them — and not getting killed by them — a bit tricky.

And I might have just bluffed my way into a room alone with one. Sometimes I'm so smart, I'm stupid.

"I'll give you five minutes to ask your questions," the man said.

He glanced at the clock radio by his unmade bed.

It was 1:35.

"Starting *now,*" the man went on. He snorted out a humorless chortle. "This way you can't say I said 'no comment.' "

"Fair enough."

I pulled out my cell, turned on the audio memo app, and held the phone out toward the man. I didn't have a little notebook or a fedora with a press card poking out of the hatband, but I could do *something* to look the part.

"You don't mind if I record this, do you?" I said.

"Oh, I prefer it! In fact . . ."

He stalked across the room and snatched up a cell phone lying on the bedside table. Lying beside it, I noticed, had been a crumpled Doritos bag and a half-empty bottle of Wild Turkey.

"I'm going to record this, too," the man said. "If *you* don't mind."

"Not at all."

He began fiddling with the phone.

"Testing testing testing. Ich bin ein Berliner. Today I consider myself the luckiest man on the face of the earth. The bombing begins in five minutes. Testing. There we go!"

A wide, wild, triumphant smile spread across the man's round face.

"There won't be any hanky-panky now, missy!" he declared.

He seemed to expect me to reply with something along the lines of "drat, foiled again!"

I was growing less and less worried that he was the killer — and, paradoxically, more and more worried that he was cuckoo for Cocoa Puffs.

"I assume you know what I'm here to ask about," I said.

The man's smile turned sly.

"Nice try," he said.

" 'Nice try'?"

"That wasn't a question."

"Oh. Okay. *Do* you know what I'm here to ask about?"

The man shrugged. "I don't know. Do I?"

He was still grinning. It felt like he was beating me at a game I didn't even know we were playing.

At least one of us was having fun.

"Are you aware that Robert Dryja was murdered last night?" I said.

The grin disappeared.

"Yes."

"So the police have already been here to talk to you about it."

The man just cocked his head and stared at me. It took me a moment to realize why.

Whatever game we were playing, it was kissing cousins with *Jeopardy!* in more ways than one.

Everything I said had to be in the form of a question.

"Have the police been here to talk to you about it?" I said.

"Yes."

The man went back to staring.

No more yes or no questions.

"How did you know Robert Dryja?"

"He was . . . a business associate."

"What kind of business?"

"Private business."

"What were you arguing with him about yesterday?"

"Business strategy."

"Why were you two in Berdache?"

"Business."

"This isn't very quotable stuff."

The man gave me a "not my problem" shrug, then looked across the darkened room at the clock by the bed.

1:37.

I had three more minutes.

The 7 turned into an 8.

Correction: I had *two* more minutes.

Time for some shots in the dark, metaphorically speaking. (I hoped.)

"Was Dryja working for you or Pichler?"

The shot found a target.

Hearing the name of the other guest Dryja had been seen speaking to — the European staying in the Presidential Suite — widened the man's eyes in surprise.

"Me. But not really. Sort of . . . both of us. But more like neither," he stammered.

"That's *really* not quotable."

"It's the best I can do." The man clamped his mouth shut. Obviously, that was all I was going to get out of him on that.

Time for another shot.

"What's a grout connector?"

"What's a *what*?"

"A grout connector. I was told you mentioned one when you were talking to Dryja in the lobby yesterday."

The man blinked at me in genuine confusion. "I have no idea what the hell you're talking about."

This shot was a clear miss. (Thanks for the non sequitur, Hector.)

I circled back to the hit.

"Is Pichler a business associate of yours, too?"

"We're in the same business sometimes. But not together," the man said tersely.

"So you're rivals?"

"Not usually."

"But you are now?"

"Yes," the man grated out. And said no more.

Silly me. I'd drifted back to yes or no questions.

It was 1:39. I might only have time to ask one more thing.

It was obvious what it should be.

"Who killed Robert Dryja?"

The man's puffy, pale face went scarlet.

"What makes you think I'd know?" he snarled.

"I thought you might at least have a theory," I started to say, but I didn't even get all the way through the "I."

"Here we go again! You people never change!" the man raged. "Back in the news five seconds, and already you're trying to pin everything on me!"

He tossed his cell phone on the bed, then started toward me, still ranting.

"Anything to sell another paper! Anything for another ratings point! Anything for another click! Go ahead! Ruin a man's life! You're just doing your job, am I right? *Am I right?*"

"Well . . . ," I said, backing away from the man as he stalked closer.

Then I had nowhere to back to. I'd bumped into the door.

"You want a quote? You want an exclusive?" the man spat at me. "I'll give you one! I'll give you one you'll never forget!"

He raised his hands. They weren't particularly big hands, but that didn't matter. They were big enough and close enough to wrap around my neck.

I knew I could probably fight the guy off, but let's face it. Anytime you're thinking that you probably *aren't* going to die is a bit of a bummer.

I was still torn between fight and flight (aka kicking the dude in the balls and trying to slip out the door) when there were four quick, crisp raps just behind me.

Someone was knocking on the door.

"Room service," GW said.

"I didn't order any room service," the man snapped.

"Really? I've got a vegan BLT and a Miller Lite for room . . . oh, my bad! This is for room 232, not 322. Sorry to disturb you."

"That's okay," the man said.

"Is there anything I can get you as long as I'm here, sir? The special today is thyme-infused rotisserie chicken served with garlic mashed potatoes and —"

"Go away!"

"You know what?" I said. "I think I'll just be on my way, too."

I kept my eyes on the man as I fumbled for the doorknob behind me.

"You still want that exclusive?" he asked me.

My left hand found the knob and turned it.

"Sure," I said as I pulled the door open.

The man clenched his fists — then popped out the middle finger on each hand.

"Screw you!"

"Now *that's* quotable," I said.

The door was open just wide enough for me to snake around it.

"Just one more question," I said when

only my head and shoulders were still in the room.

The man lunged forward.

I hopped into the hallway.

The door slammed behind me.

"How do you spell your name?" I said.

There was a moment of silence. Then —

"G-L-E-N-N B-U-D-Z-I-A-K," the man said. "I am *so* sick of seeing it mangled."

"Thank you, Glenn."

"Screw you!"

I turned to GW. He was looking at something behind me.

"I think she's noticed I don't have a vegan BLT," he said.

I followed his gaze.

The gray-haired woman two rooms down was peeping out into the hallway again. When I turned toward her, she popped her eyes and disappeared.

"How much you wanna bet she'll be calling the front desk in about three seconds?" GW said.

"Zero dollars and zero cents," I said. "Come on — let's find the back way out of this place."

"So," GW said as we hurried down the emergency exit stairwell, "did you learn anything other than how to spell the guy's name and not to go into hotel rooms alone with him?"

"Apparently Dryja was sort of working for him but sort of working for Pichler but sort of working for himself."

"Working on what?"

"Business."

"Why were they all here?"

"Business."

"Any clue as to why Dryja was murdered?"

I shrugged. "Business?"

"Great," GW said. "Sounds like 'screw you' was as specific as the guy got."

"Pretty much."

"Well, I'm *so* glad you risked your life for that. That was *so* worth it."

"Don't make me quote Budziak to you."

"What? Screw me? Screw *you,* Alanis. That was scary."

We pushed through the double doors at the bottom of the stairwell. The light outside was blinding.

"Now's the part where you apologize and promise not to take dumb chances like that again," GW said as we stood there blinking the sun-baked world around us into focus.

"I apologize," I said. "The parking lot's this way."

I started around the side of the building.

GW followed.

"I think you left something out there," he said.

"Hey, you didn't mess up the ignition when you took my car, did you? I don't want to have to stick a couple live wires together every time I want to go to the store for groceries."

"Don't change the subject."

My phone started playing Blondie's "Call Me." I was getting a call.

"Sorry. I've got to take this," I said before I even saw who it was. The caller ID could have said *B.S. TELEMARKETING INC.* and I would have picked up.

Instead, it simply said *UNKNOWN.*

So I wasn't lying. I did have to take the call.

I pushed *ACCEPT* and put the phone to my ear.

"Alright, Biddle," I said. "What the hell have you gotten me into?"

COPPE
COUPES
10
CHALICES
COPAS
KELCHE
BEKERS

Forget the pot of gold or the Lucky Charms or the magical world of Oz or whatever else it is you think might be over or under or at the end of the rainbow. The reward waiting beneath this one is nothing less than domestic bliss. Family, love, contentment — it's all yours . . . so long as you find that perfect spot along the riverbank. But don't forget: a rainbow's not a road map, it's just light bent by water; an illusion. And in the clear, strong, straight light of day, it can fade away fast.

Miss Chance, *Infinite Roads to Knowing*

At first, Biddle played dumb. Which isn't the best role for him if I'm the audience. He might be the Daniel Day-Dryja of con men, but no matter how method he goes with his performance, he's not going to convince me he's thick.

"Honest, Alanis — I don't know what you're talking about," he said. "Has there been some kind of trouble?"

"I'm starting my car as we speak, Biddle. Tell me where you are so I can come look you in the eye when you say that."

Biddle sighed.

"I should've known better," he said. "You would've seen through me when you were ten."

"Damn straight I would've. *Where are you?*"

"Tell you what — what's the scummiest diner with the crummiest location in town?"

I thought that over as I pulled out of the

hotel parking lot. I didn't have to dine with roaches and rats anymore. (When I'd first gone on the run from my mother years before it was usually all I could afford.) Yet I still had an inexplicable fondness for classic American hole-in-the-wall grease pits. Maybe they represented freedom to me. Or maybe I just like grease.

"Shanna's Home Cookin'," I said. "It's on the south side, almost a mile off the highway. The specialty of the house is salmonella, and every entrée comes with a complimentary side order of mouse droppings."

"Twenty minutes," Biddle said.

He hung up.

"Don't knock Shanna's," GW said. "If it weren't for their four-dollar breakfast special, I would've starved to death two dozen times by now."

I turned the car south.

"Well, get your four dollars ready," I said. "Because that's where we're going."

I called the White Magic Five and Dime.

"Did your old black guy call you?" Clarice asked.

"Whatever happened to 'hello'?"

"Hello. Did your old black guy call you?"

"Yes. When did you give him my number?"

"Like maybe ten minutes ago. He was really nice. Real friendly. We talked for a while."

"About what?"

"The shop. Me. You. Who is he, anyway?"

"I'm sure you asked him that yourself. What did he say?"

"That he was an old friend of yours."

"Well, there you go."

"If he's just an old friend, why didn't *you* tell me that?"

"Haven't you noticed? I like being mysterious."

"Oh, is that what you call it? Because I call it being a condescending, controlling b—"

"Big sister?" I cut in.

"No. B—"

"Brainiac?"

"No. B—"

"I've got another name for you."

"Why didn't you say so? What is it?"

"Glenn Budziak."

I spelled it for her.

"Got it," Clarice said. "Who is he?"

"I hope you and Ceecee can tell me. All I know is he's from out of town, he's connected to Dryja and some guy named Pichler, and he hates reporters."

"And he has *major* anger management issues," GW threw in.

"Sounds like it was a good thing you brought GW along," I heard Ceecee say.

Clarice must have put me on speaker phone just to spite me.

And to think *she* was calling *me* a b—.

"So what level is the sexual tension at?" Clarice asked. "Eight? Nine?"

"You know we totally 'ship you two," Ceecee added.

"Just dig up whatever you can on Budziak, alright?"

"Alanis and GW sittin' in a tree," Clarice began to sing.

I hung up before she could get to the K-I-S-S-I-N-G.

Imagine the kind of diner the Road Warrior would eat in.

Now imagine one the Road Warrior *wouldn't* eat in — because it was too grungy, even for him.

Shanna's Home Cookin' was the latter.

In the span of fifteen minutes, GW and I had gone from the classiest spot in Berdache to the crappiest.

I got out of the Caddy and looked the place over.

"You will never find a more wretched hive of scum and villainy," I intoned ominously.

"Yeah," said GW. "But you can get a stack of pancakes for three bucks."

I held a hand out toward the entrance. "Lead on."

I sat in a booth and waited for Biddle. Again. Just as I had at El Zorro Azul the night before.

Which isn't saying he was late. All he'd told me was "twenty minutes." That was when he wanted *me* there. He was probably somewhere nearby, watching, making sure this wasn't a trap with me as the bait — or the trapper.

I ordered a cup of bitter lukewarm water. (Actually, I ordered a cup of coffee. Bitter lukewarm water is what the waitress brought me.)

GW ordered a stack of pancakes and (smart man) a Coke. He'd changed back into his worn jeans, faded flannel, and scuffed boots before we came in, which was wise. Now he was dressed like every other guy in the place (except for the three or four wearing T-shirts and/or weather-beaten baseball caps). Which was why I, in my Lands' End–friendly turtleneck and corduroys, was the one getting the resentful glares. We probably looked like an ex-con being treated to lunch by his parole officer.

"Wish me luck," GW said as I dribbled two drops of cream into my cup. (That was all it took to turn the coffee as white as a big blob of Elmer's glue.)

"Why?"

"Because I'm going to the men's room."

GW scooted out of his seat and headed toward the back of the restaurant.

I didn't ask him to elaborate. I just shuddered.

"Who's that?" Biddle said.

He was slipping into GW's spot across from me, and I heard him before I saw him. When I looked his way, I got a jolt.

Not that he looked any different than he had the day before. It's just that I still wasn't used to seeing him in the here and now, real, alive. And I still wasn't used to him *old*.

"A friend," I said.

"A friend? Or a *friend*?"

Biddle gave me a wink.

"Just a friend," I snapped. "You know — someone who's always there when you need 'em? Somebody you can trust to help and never hurt you?"

"I don't believe in angels," Biddle said. "And even if I did, he sure didn't look like one."

"You're right. GW's no angel. But he *is* a

friend. That's all you need to know."

Biddle gave me a long, skeptical look, then turned to speak to our waitress as she shuffled listlessly by.

"Pardon me, young lady."

The "young lady" stopped. She was at least ten years older than me, and no one's called me young in a decade.

"Could you please bring me a cup of coffee when you have a moment?" Biddle asked her. "I thought I had enough this morning, but then I caught a whiff of what you're brewing here and I said to myself, 'If I don't get a taste of that, my mouth'll be mad at me the rest of the day.' "

"Coffee. Got it."

She sounded surly — but not as surly as when she'd taken *my* order.

I rolled my eyes as the woman walked away.

"What?" Biddle said.

"Why the line? She'd have brought you the coffee anyway. Bullshit's not going to make it taste any better."

"That wasn't bullshit." Biddle grinned. "That was a little ray of sunshine brightening an otherwise gray and gloomy day."

"Bull," I said. "Shit."

"Well, I can see this conversation's gonna be a lot of fun."

"You should've known that before you walked in the door."

The waitress returned with Biddle's coffee.

"Here you go, hon," she said as she slid it onto the table before him.

I hadn't been "hon" when I got my coffee.

"Thank you, miss," Biddle said. He brought the cup up to his face and took a big sniff. "If this tastes as good as it smells, you're going to have a new regular around here."

"Well, aren't you the old smoothie?" the waitress said, shaking her head. But she walked away smiling.

She passed GW as she went.

"You can turn off the charm, buddy," he said to Biddle. "Flattery will get you nowhere in this place."

He sat beside me and took a look around the table.

"My Coke hasn't come yet?" he said.

Biddle cocked an eyebrow at me and took a loud sip of his coffee.

"Biddle, this is GW Fletcher," I said. "GW, this is Biddle."

"I guessed," said GW.

He didn't offer to shake hands. Neither did Biddle.

"Why do we need him here?" Biddle asked me.

"Because," I said, "I'm being watched by a woman who tried to run me over last night, someone broke into and searched the White Magic Five and Dime, and a private investigator who came into the store right after you yesterday has been murdered."

Biddle either made himself or let himself look surprised. (It was Biddle who'd taught me how to maintain a stone face at all times. Once upon a time I'd been pretty good at it, but I was never as good at it as him.)

"*Who* was murdered?" he said.

"A guy named Robert Dryja. Philly cop turned PI. Know him?"

Biddle gazed down into his coffee for a moment, seemingly thinking hard.

"Never heard of him," he eventually said.

He looked back up at us and saw the skepticism on our faces.

"Really," he said.

"How about the names Pichler and Glenn Budziak? They ring any bells?"

Biddle shook his head.

Our expressions didn't change.

"Really," Biddle said.

"Okay. So you don't know them," I said. Not because I believed it but because it would be a waste of time arguing about it.

"But you do know why they're in Berdache, don't you? Dryja was following you. Why?"

Biddle sighed and took another sip of his coffee. He scowled down at the cup. It really did taste as good as it smelled, and it smelled like scorched swamp water.

"Answer the question," GW said.

Biddle glared at him and took another long, deliberate, defiant drink of his coffee. Then he put the cup down and looked at me.

"I decided it was time to wrap up some unfinished business while I still could," he said. "And I think some other people decided to wrap it up their own way."

"Oh god," GW groaned. "Please don't tell me this is a 'one last score before I retire' thing."

Biddle kept his eyes on me.

"It is and it isn't," he said. "It's an old score with loose ends I need to tie up. Once that's done, I am out of the game for good."

"And then you're gonna do — what? Spend the rest of your days writing checks to charity and helping old ladies cross the street?" GW said. *"Riiiiight."*

Biddle was still looking at me and me alone. His face was blank, but in his eyes I could see a plea: *believe me.*

"So you didn't come to Berdache because

you found out I was here," I said. "You came for business."

"Sweetie . . . I came for both," Biddle said.

I was about to tell him that his "sweetie" privileges had been revoked — I was "Ms. McLachlan" until further notice — when Debbie Harry started singing "Call Me" in my purse.

"You got a disco in there or is that your phone?" Biddle asked.

I didn't answer him. I did answer the phone.

The call was from the White Magic Five and Dime.

"What's up?" I said.

"He's an art thief!" Clarice blared so loudly she didn't even need to be on speaker phone to be heard by everyone at the table.

Biddle's eyes widened ever so slightly. For him, that was practically a spit-take.

"Who's an art thief?" I said.

"Budziak! Way back in the nineties he worked at this art museum in Philadelphia that got robbed, and even though he never got busted, everyone knows he was in on it."

"Who's 'everyone'?"

"Wikipedia. Well, sort of. The moderators took it all out, but it's in there if you go into the edit history."

"You're losing me."

Clarice grunted in frustration. How trying it must be to deal with all us old fogies over the age of twenty.

"I'll try to keep this simple," Clarice said. "We googled his name, right? And that led us to a Wikipedia page about the heist. Because it's, like, famous. But Budziak wasn't actually mentioned. So we went into the edit history. You can see stuff that people added to the article that the mods deleted — you know, because it's wrong or crazy or they're afraid of getting sued or whatever? And that's where we found the stuff about Budziak. Like, back in the day the newspapers kept hinting that someone who worked at the museum was going to be arrested, and everyone knew it was Budziak. But then nothing ever happened. The cops couldn't pin it on him. He got away with it."

"Or he didn't do it."

"Oh, come on."

"You're right. If people hinted about it in old newspaper stories that somebody mentioned on the Internet, it must be true."

"Okay, fine. I guess we've just been wasting our time. Sorry to waste yours."

"Clarice —"

"Ask her about Elvis," Biddle said.

I studied him for a moment, looking for signs he was having a stroke.

All I saw was resignation.

"What?" GW said before I could.

"Ask her what happened to your mother's velvet Elvis," Biddle said to me.

"Mom owned a velvet Elvis?"

It didn't fit her personality at all. It seemed too quirky. Too whimsical. Too human.

Yet I heard Clarice say, "Like, the painting? How do you know about that old thing?"

"So she did have one?"

"Sure. For years. And I always hated it. There was something so . . . I don't know . . . creepy about it. Mom made me promise to keep it, but I got rid of it a week after she died. I just couldn't take that big bloated dude staring at me from the wall."

"She says she got rid of it," I told Biddle.

Biddle's expression didn't change, but I could tell that took effort. I can't say he went pale; that probably doesn't happen to men who look like Morgan Freeman's slightly more spry kid brother. But if he'd been a white guy, I'm guessing he would've borne a sudden resemblance to Casper the Friendly Ghost.

"How?" he said.

"How?" I said into the phone.
"How?" said Clarice. "Goodwill."
"Goodwill," I said.
"Goodwill?" said Biddle.
"Goodwill," I said.
"Who are you talking to?" said Clarice.
"Hold on a sec." I looked Biddle in the eye. "Anything else you want me to ask her about? What happened to Mom's whoopee cushion? Where her old lawn jockey is?"
Biddle shook his head.
"Thanks for the information about Budziak. It really is helpful," I told Clarice.
"Wait. You're not about to hang up on me, are — ?"
I hung up.
"It was you, wasn't it? In the White Magic Five and Dime last night," I said. "That's why you were late to the restaurant. You waited for me to leave so you could break in and search the place. Because you want that velvet Elvis."
Biddle didn't deny it, which was wise. If he had, I might have thrown my coffee cup at him.
"Why is it so important?" I asked. "What does it mean?"
"You're better off not knowing," Biddle told me.
GW scoffed.

"Really," Biddle went on, eyes on me. "I've put you and your sister in danger. That ends now. You won't see me again until I've resolved this."

He pushed back his chair and stood up.

"But —," I began.

"*Alone,* Alanis," Biddle cut in. "There's not much left I can call family. I'm going to do what I got to to protect it."

He turned and went striding away.

"I'm trying to remember which John Wayne movie I heard that in," GW said.

"You don't buy it?"

" 'A man's gotta do what a man's gotta do?' From an old grifter like that? Please."

We weren't in a window seat — Biddle had obviously chosen our meeting place for minimum visibility, and I'd picked the booth accordingly. So I had to crane my neck to look out one of the diner's windows. I could see the parking lot, but not Biddle. He'd parked somewhere around the corner so we wouldn't spot his car.

Same old Biddle.

GW chuckled and shook his head. "He didn't even pay for his coffee."

Yup. Same old Biddle alright.

"Don't tell me *you* buy that 'you're better off not knowing' bull," GW said.

The waitress finally returned with GW's

cola. She plopped it front of him wordlessly before trudging off without asking if we wanted anything else.

"I don't know what to think about Biddle right now," I said. "But I know how we might start figuring it out."

GW took a sip of his drink and winced. Apparently, Shanna's Home Cookin' could even ruin a cup of Coca-Cola.

"How?" he said.

I started to pick up my coffee, then thought better of it and put it down.

"First you're gonna finish your drink," I said. "Then we're gonna get in my car and drive to the nearest Goodwill."

FANTE DI COPPE
VALET DE COUPES
KNAVE OF CHALICES
SOTA DE COPAS
BUBE DER KELCHE
BEKERS SCHILDKNAAP

What do you do when a fish pops out of your Big Gulp and starts talking to you: scream? Run? Film it on your cell phone and post it to YouTube? None of the above if you're the Knave of Chalices (aka the Page of Cups, aka Little Lord Fauntleroy). You just stand there in your big balloon britches and take it all in. There are times that call for action and times that call for observation and contemplation — and times that call for you to get your butt to Target and buy some pants that don't look like a giant onion. What time is it for you?

Miss Chance, *Infinite Roads to Knowing*

"So . . . he's after a velvet Elvis," GW said as I steered the Caddy away from Shanna's Home Cookin' (and Crappy Coffee and Coke). "Any idea why?"

I shrugged. "I don't think it was stolen from an art museum in Philadelphia, if that's what you're asking."

"That's *not* what I'm asking. I'm asking if you can see a connection between the heist and your old buddy Biddle and his scavenger hunt. 'Cuz I figure there is one."

"I figure you figure right," I said.

I glanced over at GW. He was smirking at me from the passenger seat.

Neither of us had to spell it out. He had his theory, I had mine, and odds were they were one and the same.

"You think if he gets what he's looking for you'll ever see him again?" GW asked.

"I don't know. He's a con man through and through, but I'll give him this much:

he's not a sociopath like my mom. He cares about something other than money — or at least he used to care about me."

"So how come he didn't track you down years ago?"

I froze my face so I wouldn't wince.

GW had hit the bull's-eye. My most vulnerable spot: the question I'd been too afraid to ask out loud myself.

"Maybe he tried to," I said. But I didn't believe it.

We were still five minutes away from Berdache's one and only Goodwill. I decided to put the time to use.

"How'd you like to try your hand at tarot reading?" I asked GW.

"Whoa. Subtle subject change."

"Not at all."

"I know. I was being sarcastic."

"No. I mean 'not at all' as in 'I wasn't changing the subject.' Look in my purse."

"What?"

The purse was sitting on the armrest between us. I elbowed it.

"There's a deck of cards in there. Take it out."

Slowly, cautiously, as if he suspected I kept mouse traps in it, GW reached into my purse.

"It's in a Crown Royal bag," I told him.

"Doesn't that mess up the readings? I mean, you don't want your deck to be buzzed."

GW pulled out the velvety purple bag.

"The cards don't mind." I held out my right hand. "Give 'em to me."

GW handed me the deck.

We were on a straight stretch of road, cruising by a grocery store and an abandoned Blockbuster on the right, a Dairy Queen and a Carl's Jr. on the left. Berdache's Times Square.

I steadied the steering wheel with my knees while I shuffled the cards.

"Uh . . . that's not how I was taught to steer in driver's ed," GW said, voice warbling.

"This'll only take a sec."

I took a moment to think about what I wanted to know. *Did Biddle come to Berdache for me or for a score?* Then I gave the cards back to GW and put my hands on the wheel again.

"Take the card off the top and put it on the armrest," I said. "Faceup."

GW did as he was told.

I looked down and saw this:

"Thanks a lot," I grumbled.

"What? Did I deal it wrong?"

"I'm not talking to you. I'm talking to the card."

"You *talk* to them? I never knew that was part of the act."

"It's not an act," I snapped.

GW put up his hands. "Whoa. Sorry."

"It *is* possible for people to be sincere, you know."

"I know that. I just didn't think someone like you would be that way about something like this."

I gripped the wheel and gritted my teeth. "What do you mean, 'someone like you'?"

A manipulator, I assumed he meant. A scammer. A swindler.

Someone like Mom. Someone like Biddle.

"You know," GW said. "Someone smart."

"Oh. Right."

I thought you were too intelligent to believe something this dumb isn't exactly a compliment, but it's not entirely an insult either. Just mostly one.

I forced myself to relax.

"It was an act in the beginning," I said. "And even now I feel like I'm faking it half the time I do a reading. But there is something to it, GW. I can't explain it. I don't understand it. It just . . . works. Sometimes."

GW tapped the Two of Swords lying faceup on the armrest. "And this doesn't work?"

I smiled and shook my head.

"It works too well," I said. "I got this spread from a tarot book I've been reading a lot since I came here. The first card is supposed to reflect the situation I'm thinking about. And do you see what it shows?"

"A blindfolded dude in a bathrobe about to cut his head off?"

"No. A *woman* thinking. The blindfold is keeping her from seeing the truth. And she's got two swords. Two options. Two possible answers. I wanted the cards to help me figure out what's going on, and all they showed me was myself being confused."

"Oh. Yeah, I can see that. That's actually kind of cool how you did that."

"How I did what?"

"Pulled some kind of meaning out of your" — I could practically hear the gulp as GW swallowed what he was about to say — "knowledge of the cards," he said instead. "So what next? Another card?"

I nodded. "This one will show an influence on the situation. Put it below and to the left of the first, faceup again."

GW dealt out another card.

"A-ha," I said.

"A-ha?"

"A-*ha.*" I pointed down at the card. "That's Biddle."

GW tilted his head to peer down at the armor-clad figure on the card.

"Looks a lot younger than Biddle. And whiter. And knightier," he said.

"He's a traveler on a quest. Looking for adventure — or something more."

"Like a big score?"

"Exactly. Except the card's reversed — upside down. Brave Sir Biddle is overconfident. He's in over his head."

GW grunted. "Fits what we know so far."

I threw him a look.

He met my gaze, his expression both challenging and amused.

So far the reading hadn't revealed anything. It just put a pseudomystical spin on what we could have already guessed.

Did the cards pull back the curtain on reality or just my subconscious? Were they a way to see beyond myself or simply look deeper in?

After months using the tarot, I still wasn't sure.

GW's smirk started to wilt.

"Uh . . . you maybe wanna look at *the road* occasionally?"

I turned my head — and had to slam on the brakes to keep from rear-ending a tour bus slowing for a stop light.

One thing I *had* learned for sure about tarot readings: doing them while driving wasn't a great idea. Still, we were two-thirds of the way through this one and hadn't learned anything new. We might as well see what the final card had to say.

The first two had gone flying off the armrest when we skidded to a stop. I told GW to pick them up, put them back in place, then deal out a third card below and to the right of the first.

"I'll do it on one condition," GW said. "Promise not to kill us."

"Cross my heart and hope to . . . I promise."

GW put down the last card. I didn't see it for a moment because the light had changed. The tour bus cruised off toward the desert and the powerful energy vortexes that supposedly swirled there. I hung a right by a 7-Eleven.

When I finally looked (quickly) down, this is what I saw:

"Huh," I said.

I drove a block in silence.

"Well?" GW finally said. "There must be more to it than 'huh.' "

"Oh, so now you want to know what the cards have to say?"

"Now I want to know what *you* have to say."

I tried to point at the card without looking at it. (The road had gone curvy, and I was taking my promise not to kill us seriously.) For all I knew, I was pointing at GW's crotch.

"This is another influence on my situation. Cups is the suit of love and compassion and emotional connections. So the queen is . . . I don't know. Super lovey, I guess. Super compassionate. Super . . . connected."

GW grunted out a "huh" that echoed my own.

"Doesn't sound like anyone *I* know," he said.

I nodded silently. It sure as hell didn't sound like Biddle.

But it had to be him, didn't it? I'd asked the cards if he'd come to Berdache for money or for me, and I'd gotten what looked like a pretty clear answer.

Both.

The Queen of Cups, though? If Biddle cared about me so damn deeply, why hadn't he come looking for me twenty-five years ago, when I really needed him? And now that he was back in my life, he was withholding, manipulating, scheming. He was still fond of me, I accepted that, but he was no Queen of Cups about it. That was overkill. Melodrama.

Can tarot cards exaggerate?

"Alright," I said. "You can put 'em away."

GW scooped up the cards.

"You learn anything?" he asked as he put the deck in its bag.

"I'm not sure. I don't think so."

GW stuffed the Crown Royal bag back in my purse.

"You got a Magic 8 Ball in here?" he said. "Maybe you should've tried that."

I was too lost in thought to come up with a comeback any wittier than "ha ha." Which was fine, because the subject was about to be changed for me anyway.

We were pulling into the Goodwill parking lot.

Berdache's Goodwill is basically 2,000 square feet of secondhand clothes, broken toasters, and Def Leppard albums packed into 1,000 square feet of underlit space. There were half a dozen other customers there, none of whom looked like Biddle and all of whom looked like regulars at Shanna's Home Cookin'. The art section consisted of a Britney Spears poster, a smattering of porcelain clowns, and a generic watercolor of an ocean sunset that would've looked right at home in a Holiday Inn circa 1976.

We looked behind the poster and the painting just in case. There was nothing there.

"Elvis has left the building," I said.

"Yeah. But when and who with?"

I started toward the front of the store. "Let's see if we can find out."

A gray-haired woman in mom jeans and a baggy, sequin-studded sweatshirt that could have come right off one of the racks nearby gave us a friendly smile as we walked up to the counter. *ASK ME ABOUT MY GRAND-CHILDREN* was written across her shirt. Her nametag said *PATTY.*

"You need help finding something?" she said.

"Something and somebody," I told her. "Was an older African American gentleman just in here looking for a painting of Elvis Presley?"

Patty's smile faded.

"Oh," she said gravely. "You're trying to find him, too?"

GW and I looked at each other. Neither of us said it, but it was clear we were both thinking it.

The cops? Already?

And it was clear we were thinking this, too:

Shit.

CAVALLO DI COPPE
KNIGHT OF CHALICES
CHEVALIER DE COUPES
CABALLO DE COPAS
RITTER DER KELCHE
BEKERS RIDDER

Behold, the bold knight setting off on his perilous quest! He has his trusty steed, his shining armor, his golden goblet of Gatorade. Everything a valiant cavalier needs to — hold on, what's up with the cup? Won't that get in the way when he's slaying dragons, battling brigands, rescuing fair maidens, etc.? Looks like Sir Gulpsalot hasn't given it that much thought. In fact, he seems more interested in what's in his cup than where he's going. If the road before him is bumpy, he might just spill his precious drink . . . or take a spill himself.

Miss Chance, *Infinite Roads to Knowing*

After a moment, I realized it might not be Detective Burby who was on Biddle's trail. Why be paranoid? It could be someone else entirely.

Like, you know, *the murderer.*

Still, I managed to keep my face totally blank, totally emotionless. (All those years watching Robert Stack on *Unsolved Mysteries* really paid off. And I suppose Biddle's training had something to do with it, too.)

"Someone else has been here looking for him?" I asked Patty the Goodwill Grandma.

"Yes — and they *just* missed him," she said. "I told them where he was going, so hopefully they've caught up with him by now."

She flashed us an attempt at a reassuring smile.

It didn't work.

"Sounds like they told you the whole story," GW said to her.

"Oh, yes. I felt so bad for him when I heard what he's going through. My Aunt Margaret got to be the same way right before the end. So stubborn, so lost. I can't believe the nursing home let him slip out. It's a miracle he got this far across town without hurting himself."

"Isn't it, though?" I said, nodding. "So . . . these people who were looking for him. Was it a woman with dark hair? And a sixtysomething man with a ponytail and a German accent?"

Patty furrowed her brow. "No. It was two of his friends from the home."

"From the home," I said. "Of course."

"I bet I know who it was," GW said. "Tall Asian guy with an eyepatch and a short Native American with a prosthetic arm; am I right?"

Patty furrowed her brow even more. Any further furrowing and she wouldn't be able to see.

"No. They were both white, about normal height. And neither of them had an eyepatch or a prosthetic arm."

"White? Normal height? No eyepatches or prosthetic arms?" I turned to GW. "Sounds like Sid and Marty."

GW chuckled as if he knew what the hell I was talking about.

"Those two," he said, shaking his head.

"Yeah. There's nothing they wouldn't do for" — I caught myself just in time; we had no idea what name Biddle or the men looking for him had used — "a buddy," I said.

"Just how many people are out looking for him?" Patty asked.

"Oh, lots," said GW.

"We can't even keep track of them all," I said. "Where did you send Sid and Marty?"

Patty looked left and right. There was nothing in either direction but junk. None of the other customers were anywhere near the register.

Patty dropped her voice to a whisper anyway.

"I made an exception for them because I made an exception for their friend. So I suppose I can make an exception for you two, too."

"We'd appreciate it," GW said.

I just nodded encouragingly.

"Well," Patty went on, voice still hushed, "when the old black man came in . . . I can still call someone that, right? An old black man?"

"I'm not offended," said GW.

I kept nodding.

"Good," said Patty. "You never know these

days. People are just *so* sensitive, you know?"

"Oh, yes. We know," said GW.

I was still nodding. And now gritting my teeth, too.

"Anywho," Patty said, "when the old black man came in, he told me he was looking for a painting of Elvis that his niece had donated to us when he went into the nursing home. Apparently it had been a birthday present from his late wife — they were both big Elvis fans — so it meant a lot to him to find it. I let him know it was against store policy to tell anyone who bought what. But then he started tearing up, so I started tearing up, and . . . well, I just blurted it out before we both could begin bawling like babies."

The woman paused and looked at us meaningfully, eyes wide.

It took us a moment to get the cue.

"You did the right thing," I said.

"What's a little thing like store policy when weighed against a dying man's cherished memories of lost love?" said GW.

I made a mental note to give him grief for laying it on thick.

"That's *exactly* what I was thinking," Patty told him with a small, grateful smile.

I crumpled up the mental note and threw

it in the mental trash.

Patty sniffled, then continued.

"That painting sat in the store for weeks. I don't think most people even know who Elvis is anymore, which is a sad state of affairs. But then this kinda fruity fella came in and . . . is that okay these days? Calling a man 'fruity'?"

"I'm not offended," said GW.

I went back to gritting my teeth.

"Well, when this guy laid eyes on that painting, it was love at first sight," Patty said. "He just *had* to have it for this new lounge he was opening in town. That's what he called it: a lounge. Not a bar, though that's all it is. One of *those* bars, too."

Patty winked at us.

"So that's where you sent the old man? To the bar?" I said quickly. I didn't want to give her the chance to ask if winking was okay these days.

Patty nodded. "He was going to go there and try to talk the owner into giving him or selling him the painting. Like I said — I usually wouldn't give out information like that. But when I saw the tears welling up in his eyes, how could I resist? And then when his friends came in and told me he was having an episode and hadn't taken his medicine that morning and could *die* any second . . . well, I had to tell them, too, didn't I? And now that you two are here . . ."

Patty refurrowed her brow. I didn't need to pull out my tarot cards to guess what was coming next.

Who are you, anyway?

"Patty, you've been a godsend," I said, backing toward the door.

GW began backing alongside me.

"If Mr. Jackson lives through the day, he'll have you to thank for it," he said.

Patty doubled down on her furrowing. It looked like her eyebrows might actually touch her cheeks.

"His friends called him Mr. Schmidt," she said.

"They're off their meds, too," I told her. "Thanks!"

I spun around and made my quickest exit from a Goodwill in thirty years. (There probably wasn't a thrift store east of the Mississippi that I hadn't appropriated at least one outfit from back in the day.)

"You do realize she never told us the name of the bar, don't you?" GW said as we pushed through the doors.

"She didn't have to," I told him.

Clarice and Ceecee had been thrilled when Berdache got its first-ever gay bar. They wouldn't be able to go inside until they were twenty-one (or until they scored their first fake IDs), but that didn't matter to them. It was a sign of progress — and that something exciting and edgy and wild was actually happening in Berdache.

Later, the disillusionment set in.

"I hear people just sit around in there and, like, drink," Clarice said a few weeks after the place opened.

"What did you expect?" I asked her. "A 24/7 rave?"

"Well," she said, "yeah."

The bar was on Berdache's main drag, Furnier Avenue, just a few blocks from the White Magic Five and Dime. It wasn't your usual small-town dive. There were no smoked windows, no neon signs for Coors or Budweiser. All you could see of the "lounge" was a plain wooden door with a sign hanging over it.

I parked across the street, in front of a mom and pop liquor store, and looked around for Biddle. He was either inside or long gone already.

"One thing I've been wondering about this place," GW said. "What's up with the name?"

Written on the sign was this:

Under the words was what looked like a fuzzy purple billiards rack, one tip pointed down.

"Tinky-Winky was the gay Teletubby," I said.

"One of the Teletubbies was gay?"

"According to Pat Robertson. Or maybe it was Jerry Falwell."

"Oh. So now he's retired to Arizona and opened a gay bar?"

"Kinda looks that way."

"Hmm. And I always figured it was Barney the dinosaur who was gay."

"Look," I said, "I'd love to sit here speculating about Barney's sex life all day, but . . . hey."

Across the street, two men were walking up the sidewalk toward Tinky-Winky's. One was balding and potbellied. The other was tall and broad-shouldered. They both seemed to be in the neighborhood of seventy years old.

I'd seen one of them before.

GW followed my gaze.

"Sid and Marty?" he said.

"I'm guessing. The bald one was in the White Magic Five and Dime yesterday. He came in right after Biddle, asked to use our bathroom, then let himself out the back."

The men stopped a few yards from the entrance to Tinky-Winky's. GW and I slouched down in our seats and watched as they talked to each other. Their clothes were generic geezerwear — loose jeans, knit shirts, white sneakers — except for the jackets they were wearing.

It was a sunny spring desert day, yet they were both dressed for Cleveland in October.

Noted.

Every few seconds one or the other would glance over his shoulder or scan the street, but they didn't seem to see us.

There was something about their wariness and the stiff, tense way they stood that struck me as familiar.

GW had the same reaction.

"They're crooked," he said. "Old, but pros."

The tall one nodded, then walked off. When he reached the side of the building, he turned.

"He's covering the back exit," GW said. "The other one'll go in the front."

I nodded. "Boxing Biddle in."

The bald man scraped something off his shoe, squinted at the sun, checked his watch, picked his nose. Then he walked through the door into Tinky-Winky's.

GW started to get out of the car.

"Wait here," he said.

"Sorry. We don't have a 'wait here' relationship."

I opened the driver's-side door and stepped out of the Cadillac.

GW hopped out on his side and raced around the car to cut me off.

"You're not going in there," he said.

"We don't have that kind of relationship, either."

I started to move around him.

He stepped in front of me.

"Alanis, listen — those guys might look like a couple of old farts, but they could be killers, and we know one of them has seen you. You'd be recognized the second you step inside."

"Which is why *I* was heading around to the back alley to keep an eye on the other one while *you* go into the bar."

"Oh. That makes sense." GW scratched his head. "You sure you couldn't just wait in the car, though?"

I rubbed my chin thoughtfully. "Hmm . . . it *is* almost time for *A Prairie Home Companion . . .*"

I darted around GW and scurried toward Tinky-Winky's.

GW had to wait for a couple cars to cruise

by before following me across the street. He caught up just as I was about to go around the side of the building.

"Don't get too close," he said.

Which was kind of ironic, as he'd snagged me by the wrist and pulled me around so we were toe to toe.

"I could say the same thing to you," I was about to tell him.

Something in his eyes stopped me. Something I wasn't sure I'd ever seen in George Washington Fletcher before.

Complete and utter sincerity.

I gently but firmly pulled my hand away from his.

"I don't need a white knight to protect me, GW," I said. "I need a slippery son of a bitch to help me."

GW might have looked hurt for a moment. It was hard to tell — the expression vanished from his face almost the moment it appeared.

He replaced it with his usual mask: a wry smile.

"Thanks for the reminder," he said. "See ya."

He turned and headed into Tinky-Winky's.

I got the impression I'd hurt his feelings, which was ironic because up until that very day I hadn't been sure he had any. Now it seemed pretty obvious that he had some for *me.*

Clarice and Ceecee would be thrilled.

Why wasn't I?

GW was smart, funny, loyal (or so it seemed), and easy on the eyes.

But he was also devious, penniless, unreliable (remember the "or so it seemed" after "loyal"?), and easy on the eyes. (In my experience, being good looking does *not* make a man more trustworthy. Not that I haven't known back-stabbing bastards with buck teeth and acne . . .)

I shook all these thoughts out of my head. Literally. I probably looked like one of those women in the old shampoo commercials who were always tossing their flowing locks to prove how full and fluffy Prell or Pert (or whatever) left their hair. Only I wasn't trying to sell anybody Gee, Your Hair Smells Terrific. I was trying to sell myself Gee, Your Brain Needs to Focus.

This was no time to stand around psychoanalyzing myself. I had alleys to creep down and shady old men to spy on, which just went to show how much I really could use some psychoanalysis.

I shook *that* thought away and started creeping quietly along the alleyway.

I wasn't creeping for long. I'd only gone a few feet when I heard voices coming from behind the building. I couldn't quite make out what they were saying at first. Then it didn't matter what they were saying because the other noises I was hearing were easy enough to understand.

The *ahhhhh,* for instance.

And the *oof.*

And the sound of someone hitting the ground.

My quiet creep turned into a sprint. When I reached the back of the building, I found the two old men kicking and hitting another old man sprawled on the pavement beside a dumpster.

The man on the ground was clutching a portrait of Elvis.

He was also, of course, Biddle.

The bald man — the one who I thought had flushed himself down my toilet the day before — reached for the painting.

"Gimme that," he said.

His partner kept kicking and hitting.

I gave myself half a second to weigh my options.

I could:

(A) Get in a fight with a couple oldsters who looked like they might break a hip if I threw a punch.

(B) Find the perfect phrase — something from their past, their heyday, perhaps — that would stop the grandthugs in their tracks.

I went with (B).

"Freeze, turkeys!" I barked.

Please remember: I had half a second to come up with something. Which is probably why I ended up sounding like T. J. Hooker.

At least I didn't call them "*jive* turkeys."

Anyway, it didn't work. There were no frozen turkeys. Both men whirled around and instinctively reached for something under their jackets.

That something, I could only assume, was not a hard candy for me or a crisp new dollar bill so I could run to the corner store and buy myself a soda. It was the kind of something that would fill me full of big, messy new holes.

"No!" Biddle cried.

Then the shooting started.

REGINA DI COPPE
QUEEN OF CHALICES
REINE DE COUPES
REINA DE COPAS
KÖNIGIN DER KELCHE
BEKERS KONINGIN

The suit of cups is associated with water — the element of emotion and intuition — so what better place for the dreamy, chalice-clutching queen to set her throne than by the seashore? Don't let her distracted look fool you, though. She's not just there to huddle under her beach blanket and stare at beverages. What looks like daydreaming could be plotting and planning. And when the moment's right, this lady's capable of shrugging off her blanket, rolling up her puffy white sleeves, and making things happen.

Miss Chance, *Infinite Roads to Knowing*

First thing I noticed: the gunshots. Naturally.

Second thing I noticed: the gunshots stopped almost as soon as they started.

Third thing I noticed: no one seemed to have been shooting at me. Neither of the old men looming over Biddle had managed to get their hands (and, presumably, the guns in them) out from under their jackets.

Fourth thing I noticed: clumps of gray feathers drifting down out of the sky like heavy snow.

Fifth thing I noticed: the sound of a woman cursing off to my right, back toward the street.

Sixth thing I noticed: how lucky I was to be alive to notice things. Because when I looked down the alley, I saw a short woman in a trench coat and fedora pointing an Uzi into the air. She wasn't hunting pigeons (though apparently she'd bagged one). The

Uzi was aimed up because she hadn't been ready for the recoil when she'd pulled the trigger.

Seventh thing I noticed: the woman was lowering the gun and taking aim again — at me.

I stopped noticing things and started diving for cover.

I leapt around the corner of the building, then ducked behind the dumpster there for good measure.

"What — ?" Biddle began.

He was cut off by another burst of gunfire. It didn't last long, ending with a startled yelp and the sound of metal clattering on pavement.

"Let's get outta here," the tall old man said.

The bald one made another grab for the velvet Elvis, but Biddle held tight.

The tall man pulled his partner away, and together they scurried off as quickly as their old knees would let them go.

The back door to the bar burst open, and GW rushed out.

"Alanis! Thank god!" he said when he saw me. "Are you — ?"

I shushed him with a finger to my lips, then crept to the corner of the building and peeped down the alley.

I saw what I expected to see: an Uzi lying on the pavement. And nothing else.

I started to sprint down the alley, hoping to get a look at the woman's license plate before she could drive off. GW ran with me.

When we were still twenty yards from the street I heard a squeal of tires. The woman was peeling out.

We kept going, but it was too late. By the time we reached the street, she was gone. I didn't have to see her leave to know what she was driving, though.

A dark blue sedan.

I turned and marched back to the dumpster behind the bar. Biddle owed me answers, and I wasn't going to wait for them another second. Or so I told myself.

He was gone, too.

The bar's back door opened again, and a lean, fortyish man with short-cropped blond hair leaned out cautiously. He had a cell phone pressed to one ear.

"Is it over?" he said. "Did you see what was going on?"

He was looking at me and GW. It was too late for us to run.

I suppressed a sigh and began to tell the man a carefully edited version of what had happened. I knew GW would be listening carefully. We had to get our stories straight before the cops showed up.

Alanis and the Incompetent Assassin

Once upon a time, a nice law-abiding lady named Alanis went to a bar with her friend GW, a nice law-abiding man. It was the first gay bar in their area, and they wanted to welcome the proprietor to the community.

Just as they were about to step inside, Alanis remembered that she had to make an important phone call, so she let GW go ahead. Before Alanis could finish dialing, however, she heard what sounded like a mugging behind the building. Being a nice law-abiding lady, Alanis went to see if one of her fellow citizens was in need of assistance.

Suddenly, a woman wearing a trench coat and a fedora appeared! She began shooting at Alanis with an Uzi! What was Alanis to do?

Fortunately, the woman couldn't control the gun, and after firing off two short bursts and murdering an innocent pigeon, she fled.

GW ran out of the bar.

"I don't know anything about firearms or

violence," he said, "but that sounded like the guns I've seen on TV. What happened?"

"I don't know," Alanis told her friend. "But I'm sure the police will quickly get to the bottom of it. They are true American heroes, and I salute their competence, dedication, and bravery."

And Alanis and GW lived happily ever after . . .

ThE END

"Bullshit," Burby said.

I couldn't remember ever hearing the baby-faced cop swear before. It felt like a Boy Scout had just given me the finger.

"Let's keep this civil and professional, Detective," said Eugene, which was ironic given what he'd said when I'd called to tell him I was being taken to police headquarters for questioning. "Civil and professional" it wasn't — yet he'd come to sit with me in the interview room all the same.

"If you want civility," Burby growled, "tell your client to start telling the truth."

"I am telling the truth," I said.

Burby glared at me across the table. Again. He'd been at it off and on for the last ten minutes.

"A mysterious woman wearing a trench

coat and an Indiana Jones hat?" he said. (I'd had to explain to him what a "fedora" is. Kids today.) "Trying to run you over, then shooting at you in broad daylight? All for no reason?"

"I didn't say she had no reason. I said I didn't know what it was."

Burby leaned back in his creaky seat and crossed his arms.

"Guess," he said.

"Guess?"

"Yes. Guess. Who would want to hurt a nice law-abiding lady like you?"

"Well, the Grandi family, for one. You know they run half the fortunetelling places around here . . . and *all* the crooked ones. They've hated me from the day I came to town."

"Because you're a competitor?"

"Because I'm nice and law abiding."

Burby rolled his eyes.

"There's also the Berdache PD," I said. "You guys have hated me almost as long as the Grandis."

Burby stopped eye-rolling and went back to glaring. "What are you suggesting?"

"I'm not suggesting anything. I'm guessing. Like you told me to."

"Well, guess something else."

"Alright. My mother ripped plenty of

people off. One of them might be trying to take it out on me. And I get some pretty off-the-wall customers sometimes. Maybe I gave one a reading she *really* didn't like, and reporting me to the Better Business Bureau just wasn't gonna cut it. Hell, I don't know — maybe she owns the local Dominos. I gave them a bad review on Yelp because they delivered a Philly cheese steak pizza when I ordered a veggie deluxe. Can I stop guessing now? You've got a description of the woman and her car. Just go find her."

Burby finally took a break from glaring at me.

He'd switched to scowling.

" 'Just go find her'?" he said. "Put out an APB on a woman in a hat and a coat in a blue car, and call it a day? It's that simple?"

I shrugged. "It might be."

Burby jerked forward and slammed his palm down on the table.

"Bullshit!"

"Detective . . . ," Eugene said in a way that was both soothing and chiding.

It worked.

Burby took a deep breath, and when he spoke again his voice was calm and even. He managed to dial his scowl back to a mere glare, too.

"This fight behind the bar," he said.

"What did you see of it?"

"Not much. Rambette started blasting at me just as I reached the end of the alley."

"So you didn't get a good look?"

"Not really. All I saw were some people struggling, then scattering."

"What kind of *people*?"

I shrugged. "It was a bit of a blur."

"Were any of these *people* carrying anything?"

"I couldn't say."

I was proud of myself for managing to avoid outright lies (though I was pushing it, depending on how you wanted to define "couldn't"). I wouldn't be able to keep it up much longer, though.

Time for a change of subject.

"Can I ask *you* a question?" I said to Burby.

He didn't keep me waiting long for his answer — just a millisecond or two.

"No."

I asked anyway.

"Do you think this might be connected to the murder you spoke to me about this morning?"

Burby cocked his head and looked at me with wary bemusement, as if he couldn't figure out if I were setting a trap for him or had walked into one myself.

"What makes you ask that?" he said.

"A man I talked to in my shop is killed, and the very next day I'm on the wrong end of an Uzi . . . ? I'd be nuts not to ask."

"It is a reasonable question, Detective," Eugene slipped in smoothly. "After what happened today, Ms. McLachlan needs to be thinking about her personal safety."

"Maybe she oughta move somewhere safer," Burby sneered. "Like back to Detroit."

Before I could say "Chicago" (Burby's insult would have packed more punch if he'd at least gotten the city right), Eugene cleared his throat in that quiet way that announces that someone is about to be the grownup in the room.

"Detective," he said, "I suggest that you answer Alanis's question as if she were any other citizen who'd just survived a murder attempt and is turning to the police for advice and assistance *in the presence of her attorney.*"

For the first time, Burby turned his glare on Eugene.

Eugene just stared back at him, expressionless, and let what he'd really said sink in.

If anything happens to Alanis, I'm gonna sue your ass.

"What was the question again?" Burby finally sighed.

"Do you have any reason to believe the attack on me and the murder you told me about this morning are connected?" I asked him again.

Burby reluctantly shook his head. "The MO was different."

"Meaning what, exactly?" Eugene asked.

"Look, I answered the question. I'm not going to start showing you crime-scene photos."

"He means the murder was more slick," I told Eugene. "Professional."

"Why do you say that?" Burby snapped at me.

"Because the murder was committed in a hotel parking lot, yet the victim wasn't found till this morning. Those aren't the kind of results you're going to get if your 'MO' is cutting loose with an Uzi you can't even hold."

Burby narrowed his eyes. "How do you know the body was found in a parking lot by a hotel?"

"I heard it on the radio," I said nonchalantly.

Two seconds of pure terror followed while I wondered if the murder *had* been mentioned on the radio yet.

Burby gave me an answer.

"Goddamn reporters," he muttered.

"Do you have any more questions?" Eugene said.

"Yes, but —," Burby began.

"Actually, I was asking my client." Burby sank into seething silence.

"No," I said to Eugene. "Thank you."

Eugene turned to Burby again. "Do *you* have any more questions?"

"Yes," Burby said through a tight, sulky smile, "but I think I'll go and find the answers myself. You can leave."

Rather than stand and make a quick escape, I leaned over and whispered in Eugene's ear. He listened, then whispered in mine. I nodded, then Eugene nodded. Then we both faced Burby again.

"If you're going to interview Mr. Fletcher now, I can just wait here while you bring him in," Eugene said. "I'm his attorney, too."

Waiting for GW and Eugene in front of Berdache's beige, boxy police headquarters would have been the smart thing to do. The assassin who was after me sucked at her job, but she wasn't crazy enough to take a shot at me there. (So far as I knew.)

But I didn't last long by the front steps of

BPD HQ. The local cops all know who I am, so they got to practice their Dirty Harry Death Glares on me as they came and went. Ten minutes of it was all I could take.

I went to get a cup of coffee and an apple fritter. If I was going to be murdered, at least I'd go out happy.

When I got back to police headquarters, GW and Eugene were standing out front.

GW looked at my coffee cup (the fritter was long gone) and gave me a mock pout. "No cappuccino for me?"

"I think I've treated you enough today." I said and nodded at Eugene. "What I'm paying him could buy a thousand cappuccinos."

I remembered the last time I was in a Starbucks and did some quick math.

"Or a few hundred, anyway."

"Hey, I wouldn't need a lawyer at all if it weren't for you," GW said.

I gave him a dubious look.

"Okay, I'd probably need one sooner or later," he admitted. "But not today."

Eugene rolled his eyes and folded his arms across his broad chest and the pink, slightly too tight golf shirt covering it.

"Alright. Enough banter," he growled. "Is there anything either of you want to tell me?"

"What do you mean?" I asked innocently.

"Tell you?" said GW.

Eugene threw up his hands. "Fine! Play it that way! But let me remind you, Alanis: despite the situations you keep dragging me into, I. Am. Not. A. Criminal. Lawyer. I am a boring small-town business attorney who dabbles in estate planning and property law. Your arch enemy in there? Burby? I shouldn't be sparring with him in an interrogation room. I should be talking him into getting a living will. On a golf course. With a beer in my hand."

"And I'm sure you will one day," I said.

"Not after you're done with me! It's a wonder I haven't been drummed out of the Lions Club already. People are going to start wondering about me. They're going to start thinking I'm shady."

I looked Eugene up and down.

Pink shirt. Banana yellow slacks. Old-school black-and-white golf shoes.

"Shady? Never," I said. "Tacky . . . ?"

Eugene swiped a hand at me and said something that sounded like "mwaaah!"

"And by the way, you're not boring anymore," I told him. "Thanks to me."

"I *want* to be boring, Alanis. I *like* boring. You should try it sometime. Boring is safe. Boring is secure."

"Boring is boring," GW yawned.

Eugene ignored him. It looked like it took some effort.

"Alanis. Really," Eugene said to me. "Is there anything I should know?"

"How to dress yourself without blinding people?" I almost said.

I swallowed it. Like the man himself said: enough banter.

"Some of it you're better off *not* knowing," I said. "And a lot of it I don't know yet myself. But if the time comes when you need to know everything I do, I'll tell you. I promise."

Eugene just looked at me for a moment, obviously swallowing a few things he could say, too.

Eventually, he nodded.

"You know, Alanis," he said, "your mother may have been a sociopath, but she never gave me headaches like you do."

I patted him on the shoulder. "That's because you care, big guy."

Eugene gave me a small smile.

"You'll get my bill Monday morning," he said.

GW and I headed back to Tinky-Winky's to get my Cadillac.

"None of the old dudes was in the bar when I went in," he told me as we walked up Berdache's main drag, Furnier Avenue. "I guess I should've gone out the back right away to see where they went, but I wanted to ask the guy behind the bar about the painting. It was the owner. He told me 'an African American gentleman' had just bought it. Said his wife was sick and she's a big Elvis fan and it would really cheer her up to see it hanging in the ICU, so the guy let him have it for ten bucks."

We walked half a block without saying anything.

GW broke the silence.

"Whatever the deal is with that painting, it's why Biddle came to Berdache," he said. "And now that he has it . . ."

He didn't have to finish the thought. I was thinking it already.

You'll never see Biddle again.

RE DI COPPE
ROI DE COUPES
KING OF CHALICES
REY DE COPAS
KÖNIG DER KELCHE
BEKERS KONING

“It’s good to be the king,” the saying goes. But that doesn’t mean it’ll always be easy. For one thing, you’ve always got to be kingly. Kingish. Kingtastic. A king can be many things — calculating, cold, selfish — but he can’t be a goofball, can’t be a spaz, can’t, in some ways, be fully human. His kingdom could be a sea so stormy it bops dolphins around like hacky sacks, but the king has to look calm and comfortable and content on his throne. Otherwise, it won’t be his throne for long. “Never let them see you sweat” could be another catchphrase for kings. Or worded another way: “Never let them know you feel.”

Miss Chance, *Infinite Roads to Knowing*

"So," GW said as I parked my Caddy in the lot behind the White Magic Five and Dime, "that's that."

"I don't know," I said. "*Is* that that?"

"Yes. It is," said GW. "Your old pal Biddle got what he wanted — whatever that really was. End of story, right? Those old dudes will follow him wherever he runs to next, and we'll never know who killed Dryja or why that Budziak guy was here or what the German, Pichler, was after. And it won't matter. It's all moot now."

"Because Biddle will be gone again."

"Right. Your troubles are . . . oh."

Some men just look like a deer in headlights when they realize that the woman they're with is about to cry. GW looked like a deer who's just realized he's wandered onto a shooting range.

He put a hand on my shoulder and offered what comforting words he could.

"Hey . . . Alanis . . . hey . . ."

At least he was trying.

I took in a deep, deep breath, as if I could suck back the tears that were about to spill down my cheeks.

And I could. The tears didn't spill. My eyes dried. I even managed to smile.

"Oh, yeah. My troubles are over . . . except for the crazy bitch who's trying to kill me," I said. "But at least I won't get sucked any deeper into Biddle's bullshit. And I won't have to figure out what to tell Clarice, either." I forced myself to laugh. "Guess I dodged another bullet. Only not quite so literal this time."

"What do you mean?"

"Clarice found an old picture my mother had of Biddle and assumed he's her father. I didn't have the heart to tell her he was killed sixteen years before she was born, so I never set her straight. Now I won't have to."

GW squeezed my shoulder. "There you go. Another silver lining."

"Yes. I can keep lying to my sister."

"Not lying. Protecting."

I nodded. GW might have started with "hey . . . Alanis . . . hey," but he'd found the right words eventually.

Not lying. Protecting. Exactly.

But protecting who from what? Clarice from confusion and disappointment? Or me from a big emotional mess I didn't want to wade into?

I patted the hand GW still had on my shoulder.

"Thanks, pal," I said. And I turned away and opened the door and climbed out of the car quickly, not looking back as I headed toward the store.

Marsha Riggs, the White Magic Five and Dime's new assistant manager, was behind the counter when I walked inside. She'd been a wallflower when I'd hired her, afraid to speak, afraid to be seen, afraid to breathe. Her abusive (and now dead) husband Bill had had a lot to do with that. But the wallflower had blossomed.

When I came in, she was happily lecturing a browsing tourist couple about her favorite and least-favorite tarot decks. She didn't just look enthusiastic; she looked luminous. The pale, mousy drudge who'd started at the shop a few weeks before had been replaced by a beaming hippie chick in an African dashiki and hemp skirt. She fit in at the White Magic Five and Dime better than I did.

"Where are the girls?" I asked her.

She flapped a lanky hand at the hall leading to the back of the building.

"They went to the office when I came in. I guess they've got some homework to do."

I nodded.

I'd assigned the homework. And now I could unassign it.

"Well, hello," Marsha said with a smile as GW stepped in behind me. "Nice to see you again."

She shifted her gaze to me, eyes slightly widened. The expression on her face was pretty easy to read.

Hubba hubba.

She 'shipped me and GW, just like Clarice and Ceecee. Unlike them, she also 'shipped me with Victor Castellanos. She 'shipped me with any unaccompanied male between the ages of twenty and seventy-five, in fact. She hadn't suggested that I hook up with Eugene yet, but I wouldn't put it past her.

"So . . . what are you two up to today?" she asked.

"Oh, you know," GW said with a shrug. "The usual."

Marsha kept smiling, though she should've known that "the usual" for me these days involved angry cops and dead bodies.

"Let's go see how the girls are doing with their project," I said to GW. "Marsha, let me know if you need any help up front."

Marsha gave me a thumbs-up and another *hubba hubba* look.

I walked quickly up the hallway, several paces ahead of GW. I knew he would have picked up on Marsha's "go for it, girl!" vibe, and I didn't want to hear what he might have to say about it.

I was out of luck there.

"Nice young lady," he said as we passed the little nook where I did tarot readings. "But I wonder if she knows we don't have *that* kind of relationship."

"Well . . ." I said.

Clarice rescued me.

"Finally — you're back!" she called out when she saw us coming. "You gotta see this!"

I practically ran the rest of the way down the hall.

"What is it?" I said.

Clarice and Ceecee were in the little office by the back door, hunched over our laptop. Clarice turned it so that GW and I could see what they were looking at.

"We started searching for stuff on that museum robbery Budziak was supposedly in on, and we found this," Clarice said. "It showed up in a bunch of different newspapers, but this is where it was first."

"I think you're in the middle of something *big*!" Ceecee said to me with a grin.

On the screen was an article that had run in *The Philadelphia Post* a few days before.

I knew it probably didn't matter what big thing had momentarily swirled around us. But, hey — I'm only human.

I started reading anyway.

DEATHBED CONFESSION COULD SOLVE DECADES-OLD MYSTERY
BY KATRINA GILVER-MCPHERSON

Michael "Big Mike" Fusillo spent the last quarter of a century denying that he had anything to do with the infamous robbery that cost the Bischoff Gallery of Fine Art nine priceless paintings. Even when eight of the paintings were found in a Kensington warehouse he controlled as one of the city's most powerful and feared crime bosses, Fusillo insisted he knew nothing about the heist.

This week, Big Mike finally changed his tune. Diagnosed with pancreatic cancer earlier this year, the frail eighty-year-old has admitted that a crew of thieves in his now-dismantled criminal organization pulled off the 1991 break-in.

"I want to clear the air," said Fusillo in a telephone interview from the State Correctional Institute at Graterford, where he's halfway through a twenty-year stretch for racketeering and tax evasion. "It's time the truth was told."

But there's a catch. Although Fusillo is at long last acknowledging his role in the Bischoff Gallery heist, he's withholding key details. His price for full cooperation: an early release from prison.

"My father is an old, dying man who poses no threat to anybody," said Fusillo's daughter, Jennifer Garlen. "He should be allowed to come home and spend his final days with his family."

Perhaps Fusillo's most valuable bargaining chip is the one piece of art never recovered after the robbery. Fusillo says he doesn't know the exact location of the missing masterpiece, Vincent Van Gogh's *Stormy Sea from Scheveningen Pier,* because a disgruntled associate made off with it around the time the other paintings were seized by police. But he claims to have come into possession of new information that could quickly lead authorities to the priceless Van Gogh.

"That painting should be back on the wall at a museum," Fusillo said. "I have the name that could put it there. The rest is up to the state."

Neither the governor's office nor the office of the state attorney have responded to Post queries about Fusillo. But Bischoff Gallery Executive Director Marta Laura Martinez is urging officials to take the ailing crime lord's offer seriously.

"*Stormy Sea from Scheveningen Pier* was once the jewel in the Bischoff collection crown, and it's been missing far too long," Martinez said. "if one of the men who took it can help put it back, we should do whatever it takes to make that happen."

According to Martinez, the painting is currently worth around $2.5 million.

There was more, but I stopped reading.

It wasn't the words that stopped me. It was the numbers. They didn't add up.

Biddle had died — as far as my mother and I were concerned, anyway — in 1984.

I ran away from my mom in 1990.

The Bischoff Gallery robbery was in 1991.

My mother was somehow connected with the robbery.

So was Biddle.

2 + 2 = 3.

There was a simple way to adjust the equation so that it worked out, I realized. An assumption that could be accounted for. A single variable that could be changed . . .

and that would change everything.

I re-ran the math. This time, I got 4.

The tears I'd managed to fight back earlier returned.

I felt a hand on my shoulder.

"Are you alright?" GW asked.

It was a step up from "hey . . . Alanis . . . hey." Practice makes perfect.

Someone cleared his throat behind us. We all turned to look.

Biddle stood in the doorway, a painting of Elvis Presley in his hands.

Clarice gasped.

Biddle looked down at her, smiled sadly, and said, "Hello, sweetie." And I knew then that I'd finally added it up correctly.

Just because *I* hadn't seen Biddle after 1984 didn't mean my mother hadn't.

My sister had been right all along.

Biddle *was* her father.

■ ■ ■ ■

Part 2
Reversals

■ ■ ■ ■

RE DI COPPE
ROI DE COUPES
KING OF CHALICES
REY DE COPAS
KÖNIG DER KELCHE
BEKERS KONING

Cups is the suit of emotion, so guess what happens when the King of Cups is reversed? That's right: the same thing that happens if you flip your Big Gulp upside down. You get a Big Splash. Everything you've been holding in — anger, resentment, tears — will come pouring out. Good luck keeping your crown on when all that's running up your nose.

Miss Chance, *Infinite Roads to Knowing*

Clarice started crying. Ceecee — who'd apparently seen the picture of Biddle and knew what it meant — wrapped her arms around her girlfriend and started crying, too. Then *I* started crying.

I managed to stop. They didn't.

"Alanis?" GW said. He still had a hand on my shoulder. It felt different now, though. Not like he was comforting me. More like he was holding me back.

I hadn't stopped crying because of my supreme self-control. I'd stopped crying because my rage had boiled up over my heartbreak.

Biddle saw it. He didn't flinch, but I could tell he was steeling himself.

"I'd like to explain," he said.

I shrugged off GW's hand and took a step toward Biddle.

Was I going to slap him? Punch him? Bust that stupid painting over his head?

Definitely not the latter. That much I decided. The velvet Elvis may have been tacky, but I had the feeling it was priceless, too. The first two options, though, were very much in play.

I brought up my right hand.

Biddle still didn't flinch. Whatever I decided to do, he seemed ready to accept.

Marsha appeared in the hallway outside the cramped, crowded little office, and I froze.

"Is everything alright, Alanis?" she asked, eyes wide. She looked at Biddle, then back at me. "He said he was a friend of the family, so I told him he could come back here to see you."

"Oh, he's more than a friend of the family," I said. "Don't worry. It's okay. We'll take the conversation upstairs."

Marsha nodded, threw a worried look at the girls crying side by side in front of the laptop, then turned with obvious reluctance and walked back up the hall.

"The stairs around the corner lead up to our apartment," I told Biddle. "But you already know that, don't you?"

Because you searched the place last night, you slippery son of a bitch, I didn't add out loud.

"Why are you so pissed, Alanis?" Clarice

asked through her tears. "What's going on?"

I kept my eyes on Biddle and held a hand out toward the door.

He nodded, silent and contrite, and started to walk out of the office.

"Wait," Clarice said.

Biddle stopped.

"You're my dad, right?" Clarice asked him.

Biddle's sad smile returned, and he nodded.

"Can I . . . hug you?" Clarice said.

Biddle put down the painting he was holding before saying, "Of course."

Clarice sprang from her seat and threw her arms around him. Biddle's arms were pinned to his sides, but he managed to bring up his left hand and pat her awkwardly on the back.

After a moment, Clarice let go and stepped back.

"Upstairs," I said to Biddle.

He turned, picked up the painting, and walked out of the room.

"I wanted the hug now," Clarice said to me, "because I'm not sure I'm going to want it later."

Smart girl.

She followed Biddle into the hall and up the stairs. Ceecee went with her. They were a couple. That made Ceecee family.

I turned to GW.

What was he?

"This ain't gonna be pretty," I said to him. "You don't have to stick around for it."

He just gestured toward the door and said, "After you."

"My name," Biddle said, "is James McDonald."

We were off to a great start. It was the first thing he told us, and I figured he was probably lying.

He'd gone by fifty different names in the time I'd known him, but none of them had been "James McDonald" or anything like it. He'd always been "Biddle" to me and mom.

He looked at the audience gathered around him in our little living room — a still-sniffling Clarice and Ceecee side by side on the couch, me sitting stiffly in a chair I'd pulled over from the dining room, GW standing with his arms crossed and his head cocked and his eyes narrowed. It wasn't a friendly crowd, and Biddle's stooped shoulders and forlorn face said he knew it.

Which I also didn't trust. The man could act rings around Laurence Olivier. If he were weeping and wailing and pulling out his hair, I'd still think he might be smiling inside.

"I met your mother in 1977," he said to Clarice. He shifted his gaze to me. "You were still just a teeny little thing. You probably don't even remember when I showed up."

I gave him nothing.

"Well," he went on, "we were in the same business, we worked well together, we got along. So we partnered up, and the next few years, we bounced around the country together. Never staying anyplace long, developing small to medium-sized projects . . ."

"You can say it," I cut in. I jerked my head at the couch. "They know what Mom was."

"Alright," Biddle said. He focused on Clarice again. "Small to medium *cons*. Nothing that would get us noticed by the wrong people. Better to have thirty ones in your wallet than one twenty some other SOB wants for himself, that was my way of looking at it. But your mother, she was ambitious. Wanted a big score. So we scouted around and . . ." He turned back to me. "Do you remember going to Philadelphia in 1983?"

"I remember living at the King of Prussia

Mall for a week. I saw *Mr. Mom* twenty times."

Biddle winced.

I didn't buy it.

"Oh. Yeah. That's right," he said. "We sort of stashed you away that week, didn't we?"

"I was stashed away a lot."

"Well . . . it kept you out of trouble. Usually," Biddle said. "While you were watching *Mr. Mom,* your mother and I were in Philly making our play. After a small con, your average citizen's usually too embarrassed by their own stupidity to do anything about it. If the take's bigger, though, they've got more reason to swallow their pride. So you look for marks who have good reason not to go to the cops."

"Crooks," GW said.

"Sometimes. And, yeah — this time that's exactly who we went after. I won't bore you with the details." Biddle smiled shyly, hinting that the details were anything but boring. "The upshot is we left Philadelphia with a tidy little bundle we'd acquired from a gentleman there — a bundle he wanted back. And if he didn't get the bundle . . . well, he'd settle for us. Nearly got us, too."

I nodded slowly.

The worst night of my life — the nightmare I thought I'd never wake up from —

finally made sense.

"In a cornfield," I said. "In Ohio."

"You know what happened after that," Biddle said.

"Wait." Clarice turned to stare at me. "You do?"

Uh-oh.

"I know some of it," I said quickly. If I talked fast enough, I might be able to skate past the *really* awkward question. "Mom and I managed to get away, but we thought Biddle — that's the name I knew him by — didn't make it. We assumed he was dead, so Mom got us the hell out of there and didn't look back. And now I'd like to hear him explain the connection between a velvet Elvis and —"

Clarice put up her hands. "Wait wait wait. When did you find out he *wasn't* dead?"

Whoomp, there it was. The *really* awkward question.

I hadn't skated fast enough.

"Yesterday," I said.

"Yesterday?" said Clarice.

"Yesterday?" said Ceecee.

"Yesterday," I said.

"Yesterday?" Clarice and Ceecee said together.

"Yesterday," I said.

"And you didn't tell me?" said Clarice.

"And you didn't tell us?" Ceecee said at the same time.

"Hey, I thought the guy was dead," I said. "I needed a little time to process."

"I didn't see you doing any *processing* this morning," Clarice said. "I just saw you running around sticking your nose into other people's messes like always."

"Yeah," said Ceecee.

I shrugged weakly. "That's how I process."

"And hold on." Clarice pointed at Biddle. "I showed you the picture I found of him weeks ago, and you didn't tell me a damn thing."

"Yeah!" said Ceecee.

"Not his name. Not who he was," Clarice went on. "Not that he was . . ."

Clarice's eyes widened as her words trailed off.

"If you thought he was dead," Ceecee said slowly, "then you couldn't have believed he was Clarice's dad. You must have thought she was wrong — that her real dad was someone else."

Clarice's stare turned into a glare.

"And you didn't tell me. *You didn't tell me.*"

"I was going to," I said. "Eventually."

Clarice pulled a throw pillow out from behind her and did what you're not *really* supposed to do with one.

She threw it.

At me.

Hard.

I let it hit me in the face. Not exactly ten *Hail Marys* and an *Our Father,* but it was all I could manage just then penance-wise.

"Wanna go grab a beer while the ladies talk this out?" Biddle asked GW.

GW just glowered at him.

Biddle sighed and turned to the girls. "Your sister was trying to spare your feelings, Clarice. She would've told you everything she knew when the time was —"

"You can shut the duck up," Clarice spat. Only without the reference to a mallard. "You have no right to lecture me. Where the hell have you been all my life?"

"Yeah," Ceecee added meekly. She had no problem giving me grief, but telling an old man to shut the duck up seemed to cross some kind of line for her.

"Which is it, Clarice?" Biddle said gently. "Do you want me to shut up or do you want me to tell you where I've been all your life?"

Clarice simmered silently for a moment, then said, "The second."

"Alright, then. It's a long story, and I'm an old man who's been standing a little too long. So I'll have to give you the *Reader's*

Digest version."

I guess that was our cue to offer him a seat.

No one took the hint.

"You'll give us the *what*?" said Ceecee.

"He means he'll finally get to the point," said GW.

Biddle sighed again, then started talking.

"The man from Philadelphia — the one who almost killed us — eventually went to prison. A lot of years had passed since that night in the cornfield, but I'd kept my distance from your mother, just in case. I didn't want to make it easy for him to find us. After I heard he'd been put away, though, I figured maybe we were finally safe. So I tracked your mother down. It took some doing. She sure could cover her tracks, that lady. But I knew her better than anyone in the world. With a couple exceptions, I guess."

Biddle smiled at us wryly before going on.

"We picked right up where we left off. Your mother — she hadn't changed a bit. I had, though." He locked his gaze on me, and his smile faded away. "I've done a million shameful things in my time, but I'm only truly ashamed of one: how we used you, Alanis. We had no business bringing up a child that way. So when your mom told me she was pregnant again . . . well, I guess that was what they call 'my come-to-Jesus moment.' Not that I'd ever come to Jesus. Or that He'd have me. But I could say no. And that's what I did."

"What do you mean, you said no?" Clarice asked.

"I mean I ran away. That quick enough to the point for you, fella?"

Biddle threw an irritated glance GW's way. It seemed like an excuse not to look Clarice in the eye.

She didn't let him get away with it.

"So you just left me with *her,*" she said.

"Yes. That's right," Biddle told her. "What else was I supposed to do? Steal you away and raise you myself?"

"Why not?"

Biddle shook his head. "Your mother shouldn't have been a mother. And I shouldn't have been a father."

"But you were one!"

Biddle had no answer for that. He just looked down at his feet — and the painting near them, leaning against the TV cabinet.

I looked there, too. It reminded me that we still hadn't gotten to the point — not the real one.

"So you ran off, and now you're back," I said to Biddle. "Why?"

"Oh my god! *Duh!*" Clarice exploded. "Because Mom stole that old painting from Big Mike Fusillo and hid it behind a picture of Elvis Pursely! You didn't figure that out already?"

"Actually, I did," I replied as calmly as I could. I jerked my head at Biddle. "But I wanted to see what *he* was gonna say before I blurted it out myself."

"Oh. Right," said Clarice, abashed.

"Presley," GW said to her. It looked like he'd already figured out the connection to the painting, too.

Ceecee, on the other hand, was blinking at us all in shock.

"Wait," she said. "What?"

"Now how'd you find out about Big Mike?" Biddle asked Clarice with a sly smile, hiding his surprise behind a display of fatherly pride.

"Oh, you know . . . the Internet and stuff," Clarice muttered.

"Really, guys. Wait," Ceecee said. *"What?"*

I tried to walk her through it fast.

"You and Clarice found a newspaper article about a Philadelphia crime boss who says an associate stole a Van Gogh from him years ago. Then Biddle — that's Mr. McDonald here — tells us he and my mother pulled some kind of scam on a Philadelphia crime boss and nearly got killed for it. In fact, Mom thought the guy *had* killed Biddle. And Biddle's been running around looking for *that.*" I pointed at the velvet Elvis and shrugged. "It's obvious, right?"

Ceecee looked down at the painting, then up at me.

"I still don't get it," she said.

Clarice patted her hand.

"That's because you're a naturally honest and law-abiding person," she said. With pity.

I turned my attention to Biddle again. "Mom didn't actually go after Big Mike for revenge, did she?"

"Does that seem so impossible to you?" Biddle said.

I thought it over.

"Not impossible. But not likely either," I said. "She'd stick her neck out for a big score. But because she *cared* about someone . . . ? I don't think so."

"Oh, you don't? Well, if you're so sure all she cared about was money, tell me this," Biddle said. "Why would she risk her life to steal something that she knew she could never sell? Why would she keep it hanging on her wall for years, hidden in plain sight?"

I thought some more, then conceded the point with a nod.

"You're right. She wasn't just greedy," I

said. "She was a spiteful bitch, too."

Biddle opened his mouth to reply.

GW jumped in first.

"Guys, guys, guys," he said. "This is the best episode of *Dr. Phil* I've ever seen, really. But could we maybe set aside the family drama for a minute while we decide what to do with that?"

He nodded at the painting.

"We can burn it for all I care," Biddle said, giving it a little kick.

"Whoa!" GW cried. "Easy with the priceless work of art there, buddy!"

"Oh, there's nothing priceless here."

Biddle gave Elvis another prod with his toe that made GW flinch. Then he bent down slowly, with a groan — we really had been making him stand quite a while — and turned the painting around. I expected to see a false back ripped open to reveal the dark swoops and swirls of a Van Gogh.

I was only half right. There was a false back — brown butcher paper stretched across the frame, now ripped across the middle. There were no swoops and swirls in sight, though.

"That painting used to be here. Your mother showed it to me once," Biddle said. "But when I looked for it there today, all I found was this."

He reached behind the thick paper and pulled out something about the size of a playing card.

In fact, it *was* a playing card. Of sorts.

It was the King of Cups.

REGINA DI COPPE
QUEEN OF CHALICES
REINE DE COUPES
REINA DE COPAS
KÖNIGIN DER KELCHE
BEKERS KONINGIN

Right-side up, the Queen of Cups is exactly who you want on the throne. She's powerful, beautiful, creative (it must have been her idea to wear curtains as a robe, right?); a noble protector of hearth and home. So what do you get when that's flipped? The creativity and power and beauty might remain — might — but the nobility drops away. Now you're being ruled by someone who looks out for number one. Which could leave the kingdom — whether that's a community or a business or a family — deep in number two.

Miss Chance, *Infinite Roads to Knowing*

I wanted to walk downstairs to the shop and reach into the fish tank in the corner and pull out the little box with my mother's ashes in it and say, "Thanks, Mom. You've done it again." Then I'd flush her damn ashes down the toilet.

I managed to restrain myself. First things first: we had another Mom-made mess to clean up. I could walk her to the john when and if we actually managed to do it.

I squinted at the King of Cups Biddle was holding up.

"Anything written on it?"

"No."

"Anything else hidden with it?"

"No."

Then Biddle had a question for me.

"Any idea what it means?"

I had the same answer for him.

"No."

I looked at Clarice and repeated the question with a cocked eyebrow.

She just shrugged.

"Are you seriously trying to tell us that Alanis's mother had a painting worth a bajillion dollars and she never sold it?" GW said to Biddle.

"Who was she gonna sell it to? This wasn't a piece of hot jewelry or a boosted car. It would have been dangerous even to look for a buyer. And anyway, she didn't steal it to sell it. She wanted a way to hurt Big Mike, and she found it. The important thing to her was that she had it and he didn't."

I looked at Clarice again. She gave me another shrug.

We were thinking the same thing.

Could Mom have been that petty?

Maybe.

"How come you didn't steal it from her?" GW asked Biddle. "You've had a couple decades to figure out how to sell it."

Biddle didn't bother pretending he was offended.

"It didn't seem worth the trouble," he said with a chagrined smile.

"A priceless painting not worth the trouble?" GW said skeptically.

Ceecee cleared her throat. After the first wave of emotion had worn off, she'd started looking more and more uncomfortable.

I couldn't blame her. She was trapped on a couch in the middle of the most effed-up family meeting ever.

She raised her hand timidly.

I gave her a nod, half expecting her to ask if she could go to the restroom.

"Maybe he didn't know it was priceless?" she said.

"Ding ding," said Biddle. "Give the young lady with the blue hair a cigar."

Ceecee stared at him, wide-eyed. "Uh . . . what?"

"I get it now," I said to Biddle. "You had no idea what that painting was really worth until you saw a news story about Big Mike. And that's when you decided to come take it."

Biddle shook his head. "Close, but no cigar for you. I saw a story about Big Mike and the painting, yes. It sure looked like some heat was headed your mother's way. So I checked on her." He looked at Clarice. "And you. When I found out your mother was dead, I knew I had to come take care of you."

"By taking the painting?" GW said.

"Yes," Biddle answered firmly. "I didn't want Clarice mixed up in any of this business. So I figured I'd get the painting and give it back to the museum. There wouldn't be any reason for people to keep listening to Big Mike after that. He'd stay in prison, the painting would go back on some wall, and I could finally introduce myself to my daughter, knowing that she was safe from my past."

I started to scoff. Then I saw the look on Clarice's face.

I would have expected her to scoff, too. She was a teenager. She scoffed at nearly everything. And now here was her long-lost con-man father saying he was finally going to look her up . . . right after he was done giving away a painting worth millions?

In the immortal words of Daffy Duck: *Ha ha, it is to laugh.*

Only Clarice wasn't laughing or smirking or rolling her eyes. She was looking at Biddle with a wary sort of wonder. Like a kid who'd stopped believing in Santa Claus seeing reindeer on the roof on Christmas Eve.

She still didn't believe in Biddle, but she desperately wanted to.

I swallowed my scoff.

"I like your plan," I told Biddle. "We should stick to it."

GW didn't actually say "huh?!?" but I could hear it in the way he stiffened and cocked his head.

"We need to find the painting and return it before there are any more . . . consequences," I said. "The first thing we need to do is —"

"Consequences?" Clarice cut in.

"Things have gotten complicated," I said.

"No kidding," Ceecee mumbled.

"Stop holding out on me, Alanis. I'm not some dumb kid," Clarice snapped. "What consequences?"

I was trapped.

She was right to be mad at me. I had been holding out on her, and that needed to stop. But dumb or not — and she definitely wasn't — she was still a kid. It was my job to protect her, both from the world and from herself.

Damned If You Do, meet my friend Damned If You Don't.

"I think it's time you were straight with her," Biddle said to me.

There are looks that can kill, and then there are looks that will slow-roast you over an open fire for a day, *then* kill you. I gave Biddle the latter. *Him* trying to tell *me* how to talk to a kid? The gall.

And the real pisser?

He was right.

"Robert Dryja? The cop turned private detective? He was murdered last night," I said. "And two men attacked Biddle today."

"Two men and someone with a machine gun," Biddle threw in.

I shook my head. "The someone with a machine gun was attacking *me.* I don't think she even knew you were there."

"Oh, for Christ's sake!" Clarice exclaimed. "There was a *machine gun attack* you haven't told us about yet?"

"Whoa," Ceecee said. "We've missed a lot."

Clarice started spinning her hands in the air.

"Details. Now," she said. *"All of them."*

I didn't give Clarice and Ceecee *all* the details. They didn't need to know that I'd bribed Hector the bellman and impersonated a journalist to talk to Glenn Budziak and let Patty the Goodwill Grandma jump to conclusions about nursing home escapees. I'd had fruitful conversations with all of them; *that* was what mattered.

"Wow," Clarice said sardonically. "How lucky that everyone was so talkative today."

"Yes," I said. "Wasn't it?"

Then I finished the story, and Clarice gave me another wow. She followed it up with, "What the hell is going on?"

Silently, one by one, she and Ceecee and

GW and I all turned to stare at Biddle.

He was finally sitting — I'd let him have my seat while I got the girls up to speed — and he looked up from the foot he'd been massaging and shrugged.

"You guys know everything I do," he said.

"You really don't know who those two old guys are?" GW asked.

"Nope."

"And you don't know how Dryja knew to come to Berdache?" I asked.

"Nope."

"And you don't know anything about the people Dryja was seen talking to at the hotel — the rich German and the blond?" GW asked.

"Nope."

"And you don't know how Budziak came to be here or what he might have been arguing with Dryja about?" I asked.

"Nope."

"And you don't know why some half-assed assassin lady would be trying to off Alanis?" asked Clarice.

"Nope."

"And you . . . um . . . you . . . you want something to drink?" asked Ceecee.

Biddle grinned. "Why, thank you, honey. I would, actually."

Clarice shot her girlfriend a glare.

"I thought I should ask something, but I didn't know what," Ceecee said apologetically. "This is all *really* confusing."

"I'll take sweet tea if you got it," Biddle told her. "Lots of ice."

Ceecee got up and went into the kitchen.

"My turn to ask a question. A rerun," Biddle said. He looked first at me, then Clarice. "You two really have no idea what this means?"

He held up the King of Cups.

"Nope," said Clarice.

"I got bupkis," I said.

Biddle shook his head, incredulous. "All the time you've spent talking about these cards, pretending you can read 'em like a book, and you don't even have a guess why your mother would leave this one for us to find?"

"We don't know that their mom *is* the one who put the card in that painting," GW said.

"Yes, we do," Clarice shot back.

"It was her," I said.

"Oh," said GW.

He gave me a look that said, *Well, dammit, then Biddle's got a point.*

I ignored it.

"There's another lead we can follow up on," I said. "One we let drop a few hours ago."

There was a moment of silence. Then GW, Clarice, and Biddle all spoke at once.

"The German," said GW.

"The German," said Clarice.

"The blond," said Biddle, waggling his eyebrows. "Just kidding. The German. 'Cuz for him we've got a name and a location, right?"

Clarice popped off the couch. "Give me a couple minutes and we'll have a lot more than that. Let's go, Ceecee!"

"But I'm not done making iced tea for your . . . for Mr. McDonald."

"Screw the tea! Come on!"

The two girls rushed out of the apartment and clomped down the stairs together.

" 'Screw the tea'? While an old gentleman sits here dying of thirst?" Biddle said, shaking his head. "Kids today."

"I did a lot worse than that when I was that age," I said. "Most of which you taught me."

" 'Old gentleman,' " snorted GW.

Biddle drummed his fingers on his knees and gave GW a sour up-and-down once-over.

"Remind me, cowboy," he said. "Who the hell are you?"

"My friends call me GW. You can call me Fletcher."

"That gives me a name, *Fletcher.* It still doesn't tell me who you are."

"Just an interested party."

Biddle smirked. "Oh? Interested in what?"

His gaze darted over to me, then returned to GW.

"Interested in protecting a friend from a manipulative old fraud," GW spat.

Biddle raised his eyebrows and chuckled. "Oh? So you're a white knight, then? Funny. You just look like a two-bit hustler to me."

GW clenched his fists, face flushing.

"We'll see who's really a fraud soon enough," Biddle went on.

GW took a step toward him.

I snagged him by the arm and began pulling him out of the room.

"Alright, boys, that's enough of that," I said. "The girls are probably just googling the German. We may as well go see what they find."

"Good idea," GW muttered.

"You're right, sweetie," Biddle said as he stood to follow us. "I think I know the answer to my question anyhow." GW started to turn to face him.

I tightened my hold on his arm and guided him toward the stairs.

"I'm not a two-bit hustler, you know," he said to me under his breath. "I never hustle for anything less than three bits."

"And I bet you're worth every bit."

GW gave me a surprisingly wistful smile.

"I hope so," he said.

Ceecee was hunched over the laptop in the office when we came in. Clarice sat beside her, scowling at the screen.

"Any progress?" I asked.

"Yeah," Ceecee said. "We figured out we were spelling 'Pichler' wrong."

"And once you spell it right, there are a *lot* of them," Clarice added. "We need to be more specific. Add 'German' to the search."

Ceecee started typing.

"If we're trying to be specific," she said, "why don't I make the search 'Pichler rich German guy stolen painting maybe murderer.' "

Clarice shook her head. "*Too* specific."

"I was joking," Ceecee grumbled.

"Try 'Pichler German collector,' " I said. "The bellman at the hotel said Budziak was yelling at Dryja about a grout connector yesterday. Maybe he misunderstood."

The girls gave me a blank look. GW did, too.

"Kraut collector?" Biddle guessed.

"That's what I'm thinking," I said. "Try it, Ceecee. Hold the kraut."

Ceecee banged out a few more words, then hit enter.

"Hey!" she said. "I think that actually worked!"

The rest of us crowded in to look at the screen. It was filled with search results, many of them article headlines.

Ever-Restless Pichler Sets Sights on German App Market

Pichler and Apple Go Toe to Toe Before ECJ

"You're Next, Zuckerberg!" Defiant Pichler Vows

All He Wants Is Everything: The Ulf Pichler Story

"His first name is Ulf?" Clarice said. She shook her head. "That poor, poor man."

"That rich, rich man," GW corrected. "Half those headlines are from *Forbes.*"

I pointed at the screen. "Go to Wikipedia."

Ceecee clicked on the link, and Pichler's Wikipedia page appeared. Just from the table of contents alone, I knew we weren't dealing with your run-of-the-mill rich German guy maybe-murderer.

1 Early life

2 Career

2.1 Ice cream truck
2.2 Sonntagnachmittagunwholsein Records
2.3 *Einhundertein Schokoladenhasen* (101 Chocolate Bunnies)
2.4 www.glucklichsittiche.de launch and Amazon buyout
2.5 Multimedia empire
2.6 Other business ventures
2.7 Dagegengeld implosion and lawsuit

3 World record attempts

3.1 Mountaineering
3.2 Ballooning
3.3 Deep-sea diving
3.4 Firewalking
3.5 Hot-dog eating

4 Politics

5 Controversies and criticism

5.1 Mother Teresa feud

5.2 Vatican streaking incident
5.3 Art and relics collection
5.4 Dalai Lama headbutt

6 Honours and awards

7 Personal life

7.1 Marriages
7.2 Palimony suits
7.3 Paternity suits
7.4 Vow of celibacy

Bibliography

References

There were pictures, too. A head shot up top showed Pichler to be a lean, chiseled blond with a neatly trimmed beard and a big grin. The caption underneath listed his age as fifty-nine. Further down were photos of him sitting in a recording studio with David Bowie, walking a red carpet at Cannes with Dame Judi Dench, shaking hands with Dick Cheney, waving from the basket of a hot-air balloon with Oprah and Deepak Chopra, and handing a painting to a dour, scowling woman who must have been *someone* famous and/or powerful.

"Dalai Lama Headbutt sounds like a band

you'd listen to," GW said to Ceecee.

"Too skate punk," she replied, twirling a lock of her electric blue hair. "I think I'd like Vatican Streaking Incident more. I bet they'd be emo."

I ignored them. I was speed reading (or reading as speedily as I could, anyway). Two subsections in particular had caught my attention: "Dagegengeld implosion and lawsuit" and "Art and relics collection."

"He's been having money problems lately," I said. "And he collects rare art — and he hasn't always been picky about where he does his shopping."

I pointed at the picture of Pichler handing over a painting.

"He only gave that one back after someone spotted it on his wall in a magazine spread," I said. "It's a Chagall that was taken from Paris during World War II. He said he bought it at a garage sale."

"They have garage sales in Germany?" said Ceecee. "That gazillionaires go to?"

Clarice put a hand on her shoulder and stared deeply into her eyes. "Don't ever change."

"What?" said Ceecee. "They *don't* have garage sales in Germany?"

"So," said Biddle, "we've got a gazillionaire who knows a thing or two about the black market for stolen paintings. Sounds like someone we oughta get to know better."

"Carefully," GW threw in. "This is a guy who headbutted the Dalai Lama."

"Actually, I think the Dalai Lama headbutted *him,*" said Ceecee.

GW took a moment to mull that over.

"That's even worse, somehow," he said.

"Don't worry. I've already thought of the perfect way to approach him," I announced. "Ceecee, is that article you were looking at earlier still open? The one about Big Mike Fusillo?"

"Sure."

Ceecee clicked on one of the tabs in her browser, and Ulf Pichler's Wikipedia page was replaced by an article from the *Philadelphia Post:* "Deathbed Confession Could Solve Decades-Old Mystery" by Katrina Gilver-McPherson.

"Damn," GW said when he saw the byline. "I was thinking the same thing you are."

I grinned.

"Oh, yeah?" I said. "Too bad you'd make a lousy Katrina."

"Devil's Ridge Lodge; your desert oasis of luxury living. How may I help you?"

"Hi. I'm trying to get in touch with

someone who's staying there. Ulf Pichler."

"I'm sorry. We don't give out guest information."

"That's okay, I understand. Tell you what: if there *is* an Ulf Pichler there and if he's staying in the Presidential Suite — which would mean he's someone who's going to be spending a lot of money there, which means you want to keep him happy — and if you have a pen and paper handy, then maybe you could write down that Katrina Gilver-McPherson of the *Philadelphia Post* — that's a newspaper — wanted to talk to him about art history — *recent* art history — and that he should call me at the number I'm about to give you."

"Um . . . we don't give out guest information."

"I know. Here's the number."

I read out the number for Biddle's (unlisted, untraceable) phone.

"Did you get all that?" I asked.

"I . . . I can't say if I do or don't."

"Fine. Thanks. Bye."

"Wait!"

"Yes?"

A moment went by in silence.

Then: "How do you spell your name?"

Five minutes later Biddle's phone rang. We

all crowded around to look at the caller ID: SONNTAGNACHMI.

"Sonntagknockme?" GW said. "What the hell does that mean?"

"I think it's the name of one of Pichler's companies," I said. "Or the beginning of it, anyway. The whole thing's too long to fit on the screen."

"The Germans," Biddle snorted, as if this was something he had to deal with all the time.

Clarice reached out and gave me a little shove. *"Answer it."*

I answered.

"Katrina Gilver-McPherson."

"Katrina! It's Ulf! How are you?"

The man on the line sounded extremely German, which I expected. He also sounded extremely cheerful, which I didn't expect.

"I'm good," I said. "How are you?"

"Wonderful now that I'm speaking to you! You have turned my frown upside down, as you Americans say! You do say that, don't you? I think I saw that on Facebook. Was it a meme, perhaps? Anyway, where are you?"

My eyes went wide.

The conversation was *not* going how I'd expected.

"I'm . . . on the road at the moment."

"Coming to Arizona, I hope! Berdache?

That's where the action is!"

"Yes. That's right."

"Perfect! We can meet for dinner and talk!"

"Okay. Good idea."

"Good? It's great! It's *fantastic*! What a stroke of luck!"

"Oh?"

Pichler laughed.

"I've been dying to meet you, Katrina!" he said. "I think you're just the person to clear this whole mess up!"

CAVALLO DI COPPE
CHEVALIER DE COUPES
KNIGHT OF CHALICES
CABALLO DE COPAS
RITTER DER KELCHE
BEKERS RIDDER

Upright, the Knight of Cups isn't exactly a man of action, despite all the armor. Just look at how he's holding the reins. He's keeping his horse to a nice slow amble so he doesn't spill a precious drop of his venti iced café latte (or whatever it is he's got in that cup). Reversed, then, we've got the opposite: the dude's finally doing something, even if it's just getting dropped on his tin-plated head . . .

Miss Chance, *Infinite Roads to Knowing*

I got to the restaurant twenty minutes early so I could choose the table and give my first line of defense, GW, time to get into position nearby.

Pichler was already there.

He was sitting alone at a table in the middle of the restaurant. The place usually would have been packed — even in sleepy little Berdache, the best/only seafood joint in town fills up on a Saturday night — yet all the other tables were empty. The only customers were at the bar running along one side of the restaurant.

"Sorry; we're not seating for dinner tonight," the maître d' said as I walked in. "Private party."

"I think I'm invited," I said.

The maître d' — who wasn't in a tux but looked like he wished he was — smiled primly. "Ms. Gilver-McPherson?"

I nodded.

The maître d' swept out an arm and stepped from behind his podium. "This way, please."

He noticed someone coming in behind me — GW — and paused. "We're not seating for —"

"I heard," said GW, heading for the bar. "I'm just here for an appletini."

The maître d' carried on toward Pichler. I carried on with him.

Pichler stood as we approached, a grin spreading across his tanned face. He looked a little older than in the pictures I'd seen — grayer and more leathery — but there was an intensity to him that no photo could have captured. His eyes locked onto mine in a bold, direct, fearless way, and his already toothy smile grew even toothier. The guy was *alive.*

"Katrina! Thank you for coming! This is so exciting! We have so much to talk about! Please, have a seat, have a seat! How was your flight? When did you get in? Isn't this town marvelous? You think there's nothing but tumbleweeds and coyotes, and then hey presto! Coffee shops and occult bookstores and seafood restaurants! At first I thought it was a mirage! Would you like something to drink? Wine? A cocktail? Champagne? I'm having the My Old Kentucky Home rye mint julep, and it is divine, simply divine! Would you like to try one? Yes? A mint julep for my friend, please! Oh, I think you're going to love it! I haven't had one this good since the last time I was at the derby!"

How could I say no to the drink? I'd been in Pichler's presence all of ten seconds and I already felt like I needed one. Or maybe it was some speed I needed, just to help me keep up.

Pichler had taken his seat again as I sat down, and he finally stopped talking long enough to sip his divine, simply divine mint julep.

I stole a sidelong look at the bar and spotted GW paying for a pint of beer. I knew he wasn't an appletini type.

Half the people around him were openly staring at me. The other half was just being more subtle about it.

It felt weird but comforting, too. If Pichler was the killer, at least he wouldn't try to off me in front of a room full of witnesses.

Then again, anyone who gets into competitive hot dog eating is capable of anything.

Pichler noticed where I was looking.

"Feels like you're in a zoo, doesn't it?" he said. "On the wrong side of the bars."

For the first time, it didn't sound like he

was shouting into an eighty-year-old's hearing aid.

"That's why I arranged for us to have a little space," he went on, still subdued. "I'm used to being stared at. I admit I actually enjoy it most of the time. But being overheard I prefer to avoid."

I nodded at our audience at the bar. "What is it you don't want them to hear?"

Pichler's "on" switch got flipped again. Suddenly, he was beaming.

"About the painting, of course! For your sake!"

For a man who didn't want to be overheard, he sure was loud.

"For my sake?" I said.

"Yes! At the moment, you've got an exclusive. A scoop! That's why you've come all this way, isn't it? You've got to seal the deal, as they say! Yes? Correct? Am I right?"

"Why are *you* here?"

"The self-same reason! And now my competitive juices are flowing! Who will find the prize first? I hope you will forgive a little trash talk, but . . . it shall be me!"

I was about to ask him how he knew to come to Berdache when a server showed up with my mint julep.

"Are you ready to order?" she asked after putting down the drink.

"Not yet," Pichler said. "My appetite is still building, and I have yet to see where it will lead!"

The server gave him a fake laugh and a puzzled smile and quickly retreated.

"So —," I said.

"So," Pichler said at the same time, "how did you know to come to Berdache?"

"I got a tip," I said. "How did *you* — ?"

"Ooo! You got a tip! Very mysterious!" Pichler cut in. "Do you know who it was from? Or was it anonymous?"

"Anonymous. How did *you* — ?"

"And you believed it?"

"It included some very convincing details. How did *you* — ?"

"Details about what?"

"How the painting came to be here. How did *you* — ?"

"So you know who has it?"

"I know who *had* it. How did *you* — ?"

"Fascinating! I can't wait to hear more! But, come — you haven't even tried your My Old Kentucky Home rye mint julep!"

"How did you know to come to Berdache?"

"Oh, simplicity itself. I got a tip!"

Pichler raised his glass in a toast.

I resisted the urge to raise mine and throw it into his face.

We clinked glasses and drank.

The mint julep wasn't divine, simply divine, but it was damn good.

I was halfway through my second sip when Pichler said, "Are you familiar with a man named Robert Dryja?"

If he was trying to get a spit-take out of me, he failed — but just barely.

The guy was asking *me* everything I'd planned to ask *him.*

"I know who he is," I said.

"You never met him? Never communicated with him? Never interviewed him for one of your articles, let's say?"

"Why would I?"

Pichler grinned and wagged a finger at me in an "I see what you did there" kind of way.

"Turning an answer into a question. I love it!" he said. "But I'm going to press a little harder. Were you ever in contact with Robert Dryja?"

I took another sip of my mint julep and reminded myself who I was: Katrina Gilver-McPherson, ace reporter. And you know what she'd be saying to herself if a source started talking to her like that?

Lois Lane wouldn't put up with this crap. And neither will I.

"You know what, Mr. Pichler? I think it's time for *me* to start pressing harder. Because — in case you've forgotten — I *am* the press at this table. And I want to know what *your* relationship with Dryja was and if he's the reason you're in Berdache. And if you don't tell me, I'm just going to keep digging until I find out — and you might not like what you end up reading the next time you see my byline."

Pichler considered me gravely for a moment . . . then burst out laughing.

"Oh, such an *amuse-bouche,* this conversation. Such an appetizer!" he said. "But now — on to the meat!"

He raised his left hand over his head and curled his fingers three times. For a moment, I thought he meant "on to the meat" literally and he was about to order dinner.

The woman who started toward us from the bar wasn't our server, though. When I turned to look at her, I found Hector the bellman's words echoing in my brain.

She had blond hair. Shoulder length. And a round face. Big cheeks, like a baby. And she was dressed like a professional . . .

It was the blond Hector had seen Robert Dryja having a drink with at the Devil's Ridge Lodge. Still dressed like a professional and with a drink in her hand again. A lemon drop, by the look of it.

As she sat down beside me, I noticed something for the first time — and wanted to kick myself for it.

The table was set for three.

"Katrina Gilver-McPherson of the *Philadelphia Post,*" Pichler said to me with a smile. He held a hand out toward the blond. "Meet Katrina Gilver-McPherson of the *Philadelphia Post.*"

FANTE DI COPPE
VALET DE COUPES
KNAVE OF CHALICES
SOTA DE COPAS
BUBE DER KELCHE
BEKERS SCHILDKNAAP

So you're a mime in a turban and MC Hammer pants who thinks fish pop out of beverages to talk to you. Congratulations: you're living in a Salvador Dalí painting. Kind of freaky, isn't it? Just wait till you see the melting clocks! If upright the Knave of Cups gives us a glimpse of unbridled imagination and the value of tapping into the subconscious, flipping him sends us tumbling into the Twilight Zone, where unbridled imagination spills over into an outright nightmare. You'll want to be careful while you're there. If you think those pants are unsettling, you ain't seen nothin' yet.

Miss Chance, *Infinite Roads to Knowing*

You know the little voice in your head people talk about? The one that whispers things like "you can do it" or "don't trust that guy" or "you already ate half a pint of Chubby Hubby . . . you may as well finish it."

My little voice turned into a very, very big voice.

Abort! Abort! Abort! it was screaming.

If the restaurant had come equipped with ejection seats, I would have used mine.

But here's the thing about the little voice in your head: you don't necessarily have just one.

So they know you were lying about being a journalist, another little voice in my head said. *So what? They're still not going to kill you in the middle of a seafood restaurant.*

You came here to get information, said another little voice. *Well . . . go ahead and get it.*

I want more of that mint julep, said yet another little voice. *Why did you stop drinking?*

The cioppino here is supposed to be fabulous, said yet another. *See if you can still get the German to pay for dinner.*

And through it all, the first little voice kept screaming *Abort! Abort! Abort!*

I shut it up with a nice, long drink.

Pilcher grinned as if he could hear the little voices, too.

Katrina Gilver-McPherson — the real blond one — just cocked an eyebrow and waited patiently for me to put my glass back down.

When I did, all that was in it was some ice and a limp sprig of mint.

I focused on the blond. She had big, round, unstylish glasses and cherubic cheeks and a pencil neck, yet she looked pretty and professional and poised.

"Pleased to meet me," I said to her. "What brings me to this part of the country?"

"A story," Gilver-McPherson said.

"Of course. How's it going?"

"Not well, actually. I've run into a dead end."

Gilver-McPherson winced.

Unfortunate choice of words.

"Robert Dryja," I said. "Was he working

for you, too?"

Pilcher burst out with a big "A-*ha*!"

"*Now* we're getting somewhere!" he said. "So he was working for you, as well?"

"Me?" I said. "No. But I know he was working for Glenn Budziak and that Budziak thinks he was feeding information to you. I suppose a private eye's integrity wouldn't cost much to a man who can give away Chagalls."

It was just a guess. All Budziak had said was that Dryja was sort of working for him and sort of working for Pilcher and really just working for himself.

It paid off. Pilcher didn't deny it. In fact, for the first time he looked capable of feeling embarrassment.

"How about it?" I said to Gilver-McPherson. "Was Dryja helping you with your story?"

"Not for money," she snapped back. "He was just a source. I do my own investigating."

"And I'm sure you're very good at it. In fact, maybe you've already figured out who else is here looking for you-know-what."

"What are you talking about?" Gilver-McPherson asked.

Pilcher tried to answer for me.

"Whoever killed Dryja," he said. He gave

me a smile that was a little less exuberant than the ones he'd been wearing before. "Assuming it wasn't you."

"It wasn't. And assuming it wasn't you or Budziak — and I'm not assuming that, actually — there's a good chance it was two men I've crossed paths with. Old-school tough guys from back east. Any idea who they are?"

Pilcher shrugged and looked amused.

Gilver-McPherson did neither. Quite the opposite: she went very still and looked very, very unamused.

"Why would you consider Budziak a suspect?" she asked me.

"Because he's in town. At the same hotel Dryja was staying at."

"Glenn Budziak is at the Devil's Ridge Lodge?" Pilcher hooted. "Oh, this just gets more and more interesting! He's a bit unhinged, that one. What a twist. I love it!"

Gilver-McPherson didn't share in the merriment.

"The old-school tough guys," she said to me gravely. "How would you describe them?"

"Well, when I say old-school, I mean *old* school: oughta-be-playing-shuffleboard-in-Florida old. One's balding, got a belly. The other one looks like he used to be a real bruiser. Both white. Ring any bells?"

"Maybe. I've been interviewing some of Big Mike's old cronies. Of course, I never let on that I was closing in on anything. But a couple of them might have figured it out."

She looked haunted by the thought.

"Or they could've just seen your article and put two and two together," I suggested. "Just because Big Mike knew who took the painting didn't mean they did. And once they figured out it, they might have followed the trail here somehow."

"Or maybe they just followed *me,*" Gilver-McPherson said. "And now Robert Dryja is dead."

Pilcher reached out and patted her hand.

"I counted two *maybes,* two *might haves,* and a *could have* just now," he said. "Don't blame yourself for anything yet, Katrina."

"Fine," she said softly. "Not yet."

She lifted her lemon drop with a shaky hand and brought it to her lips.

"Why couldn't they have followed *you*?" I asked Pilcher.

He laughed dismissively.

"You said your old-school crooks came from the east," he said. "Somehow, I don't think you meant as far east as Hamburg."

"So you came straight here from there? That's a long trip to make for a maybe, a might, or a could. You must've been pretty confident you were gonna get what you were after when you got here."

Some of the wild gleam kindled again in Pilcher's eyes.

"Oh, you are a tricky one! Put me on the defensive, then reel me in! Very good! I can see that this will go much more smoothly for me if we work together." Pilcher sighed. "If only I could be certain you're not a murderer . . ."

"I know the feeling," I said. "Frustrating, isn't it?"

"It is, it is. Of course, you can be a bit more certain about me. I mean, is the eighty-third most famous man in the world going to shoot someone to death in a hotel parking lot?"

"How do you know — ?"

Pilcher waved my question away before I could finish it.

"I spoke to the policeman who's investigating Dryja's death," he said. "Detective . . . Burpy, I believe? Furby? Smurfy? Anyway, he didn't mind sharing the general outline of the crime. You know. Seeing as I'm not even a suspect."

"Actually, I was about to ask how you know you're the eighty-third most famous man in the world," I lied.

"Oh! A *Der Speigel* poll. June 4, 2015. If you give me your email address, I'll send you a link."

"I'll take your word for it."

"I wish you wouldn't."

"Sorry. I guess you just have a trustworthy face. Maybe that's why it's so famous."

"Look, you two," Gilver-McPherson snapped, exasperated. "I'm glad you're enjoying your little dance, but that's not how I do business — especially when my business is this serious. A man is dead. Can we please cut to the chase?"

Pilcher nodded, looking contrite, though there was just enough of a smirk still on his face to suggest that he was thinking, "Awww, you're no fun."

"By all means," he said.

"Cut away," I said.

Gilver-McPherson locked an intense gaze on me through her big round glasses. It felt like I was in a staring contest with an owl.

"What are you after?" she said.

"The truth."

The eyes behind her Coke bottle lenses rolled.

"That's my job," she scoffed. "Everyone else I understand." She nodded at Pilcher. "He came for the painting."

"For the sport of hunting it," Pilcher corrected.

Gilver-McPherson threw him a "yeah, right" glower before continuing.

"Budziak wants to prove once and for all that he wasn't Big Mike's inside man for the Bischoff Gallery job. Dryja was just turning a buck. And those old crooks you mentioned — if you're telling the truth about that, and if my guess about them is right — are probably grabbing a last chance to get in on a big score. So which is it for you? The score? The sport? The reward?"

"Reward?" I said.

Gilver-McPherson gave me another long, owlish look, obviously trying to decide if I was playing dumb or coming by it honestly.

"The Bischoff Gallery's insurance company had to pay out millions after the robbery," she explained. "They still want to recoup their loss. They'll pay $250,000 to anyone who helps them recover *Stormy Sea from Scheveningen Pier.* No questions asked."

"Does that interest you?" Pilcher said.

Of course it did. But not for the obvious reason: *money money money!*

The word that was echoing through my brain like a thunderclap was *Biddle Biddle Biddle!*

"Like I said," I told Pilcher, "all I want out of this is the truth."

"Why do you care?" Gilver-McPherson said.

It was a roundabout way of asking "who the hell are you?" And I didn't intend to answer.

My best guarantee of safety was my anonymity. I wasn't going to give it up if I could help it.

And maybe I couldn't.

"See — I told you it was her!" a woman cried. "*Cielito!* How are you?"

I turned to find a tiny wrinkled woman tottering toward me with open arms. Just behind her were two men. One was the maître d'. The other was a muscular, dark-haired man with a sheepish look on his handsome face.

It was the woman's son — Victor Castellanos.

COPPE
COUPES
10
CHALICES
COPAS
KELCHE
BEKERS

Uh-oh: domestic bliss has been flipped on its head. Either you're not appreciating how good you've got it or all that good stuff just got thrown in a blender set to puree. Whichever it is, you can file the results under "Paradise Lost." If you want to find it again, you'll either need a whole new perspective or some much better luck — or, most likely, both.

Miss Chance, *Infinite Roads to Knowing*

"I'm sorry, ma'am," the maître d' was saying. "This is a private party."

Lucia Castellanos didn't slow down. (Not that she was going that fast. The woman was nearly eighty, and she took teeny little strides that probably brought her all of three inches closer with each step.)

I fought the urge to peek toward the bar to see if GW was going to head the Castellanoses off. It was too late to do it without being noticed — *very* noticed — and he'd tagged along to protect me from assassination attempts, not awkward social encounters.

"Party? Doesn't look like much of a party to me," Lucia was saying. "And anyway, we're just coming over to say hello."

"Mom," said Victor, looking profoundly miserable. "We shouldn't interrupt."

"Oh, don't be silly. We're not interrupting anything, are we?"

She was asking me, but it was Pilcher who answered.

"Not at all!" Pilcher turned to the maître d'. "It's quite alright, Richard."

Richard stopped, nodded, spun on his heel, and marched back to his podium at the front of the restaurant.

I stood to greet Lucia, and she wrapped her stubby arms around my ribs (because that was as far up as she came on me).

"I haven't seen you in ages, *cielito*!" she said, giving me a hug that would've made a boa constrictor proud. "Where have you been?"

"Here and there," I said. "Busy."

Pilcher and Gilver-McPherson shot smirks at each other. They still didn't know who I was, but they'd just learned one thing about me for certain: I was local.

"She's still busy, Mom," Victor said. "We should leave her to it."

He was avoiding looking at me or the people I was sitting with, which is why he was so surprised when Pilcher said, "Aren't you going to introduce me to your friends, *cielito*?"

No introduction was necessary for Pilcher. Victor recognized him.

I guess that can happen when you're the eighty-third most famous man in the world.

"Ulf Pilcher, Katrina Gilver-McPherson," I said. "Lucia and Victor."

Pilcher rose, walked to Lucia, and bent over (a lot) to kiss the back of her hand.

"Charmed," he said. He turned to Victor and held out his hand. "Victorrrrr . . . ?"

"Castellanos," Victor said as they shook.

He looked at me with wide eyes that said, *Is this really happening?* Lucia, on the other hand, clearly had no idea Pilcher was anything special. In fact, she narrowed her eyes and gave him a suspicious glare.

"Who are you here with?" she asked.

Pilcher furrowed his brow, confused. He held a hand out toward the table.

"My two lovely guests, as you see," he said.

"Oh," Lucia said. "So it's the three of you?"

Pilcher nodded slowly . . . then grinned as he got it.

Lucia wanted to know if he and I were there on a date.

"Yes, just the three of us," Pilcher said. "I suppose you could call this a business meeting."

"Oh. Well. We don't want to get in the way," Victor said. "Come on, Mom."

He started to turn away. Lucia didn't turn with him. She was as small as a shrub, yet suddenly she seemed to be planted there by the table as firmly as a giant redwood.

"Victor was taking me out for a nice piece of fish," she said. "What they serve us at the home you shouldn't give to a cat! But now, with your party or meeting or whatever taking up the whole restaurant . . . well, I guess we'll have to drive all the way over to Prescott and go to the Red Lobster."

Pilcher opened his mouth to answer. I knew everything he was going to say for the next minute.

First: "I won't hear of it! Please, join us!"

Then: "So how do you know each other?"

Then: "Tarot cards! How interesting! And what's the name of this shop?"

Then: "How charming! And it's right around the corner, you say? I'll have to drop in sometime. Now . . . who's ready for a nice piece of fish?"

I had to rewrite the script.

I took Lucia by the arm and started talking.

First: "There must be a Red Lobster up in Flagstaff. That would be closer."

Then: "Here, let me walk you out. I'll be right back, Ulf."

Then: "I haven't seen you in so long, Lucia! I wish I could be going with you!"

Then: "What a beautiful night! It's a shame I have to spend it talking business."

And finally: "Well, here we are! Enjoy the Red Lobster! Give me a call sometime — we'll go out together again!"

I closed the door on Victor's car. Lucia was in the front passenger's seat. Victor was standing beside me on the sidewalk.

"Did you get my messages?" he asked.

My gaze darted this way and that up the darkened street. A homicidal — and heavily armed — woman was still out there somewhere. When she made another try for me (and I knew that was a when, not an if), I didn't want Victor or Lucia anywhere nearby.

"Yeah. Sorry I didn't reply. Things have been crazy lately," I said quickly, backing away from the car. "Well, tell the lobsters I said hi."

Victor stared at me slack-jawed. "That's all you've got to say?"

"Sorry — gotta get back to my business thingie."

"Call him when you're done!" Lucia shouted from inside the car. "Maybe you kids could go out for dessert!"

I just kept backing away.

Victor shook his head, incredulous.

"Really?" he said to me. "I mean . . . you're not even going to tell me how it is you're having dinner with Ulf Pilcher?"

"Later! Bye!"

I turned and began walking toward the restaurant. As I went, I listened for the sound of another door opening and closing, an engine starting, a car cruising away.

When I'd heard them all, I glanced back. Victor and Lucia were gone.

I turned and began walking *away* from the restaurant. There was nothing for me there now but another free drink, maybe a nice piece of fish, and more opportunities to blow my cover and allow Pilcher to figure out who I was.

No, thanks. I'd learned more from the conversation than I'd given away. Time to quit while I was ahead. And anyway, I had another fish to fry.

I stuck to side streets as I made my way back to the White Magic Five and Dime, avoiding the traffic and lights along Furnier Avenue — and the witnesses and innocent bystanders. I may as well have been wearing a couple sandwich boards. Instead of *EAT AT JOE'S* it would say *SHOOT* on the front, *ME* on the back.

No one took me up on the offer, though, which was disappointing.

About a dozen steps from home, as I walked across the unlit gravel lot behind the shop, I finally heard what I'd been waiting and hoping for.

"Hold it right there, lady."

It was GW. And he wasn't talking to me.

"Like hell I will!" a woman spat back.

It was her. The assassin. I turned to see what she was coming after me with this time. A bazooka? A flamethrower?

She was at the edge of the lot, about twenty yards behind me, still wearing her trench coat and fedora. I couldn't see GW beyond her, but I knew he was back there in the shadows somewhere — far enough to make it look like I was alone but close enough to have my back. I hoped.

The woman started to pull something long and pipelike out from under the coat. For a second, I was relieved.

A baseball bat? Really? This was going to be easier than I thought.

Then I noticed moonlight glinting on black steel and dark, polished wood.

It wasn't a bat. It was a shotgun. And in about half a second, it was going to be pointed at me.

COPPE
COUPES
9
CHALICES
COPAS
KELCHE
BEKERS

Pay no attention to that man behind the curtain! Oh, you can't see him anyway? Well, he's there, all right: the Nine of Cups sometimes tells us that the curtains have fallen away and what's hidden is revealed. But let's pay attention to that man in front of the curtain instead. Look at the self-satisfaction on the big lug's mug, all because he got his cup collection lined up just so. Reverse the card and the cups come crashing down. It's a mess — and an opportunity. Before Big Boy there starts picking up his cups, maybe he'll finally notice that they're made to be filled — and his hold nothing.

Miss Chance, *Infinite Roads to Knowing*

Say what you will about Yosemite Sam, at least he had the decency to let Bugs Bunny make peace with God before blasting away at him.

There would be no "Say your prayers, varmint!" for me, though. Just the blasting.

I didn't have time to either stop the woman or escape the spray of buckshot she was about to send my way. Apparently, GW was too far off to do anything, too: I heard him say "hey!" somewhere behind her, but he didn't hurl himself on her before she could get her shotgun leveled at me.

Fortunately, Biddle did — though "hurl" would be a charitable way to describe how he wound up on top of her. More accurately, he climbed out from behind the wheel of my black Cadillac, where he'd been keeping an eye on the Five and Dime, staggered stiff-legged toward the woman (he'd been sitting for ovcr an hour by that point), stumbled, and fell on her.

They both went down.

Miraculously, the shotgun didn't go off.

"Ow!" the woman cried. "Goddamn it, that hurt!"

"Gimme that," said Biddle, latching onto the shotgun barrel — which was now aimed straight at me.

"Leggo!" the woman barked back.

They began rolling around on the ground, jerking the shotgun back and forth. I hopped this way and that, yet somehow no matter who had the upper hand, I stayed in the shotgun's sights. If the woman just pulled the trigger, I'd be shredded. Yet all her attention was now on Biddle.

"I said leggo!"

"I said gimme!"

"Leggo!"

"Gimme!"

"Leg *go*!"

"Gim *me*!"

GW finally came charging out of the darkness to yank the shotgun away from both of them.

"Should we call the police?" I heard Ceecee say.

I turned to find her and Clarice watching wide-eyed from the back door of the White Magic Five and Dime.

I looked up and down the block and saw no sidewalk gawkers, no silhouettes in windows, no cars driving past.

"No," I said. "Not yet."

"Come on," GW said to the woman on the ground. "Inside."

Biddle tried to push her up — she was more or less lying on his chest — but she slapped his hands away.

"Watch the mitts, buster," she said.

The voice sounded familiar now that she wasn't shouting "gimme!" I stepped closer and noticed a sickeningly sweet scent.

White Diamonds.

"Oh, god," I said. "It's her."

"Who?" said Biddle.

He grunted and groaned as the woman wriggled into a sitting position using him as her seat, then slowly pushed herself to her feet.

"Shut up," the woman snarled. "I don't weigh that much, ya sissy."

GW sniffed the air as she began to move past him, headed for the back door.

"Oh," he groaned. "I should've known."

"No way! It's her, isn't it?" Clarice said as the woman approached her.

Ceecee looked like she wanted to run off and find her autograph book.

"She's real!" she squealed. "Wow!"

"Why does it feel like everyone knows something I don't?" Biddle said.

I walked over, stared down at him a moment, then offered him a hand.

He took it.

"Because," I said as I pulled him up off the ground, "everyone knows something you don't."

"Well, that sure is helpful."

I held on to Biddle while he got steady on his feet.

"Thanks for jumping in to help like that," I told him.

"That's what I'm here for, sweetie," he said.

I still wanted to believe him. And I still didn't.

I unclasped his hand.

He held onto mine for an extra second before letting go to brush the gravel dust off himself.

"Let's go upstairs," I said, "and I'll explain everything."

Ceecee and Clarice gaped at the wrinkled little woman sitting at our dinky dining room table. A moment before, Biddle had taken off her trench coat and fedora. (Him: "Allow me, madam"; Her: "Screw you, slick.") Underneath, she'd been wearing a powder blue pantsuit and pearls, and her snow-white hair was perfectly permed.

"She looks like somebody's grandma," Ceecee said.

The old woman scowled at Ceecee's short blue hair. "Better than looking like a Smurf."

"Smurfs don't have blue hair," Clarice said.

"Better than looking like a little punk freak, then," the woman shot back.

Clarice shook her head and clucked her tongue. "That's not a very smurfy thing to say."

"Screw you, too."

Biddle pulled a ring of keys from the woman's coat and tossed it on the table.

"No ID, no other weapons," he said. "Just this."

GW walked over, snatched up the keys, and headed for the staircase.

"Be right back," he said to me. "You fill in the old-timer."

"Old-timer?" the woman growled.

"I believe he's referring to me," said Biddle.

"Oh." The woman swiveled in her seat to glare at GW. "Hey! Pretty boy! Put a scratch on my car, I'll scratch out your eyes!"

GW gave her a wink and a thumbs-up and

started down the stairs.

"So, Alanis," Biddle said. "Just who is our charming guest?"

"She calls herself 'the Fixer,' " I said. "She's a wannabe hit- . . . person."

"Wannabe?" the woman spat.

I ignored her.

"I crossed paths with her a few weeks ago. She was mixed up in some trouble Marsha Riggs was in, so GW and I tracked her down."

Ceecee cleared her throat.

"With some help from the girls," I threw in.

"We found her, basically," Clarice told Biddle.

"And GW and I confronted her," I said.

The Fixer snorted and rolled her eyes. "And *I* got away! Amateurs."

"Hey, lady," I said, "I'm not the one assassinating pigeons and leaving Uzis lying around."

The old woman's shoulders sagged, and some of the spark went out of her eyes. She began rubbing the gnarled knuckles of her liver-spotted hands.

"It's my arthritis. I can't handle the kick on those things anymore."

She moved her right hand to her left shoulder and winced.

"Feeling a little banged up?" Biddle asked her gently.

The Fixer looked up at him and nodded, then turned to glower at me.

"Well . . . ain't ya gonna offer a sore old lady some goddamn Tylenol?"

I glowered back. "I'll get you Tylenol, ibuprofen, aspirin, Southern Comfort, morphine, whatever you want . . . *after* you tell us who hired you to kill me."

The Fixer crossed her arms firmly — and winced again.

"No dice, sister," she said. "I'm a pro. I don't sell out my clients."

"If you don't tell us, it's gonna be the police doing the asking," Biddle said.

The old woman sat up straight.

"Bring 'em on," she sneered, and she smiled in a way that was both defiant and excited.

She wasn't in it for the money, I realized then. She was after the thrills. She'd been bored or lonely or depressed, so she'd found a way to inject some excitement into her life.

Some people play bingo. She became an assassin.

It takes different strokes to move the world.

"You know what?" I said to her. "I respect

that. A professional's got to have a code. Yours is you don't rat out the people you work for. That's admirable. So I've got a proposal for you."

The Fixer eyed me warily. "Yeah?"

"Yeah. Come work for *me.*"

"What?" the old woman said.

I heard Ceecee start to say it, too, but Clarice elbowed her in the side.

"I'd like to buy out your contract," I said. "Whatever they're paying, I'll double. In cash. Right now. Then *I'm* your client — and we can talk."

The woman scratched pensively at her chin. "Well . . ."

There were footsteps on the stairs, and a moment later GW appeared. He put the Fixer's car keys on the kitchen counter, beside her shotgun and shells and trench coat, and looked at the old woman with begrudging respect.

"Found her car — a dark blue Toyota Camry — parked around the corner. No registration. No emissions test. No paperwork of any kind."

"So no name," said Biddle. He gave the old woman an approving look. "I do hope you'll join the organization. We could use somebody like you."

He'd seen it in her, too. That need to do

something. Maybe be a part of something.

The Fixer cocked a silvery-white eyebrow. "There's an organization?"

I nodded. "A small one, but a productive one. I assume that's why somebody hired you, actually. We've been a little too productive for some people's comfort." I smiled grimly. "We are *not* amateurs."

The old woman looked at each of us in turn, lingering the longest, for some reason, on Ceecee. I didn't know if she was thinking "Pretty young to be part of an 'organization' " or "Looks kinda gothy . . . ooo, just like Abby on *NCIS*!"

She focused on me again.

"Two Gs, and I'm in."

I nodded, turned, and walked around the kitchen counter to the refrigerator. In the freezer was a container marked *MEATLOAF.* Inside it was around $4,000 in cash — leftovers from my mother. It had been $20,000 when I'd first come to Berdache, but I'd been using the stash to pay back Mom's marks whenever I could. The money in her old bank account had been draining slowly but surely, too. If the marks didn't stop turning up — or I didn't stop paying for my mother's sins — we'd be broke by the end of the year.

But that was a problem for another day.

Today's problem count was huge enough already. Hopefully, I could reduce it by one.

I counted out the cash I needed, then closed the container and put it back behind the stack of Hot Pockets boxes that had been in the fridge ever since I'd moved in.

I walked over and gave the money to the Fixer.

"Two Gs in cold, hard cash," I said.

"Cold and hard is right," the woman said, picking up the stiff bills. But if she was put off by my private banking system, she didn't say so. She just folded the money up and stuffed it into her slacks.

"So," she said. "Whadaya wanna know, boss?"

"Who hired you, how, and when?"

"I don't know the who. They contacted me the same way you did when you tried to trap me."

"Through your ad on Greylist.com."

The Fixer beamed. " 'If you're having trouble with someone, I am the solution. I provide killer service. It'll be a hit, man.' I wrote that myself!"

"I remember. Very clever." I rolled my hands in the air. "So they sent you an email, and . . . ?"

"And we struck a deal. A thousand bucks, five hundred up front. We set up a drop in a public place — you can bet I was careful after what you tried to pull on me — and they came through with the cash. So I got to work. When I realized you were the target . . . well, that just seemed like a bonus, given what happened last time I saw you." The old woman gave me a tight, not entirely convincing smile. "Of course, that's all behind us now."

"Do you remember the email address of the person who hired you?" Clarice asked.

"Yeah, actually: totallyuntraceable@greylist.com. Lives up to the name, too."

"When did you get the first message from that address?" I asked.

The Fixer shrugged. "Ten, eleven days ago. I couldn't move on the contract right away because my sciatica was acting up."

Biddle and I looked at each other.

The Fixer noticed.

"Hey, a lot of people have sciatica," she groused. "It doesn't mean I can't get the job done."

"It's not that," I assured her. "It's just that the timing is interesting."

"Oh, I get it!" Ceecee piped up. "That article about Big Mike only came out, like, four days ago, and that's what got everybody running around looking for the missing painting. Which means whoever wanted to have you killed probably isn't connected to the whole museum robbery thing. Right?"

She didn't notice Clarice's wide-eyed "ix-nay on the ainting-pay" stare until she was done talking.

"What?" said Ceecee.

"Museum robbery?" said the Fixer. "Big Mike?"

The old woman looked ecstatic. We *were* an organization.

"Oh," Ceecee said meekly. "Um . . . never mind."

"So . . . Fixer," I said. "Is there anything else you can tell us about the contract on me?"

The Fixer perked up even more. I was probably the first person to address her by her nom de Uzi.

"Just that the advance I got was in fresh new twenties in a plain paper bag," she said. "It didn't tell me anything about who it was from."

I nodded. "Alright, then. That's it for now. Stand by and await instructions. We'll be in touch when we're ready to move."

The Fixer looked crestfallen. "So I should . . . go?"

I nodded again. "Don't worry. You won't have to wait long. I get the feeling we're going to need your particular set of skills very soon."

That cheered her up again.

She winked at Biddle.

"See ya later, slick," she said, and she stood, hobbled stiffly to the kitchen counter, and reached for her things, including her shotgun.

GW tensed and shot a look my way.

"It's okay," I told him. "She's one of us now."

"Whatever you say . . . boss," he said. But he went back to eyeing the Fixer warily as she put on her trench coat, slipped her keys and shells into the roomy pockets, and picked up her shotgun.

"Pleasure doing business with you," she said.

She turned and started toward the stairs. None of us said a word until we'd heard her go all the way down the steps, through the office, and out the back door.

It was a long wait.

"The Grandis," Clarice said the second the door closed. "I bet ya anything they hired her."

"I wouldn't take that bet," I said.

"Who are the Grandis?" Biddle asked.

I sighed. "Some of Mom's old competitors. Grifters with tarot parlors. At first they assumed I was here to horn in on their action the way she had, so they tried to kill me."

"Us," Clarice cut in.

"Later," I went on, "they figured out that I didn't want to *steal* their kind of business, I wanted to *end* it." I flapped a weary hand at the stairs the Fixer had just gone down. "So they tried to kill me."

"They're evil," Clarice said, "but they're consistent."

Biddle looked from her to me and back again. "I didn't know you had that kind of trouble here."

"Me neither," said GW, his expression both concerned and strangely exasperated.

"Hey, sorry if I haven't kept everyone up to date on who's out to kill me. Things have been a little kooky lately, what with dead people turning up alive and live people turning up dead and finding out my mother used to keep a million-dollar painting behind a velvet Elvis. But I'll be sure to put it all in the next Christmas newsletter so everyone feels in the loop."

"Speaking of keeping people in the loop," Biddle said, walking toward the dining room table, "how'd it go with the German tonight?"

He slowly lowered himself into the chair

the Fixer had been in and crossed his arms and legs.

The message was clear: he wasn't leaving until after he'd heard everything . . . and probably not then, either.

We'd just dealt with one threat. Now it was on to the next. Together.

It was late. I was tired. So I didn't fight it.

I told him — and GW and Clarice and Ceecee — what I'd learned. And when I was done, we discussed how we'd move forward in the morning.

We had a painting to find and a killer to catch — and an organization to do the finding and catching.

KELCHE
BEKERS
COPPE
COUPES
8
CHALICES
COPAS

Hey — not so fast, Jack! We see you trying to leave the party without saying goodbye. You got those golden cups set up so nicely, and now you're going to slink off into the hills before we can even start drinking from them? No way! Get your leotarded butt back here and grab yourself a chalice. The party's just getting started, bub, and you're the guest of honor.

Miss Chance, *Infinite Roads to Knowing*

We all had our assigned roles as part of the plan. It wasn't going to be easy for any of us, and the first part was the hardest.

Go to sleep.

Not. Happening.

I'd tried to strong-arm the girls into going to Ceecee's for the night, but her parents weren't as laissez-faire (or, depending on your outlook, negligent) as me: their daughter's girlfriend wasn't welcome to pop in for impromptu sleepovers. Since Ceecee refused to leave Clarice's side — "Not until, like, the weirdness blows over," she said (making the perhaps naïve assumption that it eventually would) — the sleepover would have to be at our place. And it wasn't going to be a girls-only pajama party.

GW and Biddle were staying the night, too. "Safety in numbers," as they say. "Keep your friends close and your enemies closer." And your frenemies closest of all.

I still didn't believe Biddle was in Berdache because he suddenly wanted a World's Greatest Dad mug. And I couldn't get over the worry that GW was too good to be true. A professional ne'er-do-well is suddenly there-doing-well just because . . . why? He liked me? And he's damn cute to boot? I still couldn't accept it, for some reason.

Part of the reason was lying on my couch with my favorite pillow under his head.

"Was I snoring?" Biddle said.

"No. You weren't even asleep."

"I know. But you're standing there looking at me like you're angry."

"I'm in my forties and I've never been in a relationship that lasted more than six months," I could've said. "You don't think I've got a right to be angry?"

But it wasn't the time or place to talk out my trust issues, and he wasn't the person to talk them out with.

"Sweetie, 'trust me' is just another way to say 'bend over,' " Biddle told me when I was waaaaay too young for "bend over" talk.

"I'm not angry," I lied. "I just can't sleep."

"Oh, I get it." Biddle nodded at the bedroom door behind me. "*He* snores."

On the other side of the door GW was stretched out on my floor with my best comforter and my second-favorite pillow.

("If I can't get the couch, I'll take this," he'd said as he settled in for the night. "You know . . . as long as there aren't any other spots available." I'd turned out the light.)

"I don't think he's asleep either," I told Biddle.

"I'm not!" GW called out.

"Neither am I!" said Clarice.

I waited for Ceecee to chime in. All I heard was a muffled rasping sound.

Apparently, of all of us, *she* was the one who snored.

Biddle sat up and patted the cushion beside him.

"Let's talk," he said.

Instead of sitting with him, I lowered myself to the floor on the other side of the coffee table, by the couch. I crossed my legs, then my arms.

"Let's say we actually manage to catch the killers and return the painting. We get the danger behind us," I said. "Then what?"

"For me?"

"Yeah, you. And me. And Clarice. *Us.*"

Biddle shrugged. "I guess we see if there can be an *us.*"

I had to give him credit for not saying the equivalent of "we hug and go out for ice cream." He wasn't going to pretend it could be easy.

Half an hour before he'd said goodnight to his daughter for the first time in their lives. She'd given him a weary, wary look, mumbled "Yeah . . . 'night," and darted off into her bedroom, not quite slamming the door behind her.

Maybe the day would come when it didn't feel awkward and weird having him around. But for that to happen, of course, he'd have to *be* around.

The quarter million the insurance company was offering for the painting wouldn't buy Biddle a new daughter. It could buy him a lot of fun ways to forget her, though.

A tarot deck was on the coffee table beside my dog-eared, coffee-stained copy of *Infinite Roads to Knowing,* my go-to tarot guidebook. I picked up the cards and started shuffling them.

"A little bedtime reading?" I asked, jerking my chin at the book.

Biddle nodded.

"Interesting stuff," he said guardedly. "You do all that highlighting and underlining?"

"That was me. Like you say — interesting stuff."

"I guess you had to learn the business quick when you took over the operation."

"It's not an operation; it's a store. And

yes, I did have to learn quick. But that's not what makes the tarot interesting."

Biddle's bushy gray eyebrows shot up high on his forehead. "Oh?"

I could hear what he was thinking — echoes of things he'd said to me decades before.

There's only one thing superstition's good for, sweetie — separating super fools from their cash super fast.

Heaven, God, good vibes — it's all just gold at the end of the rainbow. While the suckers are off looking for it, I'll fill my pockets with the gold they left lying right here.

You know why I'm so good at what I do? Because I don't believe in anyone or anything . . . including myself.

I'd been hearing it all in my head for years. Carrying it in my heart — and letting it weigh that heart down and shrivel it.

Maybe it was finally time for a new voice in my head: my own.

"There's something to it," I said. "The cards . . . work. In their way."

Biddle smirked. "So you've become a true believer."

"No. I'm just letting myself believe for a change."

I resisted the urge to glance back at my bedroom door.

I assumed GW was still awake, listening. My next words were for him as much as Biddle.

"Believing in something isn't easy for me. You and Mom made sure of that. But I'm working on it."

Biddle sighed, deflated, the smirk sliding off his face.

"I was always looking out for you, sweetie. Trying to teach you what you'd need to survive," he said. "And I'm still looking out for you — and Clarice. I hope you can believe in that."

I wanted to believe. I wanted to have faith. I wanted to have hope.

But now?

With *him*?

I stared at Biddle for a long, quiet, still moment. Only one thing moved or made noise. It was me — and it took me a moment to realize I was even doing it.

I was still shuffling the cards.

I held out the deck to Biddle.

"Help me believe," I said.

Biddle looked at the cards, then at me, then back at the cards.

"Go on," I said. "Take 'em."

"Alright."

Biddle reached out cautiously, as if I were offering him a hand grenade or an arsenic cupcake.

"Now shuffle . . . and think," I said once he had the deck. "If you could ask one question about the situation we're in, what would it be?"

Biddle began slowly shuffling the cards.

"Ask who?"

"The universe, I guess."

Biddle's smirk returned.

"Alright. Is 'what the hell's gonna happen?' too vague?"

"Not at all."

I began clearing the coffee table, pushing aside my copy of *Infinite Roads to Knowing* as well as half-empty glasses and dirty bowls and crumpled junk food wrappers. (I was living with a teenager, remember?) Then I held out my hand.

"Gimme."

Biddle handed the deck back.

I began laying out cards.

"I know it's late and it's been a long, weird day and we're tired, but I don't think we want to skimp on this reading," I said. "Let's do a full Celtic Cross."

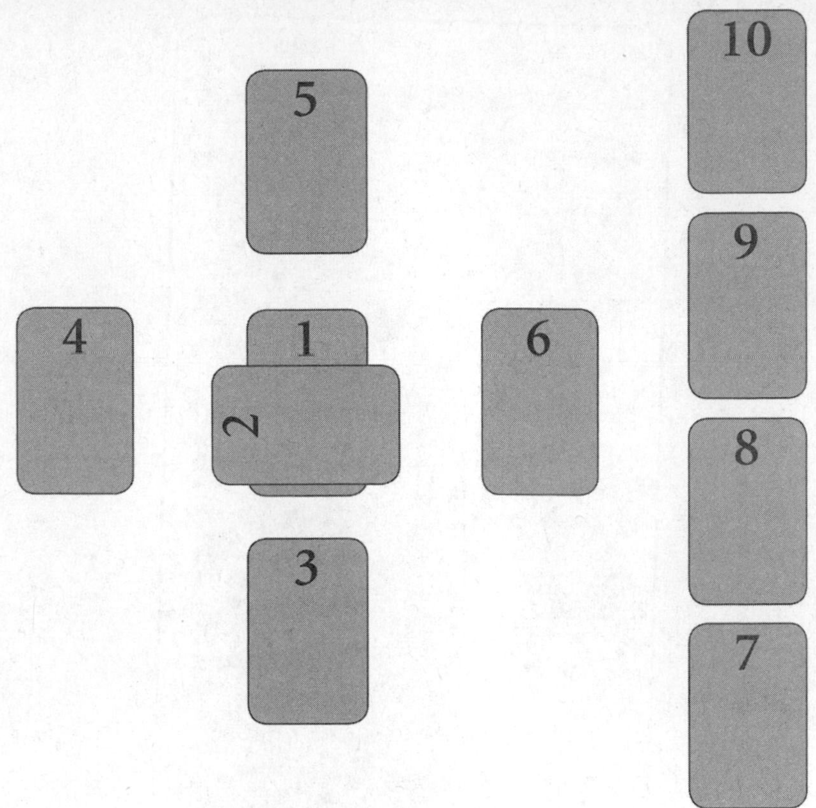

"So . . . what the hell's gonna happen?" I said once the cards were in place. "Let's see what we see." I turned over the first card, the card at the center of the spread.

"Who's that?" said Biddle. "And is he holding what I think he is?"

"That's the Magician. And I don't know what you think he's holding — and I don't want to know — but that's his wand. He's casting a spell, setting something in motion. The card in this position represents your current situation, preparing to take action. Seem accurate?"

"Sure," Biddle said, still smiling skeptically. "Right on target."

"I think so, too. Now, the next card is a little harder to explain. It's going to be something that's working with the first or against the first, amplifying it or blocking it."

"Lot of wiggle room there."

"Well . . . it depends on what's there."

I turned over the second card, the one that had been laid over the first to form the cross at the heart of the spread.

"Ooh," I said. "The World. That's big."

"Oh, yeah?" Biddle looked down at the card and chuckled. "Well, I do admit I like the lady. The rest of it reminds me why I only dropped acid the once."

"Yeah, it's a weird one. We don't have to get into the animals. The important thing is the loop. It's a cycle. The Magician is the first numbered card of the major arcana, which are the most powerful cards in the deck. The World is the last. Put 'em together, and it looks like something's about to come full circle."

Biddle peered down at the spread again.

"Oh, absolutely," he said sarcastically. "It's plain as day, isn't it?"

I shrugged. "It can be if you learn what to look for. Moving on to the root of the situation . . ."

I turned over card #3, the card beneath the first two.

"Money?" said Biddle. "Score one for the universe."

"It's a little more than just money. See the scales the rich guy's holding? He's trying to figure out what's fair, but he's giving all his coins to one person. The other beggar's getting bupkis. There's a lack of balance. Someone feels like they got cheated."

Biddle scoffed. "Well, that ain't me. You

know what I think about 'fair': no such thing. The universe doesn't owe me a dime, and I know it. That's why I've always had to go get me my dimes for myself."

"The coins on the card don't have to represent money, Biddle. They can be any kind of reward. Security. Love. Family. You've never felt like you deserved any of that?"

Biddle scoffed again, but it seemed forced this time. False.

"No such thing as 'deserve' either." He tapped a finger on the coffee table. "Next."

"Alright. This'll reflect on the recent past."

I turned over the fourth card in the spread — the one to the left of the first two.

"The recent past, huh?" Biddle said. "Well, I don't remember taking any boat rides lately. And if it was with a bunch of swords, I think I'd remember it."

I didn't play along.

"Something painful has happened," I said flatly. "A loss. A death. You're moving beyond it but taking what you've learned with you."

"That's really what that card means?"

I nodded.

"Oh," Biddle sighed.

There was no need to discuss what pain he might be moving past.

He hadn't been with my mother in years, yet she still meant something to him.

"What next?" he said.

"Funny you should ask. That's exactly what the next card is about: where this could all be heading — a possible outcome."

I flipped the card directly above the first two, card #5.

"Judgement reversed," I said.

Biddle whistled.

"I've never been too fond of being judged," he said. "Damn judges never seem to see things my way."

"This isn't that kind of judgement. It's Judgement Day. A day of rebirth and renewal. A new start."

"You don't say? The way I was brought

up, Judgement Day meant all the bad people got thrown in a furnace."

"This is more of a feel-good Judgement Day, except it's upside down."

"What does that mean?"

I shrugged. "Maybe it doesn't work out . . . or maybe someone decides they don't *want* a new start."

Biddle cocked his head and eyed me silently a moment.

"You know, I think I'm starting to see why you've taken to these cards," he finally said. "What do they show next?"

"The near future," I said. "Which might just look like this . . ."

I turned over card #6, the last card in the cross section of the spread.

"I'm gonna go to the circus and steal the sword-swallower's stuff?" Biddle said. "Hey . . . come to think of it, I did do something like that when I was a kid."

"That's not quite what we're seeing here. Swords is the suit of conflict and action, and that guy's in the thick of it. But he's being tricky about it: he has a plan. Like you say, he's stealing swords, putting his enemies at a disadvantage by using his brains."

And he's on his own, I didn't add. *He works alone.*

The card put a small smile back on Biddle's face.

"My kinda guy," he said.

"The next card is you, too. Your self as it relates to the current situation."

I flipped card #7, the bottom card in the vertical row on the right side of the spread.

"*Not* my kinda guy," Biddle said. He peered at the card. "Or gal. It's hard to tell when everybody's in those big ol' muu-muus."

"The gender doesn't matter."

"It does to me! I don't wanna be some pasty white lady."

"(A) There's nothing wrong with being a

pasty white lady. I oughta know. (B) This isn't Dungeons & Dragons. You're not being assigned a character. It's the situation that matters."

"So what situation is this? Moping under trees while ghosts try to get you drunk?"

"No. Being offered a gift you're too self-absorbed to see. Cups is the suit of feelings and relationships, so that's what you're missing out on. There's a real emotional connection you could make, but you're not even looking at it. Your mind's on something else."

"Sounds like an accusation, the way you say it."

I spread my hands out over the cards. "I calls 'em like I sees 'em."

"I guess you do. Which gives you a lot of control over what the cards supposedly say, am I right?"

"*That* almost sounds like an accusation."

"Nope. Just an observation." Biddle reached out and tapped the unflipped card above the Four of Cups. "That one next?"

I nodded.

"What's it supposed to show?"

"What's going on around you, affecting you. Whether there's someone who might have an important influence on how things'll turn out."

"Oh, yeah? Well, let's see the son of a bitch, then."

I turned over the card — and Biddle's eyes went wide.

"Him — the guy on the card we found in Elvis," Biddle said. He looked up at me, eyes tightening into a suspicious squint. "Very cute."

"Hey, you shuffled," I reminded him. "I didn't even have a chance to stack the deck."

Biddle grunted, unconvinced, then looked back down at the card again. "Tell me what it means."

"In this position? A strong or successful person, probably a man. Someone who's done well in business or law or something like that. Mature. Deep feelings — it's Cups again — but he keeps that under wraps. A 'still waters . . .' kind of guy. Someone who could help you head in the right direction — if you ask him to."

"Wonderful," Biddle said. "So who the hell is he?"

"How should I know? The cards don't have names and addresses on 'em. That description didn't sound familiar?"

Biddle snorted. "I don't usually hang around strong, silent, successful business-men. The opportunities I'm looking for are with the weak, loud, desperate ones."

"What about the German? Pilcher?" Clarice called out.

"Go to sleep!" I called back.

"What *about* the German?" Biddle asked me.

"Sounds like you're starting to take this seriously," I said.

"Well . . . it couldn't hurt to consider

every possibility. Could it be him?"

"I don't know. I suppose. If he's not the killer, that is."

"What did she say?" Clarice yelled.

"Maybe! If he's not the murderer!" Biddle answered.

Clarice grumbled something that might have been "Oh, *that's* helpful . . ."

"Just two cards left," I said to Biddle. "Shall we see if there's an answer to your question?"

"Oh, don't try to make it dramatic. This ain't *Family Feud.*"

"Alright, alright." I reached for the second-to-last card. "Survey says . . ."

"Oh, *that's* helpful," I groaned.

"You sound like your sister," Biddle said. (His hearing was pretty sharp for a man without a black hair left on his head.) "Why the grousing?"

"It's just unclear, that's all. The Nine of Cups shows a guy who thinks he's got everything set up just the way he wants. But reversed, it all goes screwy. Everything comes undone. The plan falls apart because of overconfidence."

"Sounds clear enough and bad enough. We're screwed — according to this, anyway."

"Maybe. But it could be telling us exactly the opposite."

"That we're . . . *un*screwed?"

"Yeah. See the curtains behind the guy? That's something he's not seeing — a factor he's not taking into account. But, again, reverse it, and it all changes. The curtains flip over, and whatever's behind them is revealed. The cat — whatever it is — is out of the bag."

"So either our plan falls apart entirely or it uncovers a big secret just like it's supposed to?"

"Pretty much."

Biddle scowled. "Good thing I don't believe in any of this. Otherwise, I might be annoyed. What's the card in that spot supposed to be talking about, anyway?"

"Hopes and worries."

"Hopes and worries?"

I nodded.

"Well, what the hell's the point of that?" Biddle said. "I know what my hopes and worries are. 'It might work!' 'It might not work!' I don't need any crazy cards to tell me that."

"It's really as simple as that for you? Those are your hopes and worries?"

"Tonight? Yes!" Biddle pointed at the last unturned card. "What's that one gonna be about? What I'll want for breakfast?"

"The outcome."

"The outcome? That card's gonna show us the outcome?"

"It's supposed to."

"Why'd we even bother with all these other cards, then? Flip it!"

I flipped it.

"Let me try," Biddle said. "The Fool usually means you're being a fool. But this one's upside down — 'reversed,' like the last card — so now it means the opposite: we're not being fools; we're being slick. *Ta-da!* We're getting us a happy ending!"

Biddle flashed me a triumphant grin . . . then finally noticed the somber look on my face.

"No?" he said.

I shook my head. "No. The Fool isn't just a fool. He's someone starting off on a new adventure, a new life. He's a little reckless about it, but it can be a good thing. He's taking a chance, and it might pay off big. His whole world could be transformed."

"So upside down means what? He and his dog go over that cliff they're walking toward?"

"Maybe. Or maybe he chickens out and doesn't start his new adventure after all. He and the dog go home and watch *Judge Judy.*"

"I'm not chickening out of anything."

"Then maybe the other interpretation fits."

"So I'm going over a cliff."

"Maybe."

Biddle shook his head and laughed.

"All that for a pile of maybes," he said, waving a bony, wrinkled hand at the spread. "*Maybe* we should've just flipped a coin fifteen minutes ago. Would've been clearer . . . and a whole lot quicker."

"Some questions can't be answered clear and quick."

Biddle laughed again.

"Then comes the pitch for an even longer

reading at twice the price," he said.

"I'm not making a pitch."

I swept the spread up into the rest of the deck and got to my feet.

"Aww, now I made you mad," Biddle said, trying to suppress his smile and not quite succeeding. "I'm sorry. I just don't get it. How you could fall for this stuff after everything I taught you . . ."

He had the good sense to stop there. My glare told him what I might do to him if he didn't.

"Good night, Biddle," I said coldly.

"Good night."

"Good night!" Clarice said.

Ceecee was still snoring.

"Good night, Clarice," I said.

"Good night, Clarice," said Biddle.

I turned off the light as I walked away, leaving him — and me — in total darkness.

I'd hoped the reading would give me some new insight into him — help me feel comfortable trusting him. But it seemed like all I got out of it was, "Yup. Biddle's still Biddle."

Learning to trust wasn't going to get any easier.

I walked into my bedroom and found GW going through my purse.

I cleared my throat.

"Your phone just rang," GW said without looking back at me. "Or do you say a phone 'rang' when it starts playing some old disco song?"

"Blondie wasn't disco."

"Some old New Wave song, then. Anyway, I assumed it was a call, maybe something important, so I started looking for . . . ooo, perfect!"

He took a box of Tic Tacs out of my purse, helped himself to a couple, then went back to rifling through my things.

A moment later he pulled out my phone.

"Here we go," he said. "Three missed calls, two messages. All from Victor Castellanos. Oh, well. Guess it wasn't important after all."

He tossed the phone back in the purse.

I wanted to argue, to tell him that the calls *were* important in their own way, but I was suddenly too exhausted to stick up for poor Victor. I was too exhausted to *stand.*

I started shuffling toward my bed.

"Tic Tac?" GW offered as I staggered past.

"No, thanks."

"You sure? Might come in handy."

I wasn't looking at GW, but somehow I could tell he was waggling his eyebrows.

I collapsed on the mattress and buried my face in my third-favorite pillow. Without looking over, I groped around the bedside table until I found the lamp there. I turned it off.

"Okay. Well. I'll just hold onto these — in case you change your mind," GW said.

The Tic Tac box rattled in the darkness.

"You do that," I murmured, sure I was going to fall asleep any second.

I heard GW stretch out on the floor again. After a while he rolled over on his side. A little after that he switched sides. Then he did it again. And again. Every time he fidgeted, the Tic Tacs shook.

It wasn't just weariness that kept me from talking to him, asking him what was on his mind, why he was even there. It was wariness. I was afraid of . . . something. And not even the stuff I should be afraid of, like crossing paths with a killer or knowing a whole family of scumbags wanted me dead.

GW rolled over yet again.

"You still awake?" he said.

"No. How about you?"

"Nah. Me neither."

He rolled over again.

"You remember when you did a tarot reading for me?" he said. "After we first met?"

"Sure."

"Interesting stuff."

"Sure," I said again. I could barely remember it, actually.

"Cutting myself off from other people," GW said. "Being chained to the past. Looking for a new direction."

"Sure."

"Different cards tonight, weren't they?"

"Sure." I stared into the darkness a moment. "Wait," I said. "What?"

"Different cards. Than the ones you got just now with Biddle."

"Yeah, of course they were. You're different people."

"That's what I'm saying. I'm glad to hear *you* say it."

The Tic Tacs rattled one more time, then the shaking stopped, and soon the heavy breathing began.

GW was asleep.

And I was still awake. *Very* awake now. Damn it.

I rolled onto my back and stared up at the ceiling, seeing nothing, until my eyes ached.

So GW wanted to tell me he wasn't Biddle. I knew that.

Or did I? Was that what I'd been afraid of? Trusting someone who'd hurt me? Being somebody's patsy? Their pigeon?

Their *fool*?

I remembered the last card of Biddle's

reading. The Fool reversed. It was a card I knew well.

It was me.

Did it pop up in the reading as a message for me? An indication that Biddle was literally turning my new life upside down? If so, I had a message for the cards: *tell me something I don't know.*

Or was the flipped Fool a warning to Biddle? Upright, the Fool represents a first step toward a second chance at life. Reversed, maybe, he'd be the *final* step — and that life would soon be over.

I kept staring into the blackness — worrying about Biddle, worrying about GW, worrying about Victor, worrying about myself and Clarice and Ceecee and the White Magic Five and Dime and terrorism and global warming and *everything* — until the blackness finally swallowed me and the worrying stopped. For a while.

COPPE
COUPES
7
CHALICES
COPAS
BEKERS
KELCHE

Sorry, dream lady. Sorry, dream dragon. Sorry, dream snake. Sorry, dream laurels and dream riches and dream castle. Sorry, dream Ku Klux Klan member (or whoever that is under that sheet); it's wakey-wakey time. Because it's go time. No more snooze button, no more dreaming: it's all about action now — making those dreams come true! But be careful. Dragons and snakes and Klansmen don't usually pop up in happy dreams. Better be sure you're not about to make a nightmare come true.

Miss Chance, *Infinite Roads to Knowing*

It was the first day of school and already there was an exam and I wasn't even sure what classroom I was supposed to be in and *oh my god* I wasn't wearing pants. Or a skirt. Or a shirt. Or underwear.

Debbie Harry saved me.

The ringing of the morning bell turned into the power chords that kick off "Call Me." Then Debbie started singing, and I was transported from the halls of Anxiety Dream Junior High School to my bed.

I was on my back, a trail of drool running down my left cheek. I blinked, rolled over, fumbled for my purse, and pulled out my phone.

The call was from Victor Castellanos.

"Shit," I sighed.

"Victor again, huh?" GW said from the floor nearby. He put his pillow over his head. "He can leave another message. I'm still sound asleep."

I sat up and took the call.

"Victor. Hi."

"Hi, Alanis. I hope I didn't wake you up."

"Oh, no, no. I've been up for hours."

"Liar," GW muttered from under his pillow.

"I'm glad you called," I said. "I owe you an apology for last night. You and Lucia just caught me at an awkward moment."

"I could tell."

Victor paused as if there was more he expected to hear. An explanation, maybe.

I gave him the only one I could.

"It's kind of complicated."

"I bet."

There was another pause. A long one.

"Anyway," Victor finally said, "I wanted to let you know about a weird call I just got."

"Oh? Weird in what way?"

"Weird in a guy-with-a-German-accent-asking-if-I-know-a-woman-who-meets-your-description kind of way."

Damn, I thought. *Pilcher got Victor's name out of him last night, and now he's trying to use him to get to me.*

But all I could say was, "Yeah. That *is* weird."

"I'm pretty sure it was Ulf Pilcher."

"Yeah. Probably. What did you tell him?"

"That I was busy with something and

couldn't talk just then. He's calling me back in ten minutes."

"So you could check in with me first. Thanks, Victor," I said. "You wouldn't mind covering for me, would you?"

"Covering for you?"

"Pretending you don't know me. It must have crossed your mind to try it once or twice."

I forced out a chuckle so phony it made me cringe.

Victor didn't join in.

"I can do that," he said.

"Thank you."

Yet another pause — the longest yet. So long I was about to say "Victor?" when he broke the silence.

"Are you going to tell me what's going on?"

"Don't worry about it," I tried to say casually. "There's nothing you can do."

"Ouch," said GW.

Victor didn't say it, too, but I could hear it in his voice.

"Fine. Good. Alright, then. Bye, Alanis."

"Bye, Victor. Talk to you later."

He hung up between "to" and "you."

"Told you to let it go into voicemail," GW said.

"Shut up."

"So Pilcher was nosing around after you?"

"I said shut up." I was going into voicemail. Bringing up the message Victor had left me two days before, after I'd called him for help. Things had been so crazy I hadn't even listened to it yet.

"Alanis, hi," I heard Victor say. "After we spoke, I realized . . . you're in trouble again, aren't you? Something's going on. I'm sorry I was so dense about it. Please call me back. You know I . . . you know I care about you, right? Whatever the problem is, I want to be there for you."

End of message.

And since receiving it, I'd blown off Victor — refused to tell him what was happening or how he could help — not once but twice.

End of relationship.

I dropped the phone on the bed and buried my face in my hands.

"I would ask if you're okay," GW said, peeking out from under his pillow hidey-hole, "but I'm busy shutting up."

"Keep up the good work," I grumbled.

Action. That was what I needed. Distraction.

We'd made a plan the night before. It was time to set it — and me — in motion.

I got up and marched out of the bedroom.

"Alright," I said, "let's do this thing."

But there was no one to do anything *with.* Biddle wasn't there. The comforter he'd slept under had been folded neatly and left at one end of the couch, my favorite pillow atop it.

The door to Clarice's bedroom was open, so I walked over and looked inside.

Clarice and Ceecee were gone, too.

"Goddamn it," I said. "What are you up to now, Biddle?"

"Doughnuts."

I turned to find GW leaning in the doorway to my room, clothes wrinkled, hair bedhead (or maybe that should be floor-head) wild.

"I heard the old man start moving around maybe half an hour ago," he said. "The girls got up not long after that. They talked a little bit, then he took 'em out to get doughnuts."

"Or so he said."

GW gave me a sleepy, puzzled look. "What do you mean?"

"I mean we've got a plan that could lead us to a million-dollar painting — a plan that involves all of us — and Biddle slips out with the girls before we can get it rolling? Who knows what he's telling them right now? 'We should keep Alanis out of danger.' 'That GW can't be trusted.' 'We need to do this on our own.' 'It'll be fun!' Dammit, I bet you at this very moment they're —"

"Wake up, slackers!" Clarice hollered downstairs. "Let's do this thing!"

Ceecee woo-wooed.

"You bet they're . . . coming up the stairs with doughnuts?" GW finished for me.

"Yes," I said. "That is exactly what I was about to say."

Biddle and the girls came up the stairs with doughnuts.

"Still like jelly filled?" Biddle said when he saw me.

"Not since 1987," I told him.

"Then it's time you gave 'em another chance."

He reached into the white paper bag he was holding, took out a doughnut, and tossed it to me.

Jelly filled. Strawberry. It was a good thing I caught it or the wall behind me would have looked like something from a crime scene.

"Got a call for you this morning," Biddle went on. "Don't know if it changes the plan or not."

He put the paper bag on the kitchen counter and pulled his cell phone from his breast pocket. After fiddling with the phone a moment, he walked over so I could see the screen.

He'd put a voicemail message on speaker. There was no name. Just a number with a 724 area code.

"Philly," Biddle said.

A woman started talking.

"Hello. This is Katrina Gilver-McPherson. Ulf Pilcher gave me this number. I wanted to call to apologize for last night. I don't blame you for ditching us the way you did. The whole set-up was . . . high handed. Insulting. I'm sorry. I'd like to try again, just you and me. I don't know how you fit into all this, but don't think I have to be in your way. I just want the story. Maybe we could help each other. Call me. It'll go better this time. I promise."

"What do you think?" Biddle asked when the message was over.

"Change the plan?" said GW.

I mulled it over a moment. Biddle watched me in a way that said he already knew how he'd play it. He just wanted to see if I'd come to the same conclusion.

"No. We don't call her yet," I said. "I was able to get more out of her than she got out of me last night, but I doubt I could do that to a reporter twice in a row. If we want to stay out of her next story, we shouldn't talk to her until we've got leverage."

"Information to trade," said GW. "Which is what we're going after today anyway."

A sly smile tugging up one corner of Biddle's mouth. We'd both passed his little test.

"So we stick to the plan and stay focused on our suspects," he said.

"And maybe bring the reporter in when a middleman's gonna come in handy," said GW.

I nodded. "Bingo."

"Oh my god," said Ceecee. She pointed at us with a bear claw she'd fished from the doughnut bag. "Is it okay to say it's weirdly scary to watch you guys talk sometimes?"

"Not scary," said Clarice around a mouthful of danish. "Inspiring."

I glowered at her. "Not inspiring."

I couldn't think of the right adjective to replace "inspiring" with, so I just went on glowering as I took a bite of my jelly doughnut.

Biddle had been right.

I liked it.

We ate our doughnuts.

We went over the plan again.

We split up.

Ulf Pilcher answered my call half a second into the second ring.

"Is it you? Is all forgiven? Can we try again?" he said.

"All is forgiven," I told him, "if you buy me breakfast."

"Of course! You didn't get to dine with us last night, did you? I owe you a fine meal!"

"Just you and me this time."

"Yes, yes — of course!"

"No tricks."

" 'No tricks.' I love that! Just like in the movies!"

"No. Tricks."

"Certainly! You have my word! No tricks! Now — did you have someplace in mind for this private breakfast of ours?"

I couldn't help but smile.

"I'll give you the address," I said.

Pilcher wouldn't get to our rendezvous spot before me this time. I'd called him from there. Which is why I had a front-row seat when — for the first and last time, I assume — a gleaming Maserati GranTurismo parked in front of Shanna's Home Cookin'. Add up the value of every other car in the lot and maybe you'd have the down payment on the one Pilcher was driving. Maybe.

Pilcher got out of his Maserati, looked around at the ancient Hyundais and Datsuns and pickup trucks all around him, then beamed and waved when he noticed me watching from my booth inside.

The other customers turned to stare as he came striding into the restaurant. I didn't get the feeling anyone recognized him. They just weren't used to seeing grinning men with ponytails and Don Johnson's old wardrobe (white suit, mauve T-shirt, white bucks) in that part of town.

"It is so good to see you again!" he said as he slid into the seat across from me. "I worried that my blunder yesterday had scared you away for good! What do you recommend here? Do they have a cheese platter? It has been days since I had a decent *rauchkäse.*"

I pushed the menu in front of me across the table to him. "You're out of luck on the cheese platter. But if you want something scrambled, fried, or toasted, they can probably hook you up."

Pilcher started to open the menu, then closed it again.

"I guess I'm not *that* hungry," he said. "You?"

I shook my head.

"On to business?" Pilcher asked.

I nodded.

"Fine! I like that! I did have hopes for the

rauchkäse, but such is life. We move on! So . . ." Pichler clapped his hands together and gave them a rub. "Who are you, and where is the painting? Feel free to skip the first question if you're willing to answer the second."

I had to laugh at the bluntness of it.

"We are getting right down to business, aren't we?" I said.

Pichler shrugged. "Apparently, we didn't come here for the bacon and eggs."

"Fair enough. Who am I? I'm not telling. Where's the painting? I don't know."

"That doesn't get us very far. Let me try again. Why — ?"

The surly waitress who'd served me, GW, and Biddle the day before stepped up to our table, notepad in hand.

"What'll ya have?" she asked without looking at us.

"Privacy, preferably," said Pilcher.

The waitress shot him a glare, obviously wondering if she should be offended.

"What?" she said.

Pilcher reached inside his suit and pulled out his wallet. It was small and sleek and black, yet when he opened it a wad of bills practically came bursting out. He pulled one out and put it on the table before the waitress.

Benjamin Franklin looked up at her with his prim little smile.

One hundred bucks. The bill was so clean and crisp it looked freshly ironed.

"You can either bring me all the food that will buy or you can pour me a glass of water and keep that as the tip," he said. "And the water you can drink yourself."

The waitress stared at the money, pop-eyed, before sweeping it up off the table.

"One glass of water, hold the water and the glass," she said. "Coming right up."

She turned and walked away.

"Is that what I should be trying with you?" Pilcher asked me. He spread his wallet wide so I could see just how packed with cash it was. "Would you like it? I don't know how much is in here, but it's a lot. Tell me what I want to know, and it's all yours."

"I wasn't lying before. I don't know where the painting is, and I won't tell you who I am."

"Fine. Disappointing, but fine. I'm sure there are things you *can* tell me, though. Helpful information you could share."

Pilcher ran a thumb over the bills. It made a sound like the purring of a cat.

"Put it away," I said.

Pilcher sighed and slumped.

"Then there is nothing to talk about," he

said as he slipped the wallet back inside his suit.

"Oh, I didn't say you couldn't buy information from me. It's just that I don't want money."

Pilcher brightened again.

"Information! A trade!" he said. "A little of the old 'I'll show you mine if you show me yours'!"

I nodded.

" 'I'll show you mine' . . . I hope that wasn't offensive," Pilcher said.

"I'm not offended."

"One must be so much more careful with one's words these days."

"It's okay."

"It has gotten me into trouble more than once."

I cleared my throat. "On to business?"

"Yes! Quite right! Of course, usually I would say ladies first — no offense, I hope — but in this instance I think the more chivalrous gesture would be for the gentleman to go first. Ask me anything."

"Why did you come to Berdache?"

"Because Robert Dryja told me *Stormy Sea from Scheveningen Pier* was here, and I should come quickly if I wanted to be on hand when he recovered it. See? I can be forthcoming! Now it's your turn."

"But why would — ?"

Pilcher wagged a finger at me tut-tut style. "*Ah-ah-ah!* Tit for tat," he said. "No follow-up until you've answered a question for me."

"Alright, fine. What do you want to know — other than where is it and who am I?"

Pilcher began tapping the wagging finger against his chin.

"Hmm. How best to phrase it? I don't want to waste my question, and there's so much I want to learn about you! I already know that you're from here. Your friends in the restaurant last night made that plain. And that leads me to think you're not an outside professional, like Dryja, though you're certainly cagey enough to be one. So how did you get involved in this business with the painting? That's not my question, by the way! I'm just thinking out loud. I should be more direct, but a yes or no question won't do. I can't make it that easy for you. So . . . oh, what the hell. How did you get involved in this business with the painting?"

I eyed Pilcher, wondering how much of his eccentric goofball shtick was an act. It was hard to picture such an excitable dork building a multimedia empire in Germany. On the other hand, it was just as hard to picture him pumping bullets into Robert Dryja in a parking lot. Which didn't mean he wouldn't pay somebody else to do it. But why come all the way to Berdache looking for the painting, then have Dryja killed before he can get his hands on it?

I decided not to trust Pilcher, exactly, but to take him at face value. Up to a point.

"The painting was stolen from Big Mike Fusillo by a relative of mine. I don't know where it's hidden, but I'm trying to find out because I want the damn thing sent back to the museum. Someone's already died because of it, so until it's returned, I have to worry about my family. How was that?"

Pilcher applauded softly. (The people in the booths around us weren't staring anymore, so it was smart not to give them reason to start again.)

"Bravo. Marvelous." Pilcher kissed his fingertips. "That could not have been a more perfect answer. Not only do I suspect it's true, it would mean that we don't have to be working at cross-purposes. Finding and returning the painting would benefit you, and finding and returning the painting would benefit me."

"Why would returning it help you? Don't you want it for yourself?"

Pilcher shook his head. "It's complicated."

"Then explain it."

"Well . . . that's more of a command than a question, but I'm game so long as our quid pro quo is still in effect."

"It is."

"Alright. I will explain. But first . . ."

Pilcher stretched his right hand toward me, every finger but one curled into a fist.

"Pinky promise you won't tell Katrina Gilver-McPherson or any other journalist what I'm about to say."

"You want me to pinky promise?"

Pilcher nodded. "It's actually an ancient Japanese tradition. The *yubikiri.* The finger cut-off vow."

"Um . . . okay, then. I guess that makes it legit."

I brought up my hand and wrapped my pinky around Pilcher's.

"I promise not to tell any reporter what you're about to say."

I started to pull my pinky away, but Pilcher held on tight.

"Or the authorities," he said.

"Which authorities?"

"Any authorities."

"Fine. I promise not to tell the authorities, too."

Still, Pilcher wouldn't let go.

"Come to think of it, I should've just had

you promise not to tell anyone. That would cover every —"

I yanked my hand away.

"Explain."

"Alright, alright."

Pilcher looked this way and that — which was more a symbolic gesture than anything practical since he was just glancing at the parking lot and the hallway to the grimy bathrooms.

He leaned over the table and dropped his voice to a whisper.

"I need to be present when *Stormy Sea from Scheveningen Pier* is found here," he said, "because I already own it. It's been in my private collection for years."

COPPE
COUPES
6
CHALICES
COPAS
KELCHE
BEKERS

Some people get a Brady Bunch childhood. Loving, stable parents. A big house. Nice siblings (except when they rat you out for playing ball in the house). A live-in maid. Peasant boys bringing them flowers. (Not that we ever saw that onscreen, but you've got to figure it happened to Marcia at least once.) Other people get the flipside when they're kids — a soap opera childhood, maybe even a Twilight Zone childhood. They'll have a lot of healing to do later, which is what the reversed Six of Cups is all about, but at least looking back they'll see the past as it really was: without a laugh track.

Miss Chance, *Infinite Roads to Knowing*

I met up with Biddle and GW at our super-team headquarters: the back stairwell at the Devil's Ridge Lodge. It wasn't exactly the Hall of Justice — in fact, it was hot and echoey and it smelled like Pine-Sol — but it would have to do.

"Did you get much out of Hans?" GW asked. "Or is it Franz?"

"It's Ulf. And no — I didn't get much. Only the reason he's trying to find *Stormy Sea from Scheveningen Pier* and why he probably isn't the killer."

"Oh, is that all?" Biddle said. "I was hoping for a signed confession and directions to the painting."

GW and I both ignored him. I was willing to work with Biddle if it might clear up the stink he'd brought to our door. That didn't mean I had to laugh at his jokes.

"What'd he say?" GW asked me.

"Apparently he's got a thing for ultra-rare

art: not just the hard-to-find kind, the not-exactly-legal-to-own kind."

"Guess you have to get creative with your money after you buy your second yacht," Biddle said.

I kept going.

"He bought *Stormy Sea* from a black-market dealer twenty years ago . . . or so he thought. He's pretty sure now he got conned. When a 'masterpiece' goes missing, you can sell fakes to ten different collectors and get away with it because none of them can brag about owning it. Each one thinks they've got the original tucked away in their own private little gallery. When Pichler heard about what Big Mike Fusillo was saying from prison — that the painting was stolen from him by a 'disgruntled associate' who wouldn't have any connections with the underground art market — he had his people look into it. That led him to Robert Dryja, who was close to finding the painting for Glenn Budziak. He made Dryja an offer: $50,000 to pretend Pichler helped him get the painting back."

"Why'd he do that?" GW said. "Trying to make himself look good?"

I was grateful for the question: it gave me time to catch my breath.

Biddle gave me even more time by answering for me.

"Nah, man. He's trying to make good on a bad investment," he said. "If Pichler is one of the guys who finds the missing painting, he can claim later that he swapped it for a fake. Then he can turn around and sell the one he's got on the black market as the real deal."

I nodded. "You got it. He didn't feel bad about conning another collector the way he was because, and I quote, 'We're all assholes!' "

"I like the way that man thinks," Biddle mused.

"So you figure Pichler wouldn't have killed Dryja because he needed him to get his scam going?" GW said to me.

I nodded again. "That's the way I see it. Of course, he could be lying. Maybe Pichler didn't just want to *claim* he'd swapped the real painting for a fake; maybe he actually wanted to do it, but Dryja wouldn't play along. They argued about it, things got heated, Dryja knew too much, yada yada, bang bang. But for all that to work, he'd need to have come prepared. So . . . was he?"

GW and Biddle shook their heads.

"You gave us plenty of time to search Pichler's suite," GW said, "and there was no painting there except for the one on the wall."

"And you better believe we checked that one inside and out," Biddle added. "No gun in the room, either."

"So Pichler probably didn't bring the fake with him," I said, "which would make sense if what he told me was true. And if that's the case, he not only wouldn't want Dryja dead, he'd really *really* want him alive. Without him, he's got nothing to go on."

"Isn't it the same for Budziak?" GW asked. "I mean, we know he was pissed that Dryja had tipped off Pilcher, but he still needed him to get the painting and clear his name."

Biddle shrugged. "Maybe the guy lost his temper and did something stupid. It happens a lot — all the time, even."

"Yeah, and Budziak is an edgy, edgy man. I could see him Hulking out and killing somebody," I said.

I clapped my hands together and started up the stairs.

"Let's go say hi."

"Let me knock on the door," Biddle said in a low voice as we walked up the long hotel hallway toward Budziak's room. "You and pretty boy hang back."

"Pretty boy?" said GW, looking both offended and, despite his attempt to hide it, pleased.

"Why should you go to the door?" I asked Biddle.

"You talked to this Budziak character once already. If he's in his room, he's gonna remember you."

"So? I'll just pretend to be a reporter again. Maybe I can draw him out for a cup of coffee or something. Worked once today."

"What reporter did you pretend to be yesterday? Katrina What's-Her-Name? Like you tried with Pilcher last night?"

"No. I didn't even know about her yet when I talked to Budziak. I pulled some other name out of my ass."

"Which was — ?"

I opened my mouth to answer.

I closed it.

If I'd opened it again just then, all that would have come out was a grumbled "son of a bitch."

Biddle gave me a knowing look.

Always pick names that are easy for people to forget, he used to tell me, *but easy for you to remember.*

I'd made a rookie mistake he'd warned me about nearly forty years before.

I had no idea what name I'd given Budziak.

"He probably won't remember what I called myself either," I said lamely.

Biddle went right on giving me the look.

"I felt bad enough letting you go talk to Pilcher by yourself," he said. "I'm not gonna let you go knocking on Budziak's door now. For all we know, the guy's sitting in there polishing the gun he used to shoot Dryja."

The three of us stopped by the elevators, about thirty yards from the door to Budziak's room. I looked up and down the hall — empty — then turned and searched Biddle's face, hunting for some clue to what he was thinking. Of course, all I saw was what Biddle presumably wanted me to see: concern.

Was he just angling to get into the room first?

Was he hoping the painting would be there — and that he could make off with it somehow?

Did he *want* Budziak to be there so he could talk to him away from us and cut some kind of deal?

None of it made much sense. We were on the third floor. Once he was in Budziak's room, there was nowhere for Biddle to go but out the window — and then straight down from there.

Which meant the simplest explanation was probably the right one: Biddle was putting himself between me and a possible murderer. He was actually looking out for me.

Or he wants you to think he is, a voice in my head said.

I told the voice to shut up. All this second-guessing was giving me a migraine.

"Room 322," I told Biddle.

Biddle nodded, then turned to GW.

"Gimme your little toy," he said.

GW reached into a pocket and pulled out what looked like a dry-erase marker.

"You sure you know how it works?" he said. "You only saw me use it once."

"I learn quick."

Biddle took the marker, slid it into his shirt pocket, and turned to go.

"Don't break it," GW said. "That thing cost me two hundred bucks."

Biddle just waved his free hand without looking back.

"Not that I ever plan on using it again," GW added for my benefit. "Unless I really have to. For a good cause. Like this."

He looked over at me.

"Shush," I said.

He shushed.

Beyond him, Biddle was stepping up to

room 322. The little *DO NOT DISTURB* sign was on the door handle again. Biddle glanced down at it, then knocked.

There was no answer.

Biddle knocked again.

"Maintenance," he said. "I've been sent up to check your phone line. Been told calls aren't getting through."

Nothing.

Biddle tried another knock.

"Mr. Budziak?"

Still nothing.

Biddle gave the hallway a quick this-way-and-that once-over, pulled out the marker, and popped off the top. Then he lowered the marker so it was beneath the door handle's brass housing and inserted it in a slot hidden on the underside.

There was a series of dull clicks as the microcontroller in the "marker" tried to convince the lock it was a master key. After a few seconds, it succeeded.

There was one last click, a little louder than the others, and the light on the lock must have gone green because suddenly Biddle was turning the handle and pushing the door open.

"Mr. Budziak?" he said as he moved slowly into the room. "You there? Don't mean to intrude, but I've really gotta look at that line."

His voice trailed off as the door swung closed behind him.

There were no shouts or screams or gunshots after that. Our B&E was going according to plan.

I let out a breath I hadn't been aware I was holding.

"Alright," I said. "If Budziak comes back, I'll stall him. Loudly. You get down there and help Biddle search the room."

"Help him search or keep an eye on him?"

"Both, of course," I was about to say.

"Any good sushi around here?" I said instead.

The sound of an approaching elevator had convinced me to change the subject.

"Nope. No bad sushi either," GW said. "No sushi at all in Berdache."

The elevator stopped.

"There's a place a few miles up 179, in Sedona," GW went on as the doors started to open. "I don't know if it's good or bad, though. I'm not a sushi guy."

"How about Korean barbecue?" I said.

There were footsteps behind me, and I threw a casual glance over my shoulder to see who was coming out of the elevator.

"Look!" a high-pitched voice exclaimed. "It's the woman who yells bad words!"

The pigtailed five-year-old who'd overheard me cursing when GW borrowed my car the day before — Miley or Jewel or something like that — was pointing at me. She looked happy to see me. She was probably hoping I'd say "shit shit *shit*!" again.

Her mother and father grabbed her by the wrists and practically dragged her past me.

"It's not polite to stare," Mom whispered to her.

"Let's hurry to our room and see if Elmo's on," said Dad.

The little girl kept her eyes locked on me as she was swept past.

"You know, *shit* isn't really that bad," she told me. "Daddy said it twice this morning."

"Brittany!" Mom gasped.

Yeah, that was it. Brittany.

I waved goodbye to her as her parents jerked her around the corner and stomped off up the hall.

GW shook his head and clucked his tongue. "Just when you think you know someone. You're the Woman Who Yells Bad Words?"

"Aw, hell no," I said. "Little bitch must be thinking of somebody else."

"Even so . . . the parents might call the front desk to complain."

I pictured Mom and Dad's pinched, pale faces. They did look like the kind of tight-asses who'd carp to management about uncouth behavior in the halls. It's a good way to finagle free passes to the breakfast buffet.

"You're right. We'd better both get out of sight, just in case," I said. "Come on."

I led GW to room 322 and knocked softly on the door.

Biddle didn't answer.

"Maybe his hearing's not so good anymore," GW said.

I tried again, a little louder.

"Room service," I said. "I have your egg white asparagus omelet and artisanal focaccia toast with blueberry-rhubarb compote."

The door finally opened.

"Shut up and get in," Biddle whispered.

At first I thought there was something a little flustered, almost frantic about the way he waved us into the room. But I dismissed the thought as I walked inside.

Biddle flustered? Impossible. At most he was annoyed because we showed up just as he was about to pocket something valuable.

"So," I said once the door was closed behind us, "find anything that's — ?"

Someone stepped up behind me and wrapped a hand around my mouth.

It was GW that needed muzzling, though. When we saw the mess beside the bed, he became the Man Who Yells Bad Words.

Fortunately, he only got out two (it was more of a compound word, actually) before Biddle clamped a hand over his mouth, as well.

"Shhhhh."

Not that Biddle needed to remind us to be quiet once the shock wore off.

It's one thing to get caught breaking into a hotel room.

It's another thing entirely if you're caught in a room with a corpse.

COPPE
COUPES
5
CHALICES
COPAS
KELCHE
BEKERS

Hey, Dracula! Quit your moping! Oh, boo-hoo — you spilled three cups of blood (or whatever). So what? Now isn't the time to brood over the fine mess you've made of things. It's time to count your blessings. Just look over your shoulder and you'll see you still have some: two, to be exact, just sitting there waiting to be noticed. So . . . notice 'em!

Miss Chance, *Infinite Roads to Knowing*

GW made a gurgling, burbling sound deep in his throat.

"Don't throw up," Biddle said.

"I won't." GW made the sound again.

"Don't throw up," Biddle said.

"I won't."

GW made the sound again.

"Don't. Throw. Up," Biddle said.

"I. Won't."

GW made the sound again.

The carpet in Glenn Budziak's room was already soaked with blood. Now it was about to be sprayed with half-digested doughnut, too.

"Turn around," I told GW, "take a deep breath, and picture your favorite pet."

"What?" GW said.

He made the sound again.

I took him by the arm and gently but firmly spun him so that he was facing the door and not the dead man tied to a chair in crimson-stained T-shirt and sweatpants.

"Now the breath," I said.

GW gulped in a quick mouthful of air.

"Deeper," I said.

GW nodded, then slowly filled his lungs. He held the breath a moment, then exhaled.

"Now your favorite pet," I said. "Talk to it."

GW shot me an annoyed glance, as if he might protest. But he caught another glimpse of Budziak out of the corner of his eye, shuddered, and jerked his gaze away again.

"Shiiiiit-heeeeead," he called softly, closing his eyes. "Come, Shit-head."

"Your favorite dog's name was Shithead?" Biddle said.

"My dad named him," GW said, as if that explained everything. His eyes were still squeezed tight. "Sit, Shithead. Sit."

I patted GW on the shoulder, then reluctantly turned back toward the body.

Budziak's throat had been cut. I forced myself to look for signs of torture — bruises, cuts, burns — but I didn't see anything. Whoever had killed Budziak hadn't tried too hard to get information out of him first.

"How long you think he's been like that?" I asked Biddle.

"I don't know. Maybe since last night? The

blood looks like it's been drying a while. Gone pretty crusty around the cut."

"Lie down. Roll over," GW whispered. "Who wants a tummy rub?"

"Silver lining," Biddle said to me. "We're down to two suspects, and they're working together, which means we know who's got blood on their hands."

I shook my head. "Not necessarily. I'd say we're still at three."

"Those two old goons and who?"

"Pilcher."

"You just said ten minutes ago he *wasn't* a suspect anymore," GW pointed out. His voice sounded steady now, with no gurgle to it. He was himself again.

Good boy, Shithead.

"Pilcher didn't know Budziak was in town until I told him last night at the restaurant," I explained. "It might not be a coincidence that Budziak was murdered around the same time. Maybe Pilcher's getting rid of anyone who might know why he's after the painting."

"*Did* Budziak know?" GW asked.

I shrugged. "Dryja could have told him, or maybe Pilcher just wasn't taking any chances. Either way, if Pilcher did do this, we know who he'll be coming after next."

"You," GW said.

"And anyone you might have talked to since this morning," Biddle added.

I nodded. It was long past time to get Clarice and Ceecee out of Dodge.

"So what next?" GW asked. "We can't call the cops. 'Guess what we found when we were breaking into a room at the Devil's Ridge Lodge!' Burby would just *love* that."

"Yeah," I sighed. "He'd have us on death row before Eugene was even off the golf course."

"Who's Eugene?" Biddle said.

"He was Mom's . . ."

WHAMMY!

Flashback:

The eighties. Another hotel room.

A girl sits on a bed. She's watching a game show.

On the screen, lights flash. Sound effects beep and boop.

"Big bucks! Big bucks! Big bucks!" a contestant chants. "No whammies!"

The contestant hits an oversized button.

The lights stop flashing. A foghorn sounds.

Whammy.

Game over.

Just like that.

The contestant grimaces, his rivals smirk, the audience moans.

A man walking through the room laughs. He's on his way to meet his partner.

Business.

"That's life for most people. They think they know the score, then . . . *whammy*!" the man chuckles. "Who says these shows aren't educational?"

"Bye, Biddle," says the girl.

"Bye, sweetie," says the man.

The man walks out the door.

The girl waits for more whammies.

They come.

Aside:

Whammies aren't always bad for *you.* It depends on where you're sitting.

"Alanis?" Biddle said. "You okay?"

"Maybe she's thinking of her favorite pet," GW suggested.

"I was thinking of *Press Your Luck,*" I muttered. "And I never had a pet. Mom wouldn't let me."

I shook my head. I needed to focus on the here and now or there'd be another whammy I'd really regret.

"Have you seen Budziak's phone?" I asked Biddle.

"No, now that you mention it. And I gave the place a going-over," he said. "Good thought, though. We could've checked who he spoke to last."

"That wasn't my thought. I just remembered that Budziak recorded my conversation with him. If Burby hears it, he'll recognize my voice."

Biddle spread his hands helplessly. "That's not good. But like I said, I looked and I didn't see the phone. And I don't think we wanna take the time to look again."

"No. All we can do here now is incriminate ourselves even more."

I turned and began looking around for something to put over my hand when I opened the door.

Biddle stepped past me and put his hand on the knob.

"I needed to search the room fast, and I left my rubber gloves at home," he said softly.

"Meaning your prints are all over the place already," I said.

Biddle nodded.

GW groaned.

"Hey, at least I'm keeping *your* ass out of the electric chair," Biddle snapped.

"Thanks," GW said. "We'll see how long that lasts."

Biddle swung his gaze back to me. "Can we go before there are two bodies in here?"

"Yes, please."

Biddle slowly opened the door and peeked out into the hall. When he was satisfied that we wouldn't be seen, he stepped out, waving for us to join him.

GW followed.

I hesitated.

We were leaving a dead man behind us. A *murdered* man. I hadn't really known him, yet I felt I owed him something.

A wreath was out of the question. So I offered up a whispered eulogy.

"Sorry, dude. We'll clear your name if we can."

"Come on, come on," Biddle said under his breath.

I went.

We moved quickly (but not *too* quickly) to our secret headquarters — the back stairwell — and wound our way down to the ground floor.

When we pushed through the exit to the parking lot, we found a uniformed man waiting for us — or blocking us, anyway. He seemed as surprised by us as we were by him.

"Hector is on break!" he blurted, tossing aside a small, smoldering stub that looked too white and pinched to be the butt of a cigarette.

GW and Biddle started looking around for this "Hector" the man was shouting about.

"Oh — it's you," Hector the bellman said to me, looking chagrined. "Laura Holt, private investigator."

Hector's memory was as sharp as ever. Dammit. I'd have been a lot happier if I there was a chance he'd forget me.

Just my luck: a stoner with a photographic memory.

"Hi, Hector," I said to him.

GW and Biddle stopped looking for Hector.

"Sorry if I startled you," the bellman said. "The day manager, Mr. Raffel, is always trying to catch me . . . you know. Being unprofessional."

I held up my right hand. "We didn't see a thing. Right, fellas?"

GW and Biddle nodded and smiled and generally pretended they knew what the hell was happening.

"How is your investigation going?" Hector said.

I gave him a so-so hand waggle.

"That's too bad," Hector said. "Hector will be on the lookout for anything suspicious."

"I'm sure of it. Thanks, Hector."

I led GW and Biddle away.

"What's his story?" Biddle asked once we were safely around the side of the building, heading into the main parking lot.

"He's an extremely observant bellman. Gave 'Laura Holt, private investigator' a lot of information yesterday."

"Extremely observant, huh?" Biddle said. "The cops are gonna love him."

"When he tells Detective Burby about Laura and her two friends . . . ," GW said.

He didn't bother with the "we're screwed" at the end. We all knew.

We had to finger the killers before the killers were fingered as *us.*

Hopefully, the B-Team had given us a head start.

I called the B-Team as we drove away from the lodge.

"Did you find them?" I asked when Clarice picked up.

"We tried our story out on all five places you told us to," she said. "No luck."

"Damn."

"So we tried five more."

"And?"

"Nothing."

"Damn."

"So we tried five more."

"Oh, for Christ's sake, just tell me: *did you find them*?"

"Yes!" I heard Ceecee say. "Probably! Maybe. We think."

"Where?"

"Grandpa and his loverboy are staying at the Bend of the River Motel in Cottonwood," Clarice said.

"You should've heard her on the phone with the clerk," Ceecee threw in. " 'Peepaw ran off without his medication and we think he's probably checked in under his boyfriend's name, and Meemaw says she'll forgive him if he comes home and starts going to church again, but if we don't get him his pills right away, he could have a heart attack, and please please please can't you just tell me if someone who looks like Peepaw is staying there?' "

"I don't remember the story we agreed to being so *Days of Our Lives.*"

"I'm method. I was in character. I had to follow my instincts," Clarice said. "And anyway, I was getting bored, so I decided to have fun with it."

"And it worked, so don't complain!" Ceecee chimed in.

"I'm not complaining. Did you get a room number?"

"No," Clarice said. "The clerk just put me through to the old men's room and asked me to say it was a wrong number if it wasn't actually Peepaw and Giorgio."

"Giorgio?"

"Peepaw's new boy toy. Keep up!"

"I figured it was Peepaw's new boy toy, Clarice. It's just that neither of those guys struck me as a 'Giorgio.' "

"I *really* wish I could hear the other half of this conversation," GW said from behind the wheel of my Cadillac. (The last thing we needed was for me to get pulled over for talking on the phone while driving when we were still mere blocks from Glenn Budziak's body.)

"She didn't actually talk to those scumbags, did she?" Biddle asked me from the backseat. "That wasn't part of the plan."

I fought back the urge to shoot him a glare.

Now he's got scruples about dragging a teenage girl into his schemes.

"So what happened when the clerk put your call through?" I asked Clarice.

"This old guy picks up and just says, 'What?' all grumpy. And it's hard to tell from 'what,' you know? But I think he's got an East Coast accent. Not like 'I pawked the caw not faw from the baw' East Coast, but East Coast."

"You weren't supposed to do that."

"It's alright. I just said, 'Is this Tyler's room?' And he's like, 'No,' and hangs up. He had no idea who I was. If you wanna talk to him, just call the motel and tell the guy who answers you gotta speak to Peepaw about his pills. He'll put you through."

"Alright. Good work, girls."

"Thanks," Clarice and Ceecee said together.

"Now go to Ceecee's house and stay there till this is over."

"What?" they also said together.

"You can't just kick us out of this now!" Clarice protested solo.

Ceecee backed her up with a "Yeah!"

"Look — things have gotten complicated," I said.

"They weren't complicated before?" Clarice shot back.

"Not like this. Now it's I'm-not-even-going-to-explain-on-a-cellphone complicated. I'm-trying-to-keep-you-out-of-prison complicated. *Bad* complicated."

"Then we want to help," Clarice said.

"Yeah!" said Ceecee.

"You have helped. A lot. And now you can help even more by making things a wee tiny bit less complicated."

"By getting out of your way," Clarice grumbled.

"By giving us one less thing to worry about."

Clarice kept grumbling, just more under her breath now. All I could make out were the words "stupid" and "not babies" and maybe "Elmo" and Ceecee saying, "I know! Really!"

"So you're going to Ceecee's?" I said.

Silence now.

"So you're going to Ceecee's?"

"Fine," Clarice spat. And she hung up.

"Everything alright?" GW asked me.

"The girls wanna kill me 'cuz I won't let them get killed," I explained.

GW shook his head. "Kids."

"What now?" said Biddle.

I took a deep breath. Then another. Then another, shallower, faster. Then another shallower and faster still. Then another and another and another in quick succession until I was on the verge of hyperventilating.

Sometimes I need to go method, too.

"Now," I panted, "I need to beg a motel clerk to put me through to my Peepaw."

"What?" the old man growled into the phone.

"Stormy Sea from Scheveningen Pier," I said.

"What?" the old man said again. But it wasn't a growl this time. It was a cry of surprise.

"You want it, I have it, I wanna get clear of this mess. Can we work something out?"

"What? I mean . . . I don't know what you're talking about."

Clarice had been right. He wasn't a "dese" and "dose" guy, but you could hear the Eastern seaboard in his vowels.

"Who is this?" he said.

"This'll go a lot better without names. Now — do you want the painting or not?"

There was a long pause. Then —

"Yeah. I want it."

"Good," I said. "Then this is how it's gonna go . . ."

COPPE
COUPES
4
CHALICES
COPAS
KELCHE
BEKERS

When the card's right-side up, Mopey McMoperson there doesn't see the opportunity that life is handing her. Or him. It's hard to tell. (She/he is so wishy-washy it looks like she/he can't even decide which gender to be. Hence the colorless caftan — a pretty poor fashion choice unless the message you're trying to send is "I might have genitalia but I've been too depressed to check.") Reverse the card, and Ms./Mr. McMoperson's personality flips, too. It's carpe diem time! Or at least carpe that cup. So get ready for action because the sisters (or brothers) are doin' it for themselves.

Miss Chance, *Infinite Roads to Knowing*

"You again?" the waitress said when she found me and Biddle back in our booth at Shanna's Home Cookin'. "You could just rent a meeting room at the Holiday Inn, you know."

"We like it here," Biddle said with a smile. "Such a lovely view."

The waitress looked like she didn't know whether to blush or roll her eyes. She settled for a begrudging half grin.

"So your French buddy isn't with you this time?" she said to me.

It took me a moment to realize she meant Pilcher. I guess Shanna's Home Cookin' didn't get a lot of customers from Germany. Or France. Or anywhere outside of an eight-block radius.

"No," I said. "Will his tip cover us for the table?"

"It might cover *him.* But you two . . ."

The waitress shook her head. I sighed. A

heaping plate of food was the last thing I wanted in front of me — the image of a blood-covered Budziak tied to a chair was still too fresh in my mind. But Biddle and I didn't have any hundred-dollar bills on us, and seven bucks for a burger and fries seemed like a small price to pay to stay alive.

We needed to be public but not too public, and a Holiday Inn meeting room wouldn't quite fit the bill.

I ordered the burger. Biddle opted for the special of the day — whatever that was.

"Eat it when you get hungry," he told the waitress.

Her half grin became slightly less begrudging.

"I'll be back with your burger," she told me.

"Don't rush on my account," I said.

She didn't. The burger arrived more than twenty minutes later, just before "Peepaw" (or the man I thought of as "Peepaw," anyway — he certainly wasn't any "Giorgio"). He came walking up to our booth fifteen minutes after the agreed-upon meeting time.

It was the old man who'd asked to use the bathroom in the White Magic Five and Dime two days before. The paunchy, balding half of the wrinkled goon duo that had trailed and jumped Biddle.

He'd been watching the restaurant, no doubt. Looking for — or maybe setting — a trap.

"Have a seat," I said to him.

He ignored me. He was taking a long, slow look around the diner, scouting for familiar faces and a familiar *kind* of face. The studied blasé detachment of a cop waiting for the moment to pounce.

He wouldn't see it. There were no cops. Just gray-haired couples and loud young families and a few loners who looked way too authentically skeevy even for the best narc.

The booth to one side of us was empty. In the booth on the other side was a bedraggled blond with her back to us. She was so hunched over her plate, it looked like she was about to fall asleep in her scrambled eggs.

"Where's your friend? The big guy?" Biddle said. "My bruised ribs want to say hi."

The old man ignored Biddle, too.

He was dressed like any other road-tripping grandpa, in a loose shirt and yellow cardigan and khaki slacks and white sneakers, but he had the blank face and bottomless-pit eyes of a loan shark's muscle, which was probably exactly what he'd been when he started out.

A lot of water had gone under the bridge since then, as had a lot of bodies. He didn't look like he'd forgotten how to get them there.

He finally focused on us. On *me.* "Alright, let's get this over with," he said. "Let me have it."

"No."

He let his eyebrows go up to show surprise, but his expression stayed stony.

"No?"

"No. We're not going to give it to you," I said. "We're going to give it to both of you. When you're sitting across from us. Together."

The old man showed his annoyance by tilting his head and staring at us through heavy, half-lidded eyes.

"We know there's only two of you, and we know how you operate," Biddle said. "We want to know where you both are while this goes down . . . or it's not going down. You got it?"

The old man kept staring at us.

We stared back.

He stared some more.

We did, too.

He didn't blink.

I did.

"Find someone else for the staring contest," I said. "We're leaving."

I started to shoo Biddle out of the booth.

The old man stepped over to block us. He pulled a cell phone from his shirt pocket and put it to his right ear. He didn't push any buttons. It had been on the whole time.

"Come in," he said into the phone. "Yeah, I know. Just do it."

He slipped the phone back into his pocket without hanging up.

"Thank you," I said.

I held a hand out toward the other side of the booth.

Slowly, reluctantly, the old man slid in across from us.

"While we're waiting for your buddy we can talk terms," I said.

The old man scoffed. "Terms? How 'bout you give us what's ours, we leave, and you live happily ever after?"

"Those the terms you gave Robert Dryja and Glenn Budziak?" Biddle asked.

The old man regarded him coolly for a moment, then smirked and shrugged.

He helped himself to one of my french fries.

Beyond him I could see his partner lumbering into the diner. He was Herman

Munster in a knit shirt and mom jeans — tall and broad, with skin so gray it seemed like you were watching him in black and white. Though it was eighty degrees out, he was wearing a black flight jacket. At some point in the very near future, I guessed, he was going to slip his hand inside it while glaring at me menacingly.

When he saw me watching him, he jutted out his already jutting jaw and headed toward our table with long, purposeful strides that warned anyone about to get in his way that they were making a mistake.

The first old man had obviously been tough once. The second could still pull it off.

"Sit," his friend told him when he reached the table.

"Why?" the big man croaked. It sounded like he'd been a pack-a-day smoker from birth.

"Sit," the old man snapped.

The big man sat.

"Why?" he said again anyway.

The old man jerked his head toward us. "They want to talk terms."

"Terms?" the big man rasped, incredulous.

Here it comes, I thought. And he did glare at me menacingly. (Then again, it was entirely possible that he *always* looked like that.) But instead of slipping his hand into his jacket, he reached across the table and picked up the unused spoon by my plate.

"P," the old man said.

"Here's *terms,*" the big man told me. His accent screamed *Philly!* louder than Rocky Balboa and the Liberty Bell.

"P," the old man repeated.

"Hand it over," the big man went on, "and I won't scoop out your goddamn eyeballs and feed 'em to the —"

"*Paul.* We talked about this."

The big man — Paul — threw his partner a scowl, then put the spoon down and slowly slid it across the table toward me.

I let out a breath I didn't even know I'd been holding. Paul had done a better job scaring me with a spoon than some people had with guns.

"My friend here . . . he gets a little frustrated when people make things complicated," the first old man said, slapping Paul on the shoulder. "That's why I like to keep things simple. Let me give you a for-instance: you give, we take, we leave. See? Simple."

The old man smiled coldly, baring uneven yellowed teeth.

Biddle and I exchanged a quick sidelong look.

So this was how they were going to play it: good crook, bad crook. Or, to be more accurate: bad crook, worse crook.

We'd already seen just how bad "worse" could get. It was strapped to a chair at the Devil's Ridge Lodge.

Still, we had no choice but to stick to the plan.

"I'm afraid it's not going to be as simple as you might like," I said.

"Here we go," the old man groaned, throwing up his hands and rolling his eyes. "I tried. I really did. Didn't I, Paul? I tried to be nice. I tried to warn them. Simple. Sim. Pull. That's all I asked."

Paul just kept up his menacing stare.

"We've taken some precautions, that's all," Biddle said. "We don't want to end up like Dryja and Budziak."

"No," Paul growled. "You don't."

"Paul."

The old man put a hand on his partner's shoulder again.

Paul reached back and slapped it away.

"I've waited too long for this. *Way* too long," he said to me. "Hand it over."

Before I could answer, the waitress stepped up, notepad in hand.

"More people not eating at one of my tables?" she groused. "This is a diner. *Dine.*"

She turned to face the old men.

"What'll it be?"

They just stared at her.

And stared.

And stared.

And stared.

The waitress cleared her throat and lowered her notepad.

"You know what?" she said softly. "I'm going to give you fellas a little more time to think."

She turned and left in a way that made it plain she was never coming back.

"Now where were we?" Peepaw said. "Oh, yeah. *Hand it over.*"

"We want to be clear about something first," I said. "When you get it, you leave . . . and you leave us alone. Forever."

The old man leaned back and smiled. "Yeah, sure, fine, whatever you say. We'd have no reason to hurt you once we have what we came for. Ain't that right, P?"

Paul said nothing. Paul did nothing. Paul just watched.

"You'd have plenty of reason," I said. "You'd know that we'd know who had the painting. You'd know that we'd know about Dryja and Budziak."

"We'd be loose ends," said Biddle.

The old man shrugged. "So what? I've

been living with loose ends for the last twenty-five years. I can handle a few more. Don't worry about it."

"We don't plan to," I said.

I pulled out my phone.

Paul finally reacted.

"What're you doin'?" he rumbled.

It looked like he was wondering if he should snatch my spoon back and do something nasty with it, fast.

"Don't worry. I'm not calling anyone," I assured him. "I'm just checking for messages."

I had one. From GW.

He'd headed for the Bend of the River Motel right after I'd called Peepaw in his room there.

I read his message, then looked at the men across the table again.

"You're staying in room 217, and you're driving a blue Nissan Altima, Arizona license plate 594VHB," I said. "Now that we know that, it'll just take a little more digging to get a name to go with the reservation or the rental, and that name is going in a safe place — where it's going to stay as long as *we* stay safe."

"I told you it was a setup," Paul snarled.

He started to slip a hand under his jacket.

"Paul," his friend said.

Paul didn't stop.

"It's still simple, man," Biddle said to him. "We give, you take, you leave. The only difference is you don't kill us between the take and the leave."

"That doesn't seem so unreasonable, as terms go," I threw in.

Whatever Paul was reaching for — and I had the distinct impression it wasn't a balloon animal — he got ahold of it and froze.

"They're right, Paul," the other old man said. "It's still a good deal for us."

Paul relaxed, which for Paul meant he brought his hand out from under his jacket and unclenched his jaw a bit. He still looked like he was about half a second away from busting either a blood vessel or someone's head.

"Fine," he said. "Gimme."

I thumbed a quick message into my phone and hit *SEND*.

"It's given," I said as I put the phone away again.

"What?" said Peepaw.

"Congratulations," said Biddle. "It's all yours."

"What?" said Paul.

His "what" had half the volume and twice the menace.

I talked fast before his hand went back

under his jacket.

"The painting's been slipped under your motel room door. It'll be waiting for you when you get back."

"Just one final precaution," Biddle added. "You didn't really think we'd be dumb enough to have it on us here, did you?"

The old men sat and seethed.

Obviously, they'd assumed we *were* that dumb.

"It better be there," Peepaw said. "You know what happens to people who play games with us."

I nodded solemnly. "That's exactly why we're giving you what you want."

The slightest hint of a smirk curled up the corner of Peepaw's wrinkled mouth.

He wanted to believe. Because it would mean they'd won — and that they'd done it by pushing people around.

They weren't old. Not so long as somebody feared them.

"Let's go, P," he said.

Slowly, reluctantly, never taking his eyes off us, Paul stood up. Peepaw slid from the booth to stand beside him. He started to go, then stopped.

"I'm surprised you didn't try to get any money out of us," he said.

"We figured you wouldn't have much to

give till you figured out how to unload the painting," Biddle told him. "And we didn't want to stay in business with you while you figured it out."

"So you cut bait."

The old man stood there a moment just looking at us. It was like he was at a wine tasting, testing the flavor of a new merlot. Was it a little oaky? A little buttery? A load of bullshit?

Finally, the old man nodded.

"Smart," he said. "Nice doing business with you."

He turned and walked toward the door. Paul gave us a few bonus seconds of glowering, then followed him.

When they were outside, I let myself start to relax.

When they were out of sight, I exchanged a hopeful look with Biddle.

When they'd been out of sight for a couple minutes, I turned to the woman hunched over her plate at the booth behind ours.

"Satisfied?"

The woman straightened up, swiveled around, and brushed her long blond hair out of her face.

"Absolutely," said Katrina Gilver-McPherson. "They pretty much admitted it. They're the killers. I even think I know who they are."

"Let me guess," said Biddle. "They were part of Big Mike Fusillo's crew back in the day."

"That's right. Frank Bianchi and Little Paulie McFarlane. They did time after the feds took Fusillo down. Never turned evidence against him, though they both probably could've."

"And now they figure they're owed," said Biddle.

"*Little* Paulie?" I said.

Gilver-McPherson shrugged. "Well, they already had a Big Mike."

"Makes your story even better, them being some of Big Mike's guys," said Biddle. "You call the police, tell them you spotted these old Philly hoods around town, you think maybe there's a connection to Dryja's murder, the cops pick 'em up, nail 'em for both killings, you get the scoop."

"But not the scoop I came here for."

"We're still working on the painting," I said. "Trust me — when there's a scoop to be had on that, it's yours."

"So long as you keep us out of it," Biddle added. "With everyone. Police included."

Gilver-McPherson nodded. "A deal's a deal."

"Thank you," I said. "Now you'd probably better call the cops. Bianchi and Little Paulie will be back at their motel room within twenty minutes, and when they find a velvet Elvis instead of a Van Gogh by the door . . ."

"Right. And thank *you.*"

Gilver-McPherson shook my hand, then Biddle's, then hopped up and hustled off. Before she was even out of the diner, she was punching a number into her cell phone.

When she was outside, I let myself start to relax (some more).

When she was out of sight, I exchanged a hopeful look with Biddle.

When she'd been out of sight for a couple minutes, I slumped back against the seat, sighed, and smiled.

"Mission accomplished," I said. "We're safe."

"So long as the cops don't screw it up somehow," said Biddle.

"Even Burby couldn't screw this up. We're handing it to him on a silver platter."

"We're handing him *some of it* on a silver platter. Like the lady said, we won't have the whole story till we know what happened to that damn painting."

I stopped relaxing.

Was I going to tell Biddle what I'd realized?

After all he'd done for me, did I owe him that chance?

After all he'd done *to* me, could I *take* that chance?

"What is it?" Biddle said.

He could tell something more was on my mind. I could've tried harder to hide it, but I hadn't. Some part of me had already made its decision.

It was moment-of-truth time.

"I know what happened to the painting," I said. "I've known for hours."

COPPE
COUPES
3
CHALICES
COPAS
KELCHE
BEKERS

Everybody's happy. Everybody's hammered. Everybody's doing the Hustle. And you're right there with them, happy, hammered, hustling. But this is a reversal, kiddo. So it hits you. You left the oven on. And you forgot to walk the dog. And the rent is overdue. And you have a math test in the morning. And, hold on . . . these people you're dancing with? You don't even know who they really are. Time to start looking for the exit. It turns out you crashed this party, and now for you it's over.

Miss Chance, *Infinite Roads to Knowing*

I called Eugene and said we wanted to meet him at his office.

"Why?" he said. "More trouble?"

"The opposite. I hope. I'll explain when we get there."

I called GW and said we wanted to meet him at Eugene's office.

"Why?" he said. "More trouble?"

"The opposite. I hope. I'll explain when we get there."

I called Clarice and told her not to go anywhere.

"Why?" she said. "More trouble?"

"The opposite. I hope. I'll explain when I see you."

I started to hang up.

"Oh, so you're just gonna be all mysterious?" Clarice said. "You could tell me what's going on, but no . . . I'm supposed to sit here at Ceecee's house playing Clue while you and Biddle and GW run around having all the fun?"

"We haven't been having fun."

"You know what I mean! Is there anything Ceecee and I can *do*?"

"Stay safe."

"Anything other than that?"

"Bake us a cake. Hopefully we'll have some celebrating to do soon."

"We can do a lot more than hide out and bake cakes, Alanis! We've done a lot more than that already! Stop treating us like infants!"

She was yelling loud enough for Biddle, who was still sitting next to me at the diner, to hear.

He leaned in toward my phone.

"Your sister's not treating you like an infant," he said. "And she's not treating you like a tool or a prop to make use of, either. You should be grateful for that. She's treating you like a person — one who should have a long, rewarding, *normal* life ahead of her."

Biddle leaned back, looking pleased with himself.

"Who are you, Morgan Freeman?" Clarice's voice blared from the phone. "You can blow that inspirational crap out your ass! You don't get to suddenly show up out of nowhere and start being all wise and fatherly! You wanna be a part of my life? Start by taking my goddamn side!"

"Uh . . . I think you were about to hang up," Biddle said to me.

I hung up.

Somehow GW beat us to Eugene's office. We walked in to find him sitting by Eugene's desk with a smile on his face.

"So they can't prosecute?" he was saying.

Eugene nodded glumly. He was wearing sweat-soaked workout clothes and a "how did it come to this?" expression.

"Eugene and I were just having a little get-to-know-you chat while we waited for you," GW said to us.

"Should I add it to your tab?" Eugene asked me.

GW swiped a hand at him. "Oh, come on — that wasn't a consultation. I was just making conversation."

Eugene rolled his eyes. "Fine. Tell your 'friend' he can schedule an appointment if he wants to hear more about the statute of limitations. I charge $100 an hour."

"I have a buddy who's trying to go straight," GW said to me.

"Best of luck to him," I said. "Hope we

weren't interrupting anything, Eugene."

Eugene tugged uncomfortably at the wet sweatshirt that barely stretched over his big, doughy torso.

"Just playing tennis for the first time in ten years. With another client. *Who's thinking about drawing up a new will.*"

"So we were interrupting. Sorry."

"Yet here I am because I'm sure whatever's going on with you is an emergency. Like always. Plus, it's Sunday."

"So you had nothing better to do after tennis?" GW said.

I shook my head. "So he can charge *$200* an hour."

"Oh."

GW looked like he was considering going to law school for the first time in his life.

"I don't believe we've met," Eugene said to Biddle.

"Oh, sorry," I said. "Eugene, this is . . . who are you these days, anyway? I forgot."

"James McDonald," Biddle said, moving toward Eugene's desk.

"Right. Eugene, this is James McDonald. An old friend of the family. James, this is Eugene Wheeler. Mom's attorney."

Eugene stood, and the two men shook hands.

"So you're the one in trouble?" Eugene said.

"Not anymore."

Biddle stepped back and slowly lowered himself into the only other free seat in the room.

"Age before beauty," he said to me. "My knees are too sore for me to be a gentleman."

"Well, then, who is it?" Eugene said. "Him?" He jerked his head at GW, who was rising to offer me his seat.

I waved him back down.

"No, not him," I said. "Everything's fine, Eugene."

"Then why are you here?"

"Yeah," said GW. "Why *are* we here?"

"Because this is where my mother sent us."

GW gave me a look that translated roughly as "chuh?!?"

"We're looking for something Mom hid," I explained to Eugene. "She left a clue to where it is. Probably meant for Clarice — she's the only one Mom would know could figure it out."

"The card?" said Biddle. "But she didn't understand it."

"She would have eventually. I just beat her to it. I think."

Now Eugene was giving me a "chuh?!?" look, too.

"Card?" he said. "Like a greeting card?"

"A tarot card, Eugene. Do you still have it, Biddle?"

"I thought his name was . . ." Eugene threw up his hands in defeat. "Never mind."

Biddle stuffed a hand into his pocket and pulled up a now creased and crumpled card.

I took it from him, smoothed it out a bit, and put it on Eugene's desk.

"The King of Cups," I said, tapping the card. "An older man, successful in business and perhaps the practice of law. Calm, balanced, with hidden emotional depths and creativity."

Eugene stared down at the card, then up at me.

"You think that's me?"

"I don't know about the hidden emotional

depths and creativity. But yeah, I think that's you."

"Well, thanks . . . I guess," Eugene said. "But Athena never hid anything with me. I would've told you about it."

"I know you would've — if you'd known you had it."

"We're looking for a painting," Biddle said. "Did Athena ever give you one?"

Eugene's eyes went wide.

"Yes. She did, actually."

Biddle and GW both began scanning the walls of the office. There was nothing hanging there but degrees, award certificates, and pictures of Eugene stiffly shaking hands with people I could only assume were important (because guys like Eugene don't frame pictures of themselves shaking hands with unimportant people).

"What does it look like?" I asked.

"I don't know. It's pretty generic. Waves crashing on a beach. The kind of thing you'd see on the wall at Long John Silver's."

GW and I exchanged an excited glance.

Neither of us pointed out that your average LJS isn't likely to have a Van Gogh hanging over the fryer.

"Where is it?" Biddle asked.

Eugene narrowed his eyes and shot him a "none of your business" glare. "Somewhere safe. Not long before she died, Athena told me to hold onto it for Clarice. I'm supposed to give it to her either on her eighteenth birthday or if she ever comes and asks me for it."

"So you *were* hiding something for her," said GW.

Eugene swung his gaze toward him and upgraded to a "none of your *goddamn* business" glare.

"Like I said — I was holding onto it for Clarice. Not hiding. Why would I hide a painting that wouldn't get five bucks at a garage sale?"

"Didn't you wonder why Athena would want you to hold onto it?" I asked.

Eugene shrugged. "I figured it was a sentimental thing."

I managed not to snort at the thought of my mother being sentimental.

"Well," I said, "you don't have to hold onto it any longer. We'll take it off your hands for you." Now the glare was for me.

"Like. I. Said. I'm holding onto it for Clarice."

"You won't give it to me?" I asked.

"Like. I. Said . . ."

"Alright, alright. I understand."

I turned to Biddle.

"I don't think we have any choice," he said.

I pulled out my phone and called Clarice.

"Oh, hi, sis!" she said cheerfully when she answered. "I've got something for you. Check this out!"

She hung up on me.

I called her back.

"Oh, hi, sis!" she said. "You want another one of those? 'Cuz I've got enough to last all day."

She hung up on me again.

I called her back.

"Oh, hi, sis! Back for more? Great . . . 'cuz my thumb's just getting warmed up. Here it comes!"

"Wait!" I said. "Please! Clarice, we need you!"

Silence.

Then:

"I'm listening . . ."

She listened.

She laughed.

When I asked her to give Eugene permission to hand over the painting to us, she laughed some more.

"Tell Eugene I'll be right over," she said.

She hung up.

"She's on her way," I told Eugene.

"So she wants the painting? Right now?"

"That's the idea, yeah."

"Well, it's not here."

I sighed.

"Can you go get it?" I asked.

"It's a bit of a haul."

I sighed again.

"Why don't we *all* go get it?" Biddle suggested. "Wherever it is."

"Road trip! Road trip!" GW chanted.

"How about it, Eugene?" I said.

"Fine. As long as Clarice is with us." Eugene grimaced at GW. "And he stops doing that."

"Road trip! Road trip!"

"GW," I snapped.

"Sorry."

Clarice and Ceecee walked in a few minutes later.

"Alright, Eugene," Clarice said with a grin. "I would like *my* painting, please."

"It's not here," GW told her.

"What? Well, where is it?"

"Road trip! Road trip!" I said.

It wasn't just a road trip. It was a convoy.

I didn't want Eugene to drive himself — there'd be a mileage fee on top of the $200 an hour he was already racking up — and we couldn't all fit in my mom's black

Cadillac. So Eugene went with me and GW in the Caddy, while Biddle volunteered to ride with the girls in Ceecee's shabby old Crown Victoria.

"I like that broken-down heap. Reminds me of me," he told me. "Anyway — it'll be the closest I've come to being alone with Clarice since I got here. We've got a few things to work out."

"I don't think one road trip's gonna get you far with that," I said.

Biddle shrugged. "Gotta start somewhere."

As we headed out to the cars, Eugene told us where we were going in case we got separated along the way: 58 Rockledge Road in a teeny community called Mormon Lake.

"Mormon Lake?" GW said. "What the heck's in Mormon Lake? Other than a lake named after some Mormons?"

"I have a lake house there," Eugene said.

GW looked impressed.

"So that's where you go when the hustle and bustle of Berdache gets to be too much for you?" he said.

"Sort of," Eugene growled. "It's where I go when I get tired of listening to people's bullshit."

GW got the hint. For a while. He didn't

say a word for the next ten minutes.

"So," he said once I'd turned us north onto Highway 17, "may as well pass the time with a little chitchat. Eugene, why don't you tell us more about how long the state has to file charges on nonviolent felonies? You know — so I can pass it along to that buddy of mine . . ."

The terrain changed as we drove north toward Mormon Lake. Down around Berdache the land was rocky and copper red, with sudden jutting buttes and patchy scrub. But with each mile the red faded more into green and ponderosa pines replaced the cactuses and shrubs. The buttes disappeared, and pointed peaks took over the horizon. The parched desert was giving way to mountain meadows and marshes.

We weren't on the highway for long. Most of the drive was along narrow, windy back roads. Every half minute or so, Eugene would look over his shoulder to make sure Ceecee's Crown Victoria was still behind us.

"Do I want to know why you're all making such a big fuss over a worthless old painting?" he asked after checking for the fortieth time.

"Do you remember the old phrase *plausi-*

ble deniability?" I said.

Eugene snorted out a mirthless laugh. "Forget I asked."

At last we reached Rockledge Road — or so Eugene claimed. There wasn't actually a sign for it . . . or even a road. All I saw were a couple ruts that forked off from the asphalt. But Eugene pointed at it and said, "There it is," so I turned.

"Where's the lake?" I asked, peering into the trees and brush as we seemed to cruise off into the woods.

Eugene pointed to the right. "That way. Maybe fifty yards. Maybe one hundred today. It comes and goes depending on the weather. Sometimes there's not much more out there than a big muddy pit."

"And this is where you decided to have your lake house?" GW said.

Eugene stared off into the distance. "We're in Arizona. There aren't many lake houses to choose from."

We passed a few of Eugene's other choices. One was a mobile home sitting on cinder blocks. One was an honest-to-god log cabin. The rest — three in all — were squat ranch-style homes in varying stages of decay. There were no cars or trucks in front of any of them.

"Uh . . . I know it would be hard to do,

but did we miss your place?" GW asked as we left the last house far behind us.

"I like my privacy," Eugene said.

We kept going, following the path that passed for a road.

A minute later we saw it: a lonely, dreary box with a grey shingle roof and once-white aluminum siding dingy with dirt and rust. Inside was a priceless work of art men had fought and died for . . . which was funny because from the outside you'd have thought there wasn't anything in it that didn't come from Walmart.

A rough-hewn wooden sign was nailed up by the front door. Burned into it were two words and a circle with six spokes.

Eugene's Wheelhouse

I parked in what passed for the driveway — a bare patch of ground between the house and the "road." Ceecee pulled up behind us and turned off her engine.

As I stepped out of the Cadillac, I glanced back at the other car. Biddle had the girls laughing about something as they got out. Of course. The old smoothie.

Biddle noticed me watching and smiled.

It was easy to love him again in that moment. Without words or memories or problems getting in the way.

The man was complicated. The man was *trouble.* But who wouldn't love that smile?

I let myself smile back. It felt good. A kind of good I could get used to, with practice.

Eugene led the way to the house and unlocked the front door and ushered us all in. The stuffy air inside was thick with dust and musty mildew, and when Eugene flicked on the lights I expected to see cobwebs everywhere. Yet the little house was surprisingly tidy.

There was a dining room table, a cramped kitchen, a black pleather couch, a TV (the boxy old-fashioned kind that always seemed to weigh 200 pounds when Biddle and I would try to sneak one from a motel room in the dark). Family pictures and kitschy signs ("old fishermen never die . . . they just smell that way") covered the walls. A doorway in the back led to what looked the master (and only) bedroom.

And hanging in a place of honor between a Phoenix Cardinals pennant and a bookshelf packed with ancient board games and *National Geographic*s and Louis L'Amour paperbacks: a painting of froth-frosted waves crashing onto a strip of sandy shore.

"Voilà," Eugene said.

"Shit," said Clarice.

The kid had a good eye for art — and what we were looking at wasn't it.

There was no boldness to the brush-strokes. No mania in the dark swirls of color. No madness. No genius.

No goddamn pier.

We were looking at the wrong painting. This wasn't Vincent Van Gogh's *Stormy Sea from Scheveningen Pier.* It was Johnny Generic's *I Learned to Paint Beaches Watching a Guy on TV.*

"You don't like it?" a puzzled Eugene asked my sister.

"Oh, I just love it," she grumbled back. "You got a knife I could borrow?"

GW walked into the kitchen and started opening drawers.

"Uh . . . I think she was joking," Eugene said to him.

"No," I said. "She wasn't."

"Here we go," said GW.

He turned around with a steak knife in his hand. Biddle, meanwhile, had walked over to the painting and taken it off the wall.

"Do I want to see what's about to happen or should I take a leisurely stroll down to the lake?" Eugene asked me. "For plausible deniability's sake."

"I don't think there'd be any harm in you sticking around for this part," I said. "There might not be much to see beyond the destruction of a perfectly good canvas and a perfectly crappy painting."

Biddle walked the painting across the room, flipped it over, and placed it facedown on the dining room table.

He grinned.

"It's got a false back," he announced. "Just like Elvis."

The rest of us gathered around the table.

Biddle was right. The back of the painting was covered over with brown butcher paper.

GW leaned in with the knife and started cutting along the edge of the frame.

"Please tell me your mother didn't hide drugs in there," Eugene moaned.

"My mother didn't hide drugs in there," I told him.

"Stolen money?"

"I don't think so. She hid most of that in the freezer."

"Dirty pictures? For blackmail?"

"Those are behind the pipes in the bathroom," said Clarice.

I shot her a surprised look.

"I keep forgetting to pull 'em out for you," she said blandly.

"Some of them are *hilarious,*" added Ceecee.

"Okay. We'll deal with that later," I muttered, returning my attention to GW.

He'd cut through the paper all the way down one side of the painting. He turned the blade and started down another side, making an L. After he'd gone about six inches, he stopped.

He could pull back a flap of the paper now. So he did.

Everyone leaned in and squinted.

"There's something in there, alright," said Biddle.

GW lifted one side of the painting and gave it a gentle shake, but whatever was hidden behind it didn't slide out.

"Is it poisonous or radioactive or something?" Eugene asked.

"Radioactive?" said Clarice, incredulous.

Eugene shrugged. "Well, why doesn't anyone want to touch it?"

"Oh. Good question," said Clarice.

She jabbed her hand into the slit in the paper.

"Careful!" I blurted out. "It's really old!"

"I'm *being* careful," Clarice snapped back. "I'm not some klutz who's gonna —"

There was a loud knock on the door.

"Yeeee-ahhhh!" Clarice cried, jumping straight up.

Her hand burst through the butcher paper clutching a tube of rolled-up canvas.

I let out a "yeeee-ahhhh!" too.

"Is it alright? Is it alright?" Biddle asked, wide eyes locked on the scroll in his daughter's hand.

Clarice took a moment to catch her breath, then loosened her white-knuckle grip on the scroll.

"Yeah. I think it's fine," she said. "I was just startled by the —"

Whoever was at the door knocked again.

"Wahhhhh!" Clarice said this time.

Her grip tightened on the scroll again.

"Easy! Easy!" Biddle said. He reached out for the canvas. "Why don't we put that down while *somebody* sees who's there?"

He IDed the somebody — the some*bodies,* actually — by looking pointedly at me and Eugene.

"Fine. Come on," I said to Eugene.

He followed me to the picture window looking out onto the front yard. We couldn't see who was at the door, but it was impossible to miss what he'd arrived in.

A white Maserati GranTurismo.

"What the hell . . . ?" I muttered.

"It's a drug lord, isn't it?" Eugene said. "A Colombian? From one of the cartels? I should've known better than to bring you people to Eugene's Wheelhouse!"

I started toward the door.

"Who is it?" GW asked.

"Ulf Pilcher."

"The German again?" GW said. "How'd he get here?"

"That's what I'm gonna ask him."

"Wait," said Eugene, reluctantly starting after me. "*The* Ulf Pilcher? The millionaire businessman? Is at my lake house?"

"Looks that way. Or maybe one of your neighbors is dropping by to borrow a cup of sugar. *In her Maserati.*"

The knocking started again.

I yanked the door open.

Ulf Pilcher stood frozen on the front step with his fist in the air.

"Oh my god," Eugene croaked. "It's him."

Pilcher beamed at me.

"So . . . we meet again!" he said.

I almost managed not to roll my eyes. Almost.

"How'd you find us?" I asked.

Pilcher waved the question away. "Oh, the details aren't important. What matters is that I am here to take part in a momentous occasion." He went up on his tiptoes and tried to peer around me. "Have you found it yet?"

I leaned to the side to block his view. "We don't want any part of your schemes, Ulf."

"Maybe you ought to put that to a vote.

You might be surprised by the results."

While I puzzled over that, Pilcher tried to slip past me.

"May I join the party?" he called into the house. I blocked him again.

"Listen, Ulf . . . ," I began.

The sound of another car approaching stopped me.

I looked past Pilcher and saw a Chevy Impala with tinted windows cruising slowly toward the house. It pulled up behind the Maserati and stopped.

"Who's that?" I asked Pilcher.

He looked like he wanted to high-five himself.

"My publicist," he said. "I mean, not literally, but she might as well be, given the story she's about to write. The story I just gave her. About how I helped recover *Stormy Sea* from —"

"Alright, alright," I cut in. "I get it."

"I don't," said Eugene.

I pointed at the Impala. "That's a reporter from the *Philadelphia Post.* Ulf wants her here so he can claim that he . . . oh, screw it. It's complicated. I'll tell you the whole story later over margaritas."

"Actually, you won't," Pilcher said. "There's a non-disclosure clause in our agreement."

"Agreement?" I said.

Pilcher nodded happily. "Just some boilerplate I keep on hand for these kinds of occasions. Don't worry — I brought enough copies for everyone! Once they're signed, I'll transfer the finder's fee."

"What is he talking about?" GW said, stepping up behind me.

I barely heard him. I was listening to a distant echo that was growing louder and louder. A quiet voice I'd begun to hear a moment before that was slowly building to a deafening roar.

You're an idiot, Alanis-nis-nis-nis-nis!

I turned to stare at Biddle. He'd moved to look out the picture window, Clarice and Ceecee beside him.

He looked back at me, his expression half apologetic, half smug.

The voice grew louder.

IDIOT-OT-OT-OT!

"You called him while we were driving up here. You made a deal," I said. "You slimy, sneaky —"

I called Biddle a name that was crude but technically correct, given that he'd been my mother's lover.

"Ouch," GW muttered.

"*We* called him, Alanis," Clarice said. "It was Biddle's idea, but Ceecee and I agreed.

The painting's going back to the museum anyway. Why not make a profit off it while we can? It's not like we can't use it. The money Mom left us isn't going to last much longer the way you've been handing it out to her old clients."

"So you pulled them into it with you — made them part of another scam. You haven't changed a bit, have you?" I said, keeping my glare — my *rage* — focused on Biddle. "I wish you'd stayed dead."

"Ouch," GW muttered again.

"Who are *they*?" said Ceecee, still staring out the window.

Biddle took a step toward me.

"Look, Alanis —," he began.

"Hmm. Yes. Who *are* they?" said Pilcher.

He'd turned around to see who Ceecee was talking about.

The rest of us looked, too.

There was another echo, this one not just in my head. It was four voices — me and GW and Biddle and Clarice — saying the same thing at not quite the same time.

"Shit."

"Shit."

"Shit."

"Shit."

A mini-echo followed, provided by Eugene and Pilcher.

"What?"

"What?"

Ceecee capped it with a little gasped "oh" as she realized who she was looking at.

Katrina Gilver-McPherson was walking toward the house. Behind her were two old men, one balding, one hulking.

The balding one — Frank Bianchi — reached under his Mr. Rogers cardigan and pulled out a gun.

The hulking one — Little Paulie McFarlane — reached under his black flight jacket and pulled out a gun.

Katrina Gilver-McPherson already had a gun.

She pointed it at me.

"Alright, enough fooling around," she said. "Where's my goddamn painting?"

COPPE
COUPES
2
CHALICES
COPAS
KELCHE
BEKERS

First, it's "a toast — to us." You look lovingly into each other's eyes, clink cups, drink. Then, ten seconds later, you're trying to dump your mai tais over each other's heads. How'd the relationship go so far south so very fast? Who knows? It just did. And now you've got to clean up the mess — if you can.

Miss Chance, *Infinite Roads to Knowing*

Some guys claim they laugh in the face of danger. The only one I'd ever met who wouldn't be lying was Ulf Pilcher.

The German put his hands on his hips and shook his head in disbelief and chuckled warmly, even with three guns pointed in his general direction.

"*Your* painting?" he said.

"*Our* painting," corrected Frank Bianchi.

"Yeah. *Our* painting," Little Paulie threw in.

The two men were no more than twenty yards from us, flanking Katrina Gilver-McPherson.

Pilcher chuckled again.

"*Your* painting?" he said again. "That's the plural 'your' this time. English can be so imprecise about these things."

I heard movement and muttering behind me. GW, Pilcher, and I couldn't do anything but stand there in the doorway — we were in plain sight, and the second we tried to get away the shooting might start. But for the moment Biddle and Eugene and the girls could move unseen.

I hoped they were pulling out Eugene's secret stash of AK-47s and hand grenades. Not that he struck me as the survivalist type. But if he wasn't, none of us would be doing any surviving.

I started talking to buy them time.

"Bianchi and Little Paulie there — they worked for Big Mike Fusillo, the crook behind the original Bischoff Gallery heist," I told Pilcher. "They never got a taste of the big score before all the paintings were recovered or went missing. Now here they are, old men, and the mob's retirement package probably isn't so hot. So they figure they're owed."

I turned my attention to Gilver-McPherson, who was watching me with a half smirk on her face. She seemed to be enjoying herself as much as Pilcher.

"But you? I don't get it," I said. "I mean, I know journalism's a dying field, but teaming up with a couple murderers seems like an extreme career switch."

Bianchi scoffed. "We haven't killed anybody."

"Lately," Little Paulie added.

"That's not what you said at the diner," I pointed out.

Bianchi shrugged. "You assumed we offed those guys, so we let you. We were negotiating. Gave us extra leverage."

"But if you didn't kill Dryja and Budziak, then who . . . ?"

Gilver-McPherson cleared her throat and waggled her eyebrows in a "what am I, chopped liver?" sort of way.

"You?" I said.

"Oh, don't be ridiculous," Pilcher said to me. "The reporter covering the story starts killing the people she's supposed to be writing about? No no no. That's ludicrous. Hollywood stuff."

It was Gilver-McPherson's turn to chuckle.

"You still don't get it? You didn't learn your lesson already?" she said. "Just because someone says she's Katrina Gilver-McPherson doesn't mean it's really her."

"Ohhhhh," I said.

"Whhhhhaaaaat?" said Pilcher.

"Then who the hell *are* you?" said GW.

The woman gave him a smug smile.

"Jennifer Garlen."

All three of us stared at her blankly.

"But if I were as pretentious as Katrina Gilver-McPherson," she went on, "I would be Jennifer Fusillo-Garlen."

We kept staring.

Pilcher got it first.

"Oh, yes! I see now! Big Mike's daughter!" he said. "I believe you were even quoted in Ms. Gilver-McPhersons' latest story about your father. So when you came out here, the quotee became the quoter, and I believed you without so much as a 'may I see your press card?' Bravo!"

Pilcher actually applauded.

I resisted the urge to kick his ass off the front step.

"Only Dryja and Budziak wouldn't have been fooled," I said instead. "They must've run across either you or the real Gilver-McPherson at one point or another. So you had to make sure they didn't ID you to anybody before you could get your hands on the painting."

"Something like that," Garlen said with a shrug. "I really have to thank you for letting me know Budziak was at that hotel. Would've been pretty awkward if we'd crossed paths at the wrong moment. And you hooked me up with the boys here, too. I'd heard of 'em — they're legends around the old neighborhood — but I had no idea they were in town. So I've gotta give you credit for —"

"Oh, for Christ's sake, Jenny!" Bianchi snapped. "Are we gonna stand out here yapping all day? There could be more of 'em in the house, and for all we know they already called the cops."

Garlen laughed dismissively. "Don't get your knickers in a twist, Frank. None of these little backwoods rat-holes have phone lines. And this isn't North Philly. It's Nowheresville. No one's getting a signal for a cell out here."

Little Paulie slipped a big paw into his jacket pocket and fished out a phone.

"I'm gettin' two bars," he said.

Bianchi's eyes went wide, and he pulled out his phone, too.

"I got *four*!" he said.

Little Paulie scowled down at his phone.

"Goddamn Verizon," he muttered.

"Oh," said Garlen. The smirk on her face froze for a moment, then began to melt. "Crap."

She lifted her gun and fired.

A bullet smashed into the EUGENE'S WHEELHOUSE sign, and it exploded like a plywood piñata.

Pilcher barely even flinched.

"Now, *really*!" he cried in exasperation. "There is no need for that!"

"I don't think they agree, Ulf," I said.

I grabbed him by the handiest handle in range — his gray ponytail — and yanked him backwards. He screamed something in German that definitely wasn't *danke* as I dragged him into the house and GW slammed the door — which was immediately riddled with bullets.

Bianchi and Little Paulie were shooting at us now, too.

I let go of Pichler, who still wasn't saying danke.

"That *really* hurt," he told me, rubbing the back of his head.

"Less than a bullet," GW shot back.

There was another volley outside, and the picture window burst into a shower of shattered glass.

"*Please* tell me you're an NRA member!" I turned to shout at Eugene.

Who wasn't there. Neither were Biddle and the girls.

"They snuck into the bedroom while you were getting Jenny's life story!" GW told me. "Come on!"

He grabbed me by the wrist and tugged me toward the room at the back of the house.

"Would you mind locking that?" I said to Pichler, pointing to the front door with my other hand. "Fast?"

"I suppose I could," Pichler said. "It does seem like the thing to do, doesn't it?"

He stepped back to the door and calmly began fiddling with the knob.

As I stumbled out of the room with GW, I noticed the painting we'd taken from the wall a few minutes before. It was still lying on the little dining room table, the false back ripped open.

The rolled canvas we'd found inside was gone.

The bedroom was spare. Just four walls and a double bed. No decorations, no chairs, not even a closet. And no people.

The lone window was open, the screen kicked out. GW and I hurried to it and looked outside.

All we could see were rocks and scrubby grass and, in the distance, a glinting glimmer that could have been Lake Mormon or an old Jiffy Pop tin shimmering in the sun. To the right was what looked like a low ridge. To the left were a few pine trees. That did it for cover.

Still, it was doing the trick. Biddle and Eugene and the girls were nowhere in sight.

GW stepped back and held a hand out toward the window. "You first."

I stepped back and held *my* hand out. "You first."

Pilcher came striding into the room and zipped between us.

"Excuse me," he said as he passed by.

Without missing a step, he put his hands on the window sill and went bounding out of the house. The second his feet hit the dirt he was running, his ponytail flapping in the breeze as he sprinted for the trees.

"Alright. *Him* first," I said to GW. "But now you. And hurry."

Hurry he did.

He immediately picked me up and shoved me feet-first through the window.

"Run, dammit," he said under his breath as he set me on the ground. *"Run."*

Yet I stayed to help him climb through the window — not that he really needed it. Some part of me just wouldn't go without him. Some very stupid part, my mother would have said.

She would've been right, too, I guess.

We only made it a few steps toward the trees when there was a gunshot nearby, and a spray of dusty dirt went up not three feet in front of us.

"Hold it," Little Paulie croaked, "or the next shot takes off the chick's head."

We held it.

GW took my hand and gave it a squeeze. "Told ya to go first."

"I got two of 'em over here!" Little Paulie called. "The woman and one of the guys! The younger one!"

I heard footsteps in the distance — Jennifer Garlen and Frank Bianchi rushing around the side of the house. In a few seconds we were going to have *three* guns pointed at us.

GW gave my hand another squeeze and threw me a questioning look.

Should we take off again while we still had a chance? Make a break for the lake?

I could see the water now: a swampy oval barely deep enough to skip rocks on, from the looks of it. More puddle than lake. It was maybe a hundred yards off. Close — and impossibly far.

The trees were closer but just as unreachable. Little Paulie could miss us with his first half dozen shots and still take us down before we reached them.

But what the hell? Run, and we'd probably die. Stay, and we definitely would.

I tightened my grip on GW, about to yank him along with me when I started my sprint.

"Down. On your knees. Both of you," Little Paulie snapped. He came closer until the muzzle of his gun was practically nuzzling the back of my neck. *"Now."*

Maybe he'd noticed our body language.

Maybe he'd remembered that he was an old baby boomer trying to keep an eye on a couple Gen Xers who still had some gas in the tank.

Either way, that was that. GW and I let go of each other's hands and got down on our knees.

We weren't going anywhere. Except maybe face-first into the patchy grass.

COPPE
COUPES
1
CHALICES
COPAS
KELCHE
BEKERS

Watch out, Jonathan Livingston Seagull. The Hand of Fate has flipped, and the cup that runneth over is about to squasheth thy little feathered butt. Too bad you didn't drink deep when you had the chance. Now the divine gift of happiness and healing and love has been upended, and instead of quenching your spiritual thirst, you're about to get drenched and/or smooshed. In other words, bird: you blew it.

Miss Chance, *Infinite Roads to Knowing*

"I'm sorry I got you into this," I said to GW.

He was maybe four feet from me, kneeling, obviously terrified.

And he managed to give me a small smile.

"I got myself into it," he said. "I saw an opportunity, and I went for it."

For half a second I misunderstood.

That's what the last few days had been to him — an opportunity? A chance to be in on a big score?

Then I got it.

The opportunity was *me.*

"GW," I said.

Something cool and hard pressed up against my skull, and GW's smile disappeared.

"No more talk," Little Paulie snarled.

"Oh, let her talk a *little* more. I have a question," said Jennifer Garlen.

I heard her and Bianchi walk up behind us.

Little Paulie took a step back, and the cool pressure from his gun disappeared.

"You found it, didn't you?" Garlen said. "It was here."

I looked out toward the lake. I could only hope Clarice and Ceecee and Eugene and Biddle were out there somewhere, hunkered down where they'd never be found. Talking to a group of friendly (and well-armed) hunters. Circling around to the cars — and leaving us behind while they had the chance.

They couldn't do anything for me and GW. And all I could do for them was buy a little time.

"Which *it* are you referring to?" I said.

There was a blast behind me, and a bullet plowed into the sod six inches to my right.

"The *it* that belongs to my family," Garlen said.

Another shot rang out, and this time the bullet hit the ground between me and GW.

"The *it* that could have gotten us out of that shitty neighborhood when my father got sent to prison," Garlen went on.

Bang again. This time aimed just a little to GW's left.

"The *it* the feds are still hounding us about even with my dad lying there dying," Garlen said. "The *it* I've killed two men to get . . . so why would you think you could mess with me now?"

Instead of another bang, this time there was a *click.*

"Goddamn it," Garlen muttered.

She'd really been on a roll. And now she was out of bullets.

"Hear that, guys?" I said. "She's already murdered two men because she thinks that painting belongs to her. Who's to say the killing's going to stop when she's done with us? I'd watch out if I were you."

Garlen burst out laughing.

"Nice try, bitch," she said. "But Frank and Little Paulie understand loyalty. They understand honor. They understand —"

There was another *bang.* It took me a couple seconds to figure out where it had been aimed this time . . . because it took Jennifer Fusillo-Garlen a couple seconds to topple over next to me with a hole in the back of her head.

GW and I yelped in shock.

"Paulie!" Bianchi scolded.

"Hey, the lady had a point — Jenny was a whack job," Little Paulie replied casually. "Don't tell me you weren't thinking the same thing."

"Yeah, yeah," Bianchi sighed. "When you're right, you're right."

He stepped up beside the body lying

facedown on the ground and prodded it with his toe.

"Sorry, Big Mike," he said. "But your kid was a psycho."

So much for loyalty and honor.

GW slowly raised a shaky hand. "Um . . . so we can go now, right?"

Bianchi swung his gun toward him.

"Oh, sure," he said. "As soon as we get what's coming to us."

"Hey! You out there! Wherever you are!" Little Paulie bellowed. "Bring us the damn painting or we pop your friends!"

"You can see we mean it!" Bianchi added. "We'll kill 'em!"

Their words echoed out into the trees.

There was no response.

"They're long gone," I said. "Killing us won't get you anything. You should get out of here while you still have the chance."

Bianchi and Little Paulie ignored me.

"What now?" Little Paulie said.

"How 'bout a countdown?" said Frank.

"I like it. Do it."

Bianchi cleared his throat.

"Ten!" he yelled. *"Nine! Eight!"*

"You gotta tell 'em it's a countdown first," Little Paulie said.

"They'll figure it out. *Seven! Six! Five!"*

"You should've started at twenty."

"What? Who starts at twenty? *Four! Three!*"

"Maybe they're too far away to hear you or for us to hear them. We should've given them more time. Maybe started at fifteen."

"Would you shut up about that? They've had plenty of time. *Two! One!*"

A moment of silence went by.

"Zero!" Bianchi shouted.

Echoes — "Zero! Zero! Zero!"

Then more silence.

"Alright," Little Paulie said, "which one do you think they care about less? The woman or the guy?"

"The woman does most of the talking," said Bianchi. "So probably the guy."

"Unless they're sick of the woman talking," Little Paulie pointed out. "Maybe they wouldn't mind us shutting her up."

"Guys! For Christ's sake!" GW called out. "They're debating which one of us to kill first! Do something!"

I didn't join in. Instead I closed my eyes and focused on what I guess you could call a prayer.

Don't answer. Run. Don't answer. Run. Don't answer.

Someone answered.

"I'm coming out! Don't shoot!"

I opened my eyes.

Biddle had stepped out from behind one of the trees and was walking toward us with his arms raised. One of his hands was holding a roll of canvas.

He was bringing them the painting.

And committing suicide.

He stopped about forty yards off.

"Let them go," he said.

"Give me the painting," said Bianchi.

Biddle shook his head. "Let them go."

"Give me the painting!" said Bianchi.

"Let them go."

"Screw this," said Little Paulie.

I couldn't see what he was doing behind me, but I could guess.

He was picking a target — one of the nice, easy, close ones, like me and GW — and taking aim.

"Stop! Okay! I'll give it to you!" Biddle blurted out.

"Finally," Little Paulie grumbled.

Slowly, step by reluctant step, Biddle started walking toward us again.

I wanted to warn him off. Tell him Little Paulie and Bianchi were going to kill him — kill all of us. But it was pointless.

He knew.

He and I had escaped death in that cornfield all those years ago only to face it again by a boggy, half-assed lake.

Together again. Together forever.

"This wasn't how it was supposed to go," he said to me. A little hint of his familiar old smile came to his face. "Obviously. I thought I could get the painting and reconnect with you and Clarice and not drag you into anything. I thought I could have it all. And, man . . . was I wrong. I guess I was right to stay away all these years."

"Come on, come on," Bianchi said. "Hurry it up."

Biddle kept coming toward us sluggishly, stiffly. An old man shuffling to the gallows.

"I knew you were in Chicago. Knew it for years," he told me. "Your mother tracked you down. But we decided to leave you alone. You didn't want her — you'd made that plain — and I'd just screw up whatever normal life you were trying to make for yourself. Even after your mom and I finally split for the last time, I kept my distance from you *and* your sister. You were both better off without me. Right through to now."

He'd come close enough for me to get a good look at the canvas in his hand. It was identical to the one Clarice had pulled from behind the frame earlier.

He hadn't made a switch. He was really going to hand over the painting. Bianchi and Little Paulie would take it, shoot us, leave.

The bad guys — two of them, anyway — were going to win.

At least Clarice and the others would get away. Biddle was buying them time — with his life.

"Enough with the sob story," Bianchi said. "Let's get this over with."

"I'm almost done," Biddle replied.

He was just a dozen paces away now, his eyes still locked on mine.

"I'm bad news, sweetie. I've always known it. Always known I wasn't gonna change. If I only could, things would have turned out different, and for that I'm sorry. But you've gotta give me credit for this much: at least I didn't run away just now. I'm here with you. I'm here *for* you."

What do you say to someone who's come to die by your side? "Thanks a million"? "See you in hell"? "All things considered, I'd rather be in Philadelphia"?

I didn't know. So I just cried.

Biddle was standing right before me now. Bianchi stalked over and snatched the painting out of his hand.

"Finally," Bianchi said.

Biddle slowly bent down and got on his knees, like me and GW.

"What are you doing?" Little Paulie growled.

Biddle reached out and put his hands on my shoulders.

"Saying goodbye . . . ," he said, gazing deep into my teary eyes.

He started to draw me in for a final hug, then looked up at Little Paulie.

"To you," he said. "Now!"

He flopped over sideways, pulling me with him. An explosive *brrrrraap* burst out the second we hit the ground.

"Ahhhhh!" Bianchi howled, jerking with such panicked surprise his gun flew out of his hand and arced away like a black lawn dart.

"Christ!" Little Paulie cried, staggering and clutching his chest with his free hand.

GW, meanwhile, flattened himself on the grass and pressed both hands over his head.

"Oh my god oh my god oh my god! Are people getting shot? Am *I* shot? Who's shooting?"

The gunfire stopped as suddenly as it had started, and Biddle let go of me and pushed himself up to take a look around.

"About time," he said. "I was running out of things to say. *Me!*"

"Sorry. I got lost," someone replied in a high, warbly voice. "According to Google

Maps, this place doesn't even exist."

I rolled over on my stomach and looked back toward the house.

The Fixer was standing there clutching an Uzi in her little wrinkled hands. I guess she had a spare.

"Drop it, buster, or the next burst goes into your back instead of over your head," she snapped at Little Paulie.

The big man tossed away his gun, stumbled off a few steps, and plopped to the ground, one hand still pressed to his chest.

"Hey, kid," Biddle said to GW. "Why don't you make yourself useful."

He flapped a hand at the guns lying in the grass.

GW shot him a glare but didn't argue. He pushed himself to his feet and retrieved the guns. Once he had one stuck in his jeans and the other pointed at Little Paulie and Bianchi, Biddle turned back to the Fixer.

"When I saw you standing back there, I thought you were gonna kill 'em," he told her.

"I was trying to." She gave her Uzi a little shake that almost had me hitting the dirt again. "Goddamn arthritis."

"Oh, that is just *great,*" Bianchi groaned. "One of the Golden Girls gets the drop on us, and it turns out she can't even shoot straight."

"I'm still having palpitations over here," Little Paulie said, massaging his left breast.

The Fixer jerked her jowly chin at Jennifer Garlen's body.

"They do that?" she asked Biddle.

He nodded.

The Fixer straightened her spine and narrowed her eyes. "Well, then . . . I'm sorry I missed. You just go ahead and have a coronary, Lurch. You deserve it."

I opened my mouth to speak to Biddle, but the words came out a hoarse, garbled whisper.

I took a deep breath and tried again.

"You called her when we were driving up here? After you told Pilcher where we were going?"

Biddle nodded. "Backup. In case the German tried something."

"So let me get this straight," GW said. "We almost died because you went behind our backs. And we're only alive because you went behind our backs *twice.*"

"Something like that," Biddle said.

GW gritted his teeth and shook his head.

"Son of a bitch," he muttered.

"You'll get no arguments from me," Biddle told him.

"Or me," I said.

I heard movement behind me, off toward the trees and the lake, and I looked back to find Clarice, Ceecee, and Pilcher running toward us. Beyond them, moving considerably more slowly and cautiously, was Eugene.

"Alanis! GW! Are you alright?" Clarice shouted.

"We were going crazy out there!" Ceecee threw in. "We were *so* worried!"

They stopped cold when they drew close enough to get a good look at Jennifer Garlen sprawled facedown on the sod.

"You know what? I'm just . . . gonna go . . . over here," Ceecee moaned. She spun 90 degrees to the left and started moving away on wobbly knees. "Clarice, could you . . . make sure I . . . don't fall down?"

Clarice wrapped one of her long, thin arms around Ceecee's shoulders and steadied her as she hobbled off.

"You are unhurt! Fabulous!" Pilcher said as he came jogging up. He slapped his hands together and rubbed them happily. "That became rather extreme, didn't it? But all's well that ends well, eh?"

I scowled at him. *"Rather extreme?"*

GW waved a hand at the corpse nearby. "And this is ending well?"

Pilcher didn't look at the body.

"The nice people are alive, and the not-so-nice people are either dead or our prisoner. I can think of many situations that turned out far worse," he told GW. He shifted his gaze to Biddle — and what he was still holding. "And on top of all that, the quest is at an end. The holy grail is ours!"

He held out his hand.

Biddle looked my way and gave me a resigned "it is what it is" shrug. Then he walked over and handed the painting to Pilcher.

"It's going back to the museum one way or another," Biddle said to me. "Why not send it back the way that'll spread the joy a bit, y'know?"

"I'm gonna tell the museum to be very, very, *very* sure they got the original," I told Pilcher.

He unrolled the canvas just enough so that he and only he could see what was on it.

"Oh, the museum will be careful, believe me," he said. "More careful than some other people I know."

He rolled the painting up again and gave me a grin.

So a few rich dicks who thought they'd bought a stolen masterpiece to gloat over in private were going to get screwed.

I decided I could live with that.

"Um . . . I have a question . . ."

Eugene came shambling up, looking frazzled and wary. He stopped a safe distance from the body.

"What the hell just happened?" he said. He gave Pilcher an incredulous look. "And why is *he* here?"

Before I could answer, the wail of a siren echoed out from somewhere in the distance.

"Stick around," I told Eugene. "You're about to hear the whole story."

Pilcher cleared his throat and waggled his eyebrows.

I sighed.

"Or some of it anyway," I added.

Pilcher nodded, satisfied.

His secret was safe with me.

Little Paulie, Bianchi, and the Fixer all straightened and turned to stare at the "road" leading to the house. They'd finally noticed the siren.

"Shit," Bianchi muttered.

Little Paulie groaned and began rubbing his chest even harder.

"Time to get my ass outta here," said the Fixer. She looked at me. "I'll be in touch to talk about my share of . . . whatever this was."

She scurried off as fast as her stubby old

legs could carry her.

"Got room for a passenger?" Biddle called after her.

She looked back with a leer on her face. "Goin' my way, handsome?"

"Absolutely . . . whichever way that might be."

"Well, come on, then. I wanna be long gone when Johnny Law pulls up."

The Fixer toddled off again.

Biddle looked over at me.

" 'James McDonald' has a lot of questions to answer. In a lot of states," he said. "I need to avoid all those awkward conversations. I mean, even if I talked my way out of this mess, I can't talk my way out of *everything.*"

"So you're running away."

"Not at all," Biddle said. "I'm making a strategic retreat." He stepped closer and leaned in to give me a tentative peck on the cheek. "See ya 'round, sweetie."

I pulled him in for a hug.

"No, you won't," I whispered in his ear.

I wasn't sure if it was a prediction or an order. I don't know if Biddle knew, either. He just hugged me back, then stepped away, looked me in the eye, and nodded.

"Don't forget me again, you son of a bitch," Clarice said, walking up with a trembly, teary smile on her face.

"I'll never forget you, sweetie," Biddle said.

They hugged, too.

"Get your heinie in gear!" the Fixer yelled from the other side of the house.

The siren was getting louder.

Biddle whispered something in Clarice's ear, then turned and went striding away.

He didn't look back.

"How nice that he can avoid those awkward conversations," GW said, "and just leave them all to us."

"Oh, don't worry about that," Pilcher said. "You won't have to say a thing until our lawyers arrive."

Eugene had been in a daze the last couple minutes, watching everything unfold around him with slack-jawed bewilderment. The word *lawyers* finally seemed to slap him awake.

"*Our* lawyers?" he said.

"Yes. My American legal team. We'll all want to be on the same page here, won't we?" Pilcher told him. With his free hand, Pilcher reached inside his white *Miami Vice*–ready jacket and pulled out a cell phone. "I'll call them right now. I'll need my PR team on this, too. Ulf Pilcher just recovered *Stormy Sea from Scheveningen Pier*! Someone should call Katrina Gilver-McPherson.

Um . . . the real one, I mean."

Pilcher thumbed in a number and put the phone to his ear.

"Barry? Ulf! Look, I'm somewhere in the middle of Arizona and there's a dead body and I'm holding a stolen Van Gogh. How soon can you have someone here? Splendid! All my love to Suzanne and the boys."

I could see the Fixer's dark blue Camry now. It was cruising up the rough road that continued on around Mormon Lake.

The siren was close now. It sounded like the cops were driving up to the house the same way we had. They wouldn't see the Fixer and Biddle — as long as they stopped.

"Could you make sure the police don't pass us?" I asked Eugene.

He was watching the car, too.

He was an attorney. An officer of the court. An instrument of justice. Not to mention a member in good standing of the Kiwanis Club and the Chamber of Commerce. Was he really going to help a con artist and a woman with an Uzi flee a crime scene?

He sighed, nodded, and trudged off toward the road.

"Thanks," I said.

"You'll get my bill tomorrow," he replied.

The Camry seemed to be picking up speed.

"Well, you've got to give Biddle this much," I said as I watched it. "He's a survivor."

"And he's made you rich," Pilcher said. "Or at least comfortable. By some standards."

GW had been keeping his eyes on Bianchi and Little Paulie, but that got his attention. "What are you talking about?" he said.

"Your associate. The old gentleman. Biddle, I believe? He's an excellent negotiator," Pilcher said. "Before he'd tell me where you were coming this afternoon, he upped his finder's fee to a million dollars . . . and insisted that I give half of it to the ladies here."

He waved the painting at me and the girls.

"Wait . . . what?" I said.

I spun to face Clarice.

She was ready for me with a cocked eyebrow and a smirk.

"Hey, my dad's not the only excellent negotiator in the family," she said. "Why do you think I let him call Ulf when we were driving up here?"

"Pretty slick, huh?" said Ceecee.

I could've pointed out that it was so slick it almost got us all killed. But I was thinking something else just then.

Like father, like daughter.

Biddle had found yet another way to survive — to live on. The oldest one in the book.

Through a child.

The siren was almost unbearably loud by now. The police would be showing up any second.

I scanned the horizon for the Fixer's car. It was already on the other side of the lake.

It drove behind a stand of trees and disappeared.

My sister — her father's daughter — waved at where it had been, her smile turning sad.

Biddle was gone again.

But he'd still be with me every day.

ABOUT THE AUTHORS

Steve Hockensmith (San Francisco) is the author of the Pride and Prejudice and Zombies novels *Dawn of the Dreadfuls* (Quirk Classics, 2010) and *Dreadfully Ever After* (Quirk Classics, 2011). His book *Holmes on the Range* (Minotaur Books, 2006) was a finalist for the Edgar, Shamus, and Anthony Awards for Best First Novel. For more information, visit his website at stevehockensmith.com.

Lisa Falco (Los Angeles) received her first tarot deck at the age of eight years old. She holds degrees from both Northwestern University and Cal State University Northridge, and is the author of *A Mother's Promise* (Illumination Arts, 2004).

The employees of Thorndike Press hope you have enjoyed this Large Print book. All our Thorndike, Wheeler, and Kennebec Large Print titles are designed for easy reading, and all our books are made to last. Other Thorndike Press Large Print books are available at your library, through selected bookstores, or directly from us.

For information about titles, please call:
(800) 223-1244

or visit our website at:
gale.com/thorndike

To share your comments, please write:
Publisher
Thorndike Press
10 Water St., Suite 310
Waterville, ME 04901